Startrader

Geoff Williamson

This is a work of fiction. All characters and events are fictitious, and any resemblance to actual persons or events is entirely coincidental.

2016
© Geoff Williamson
Edited by Jenny Argante and Chad Dick
Cover design by James Robinson (100% Proof Ltd)

ISBN   978-0-473-32879-5

Published by: Bowshot Media
                New Zealand
                www.bowshotmedia.com

Prologue

THE DREAM Chase Robinson is having comes regularly, and there isn't much to it. He stands on a cliff on his farm that overlooks a perfect tree-lined paddock. Detail is clear. With no stock the dew on the long grass sparkles in the morning light. On the far side, a stream tumbles over rocks, the light glinting and changing.

He knows he is waiting, but he doesn't know what for.

Tension builds inside him as he feels something drawing nearer. Silently, something large looms overhead and he ducks. When he looks up there is nothing and then the dream is over. He is now awake, heart thudding.

Chase lies looking at the ceiling and then swings his feet out, but stays sitting in his boxers on the edge of the bed, mulling over the dream. Again and again, and more lately. Most mornings now; always at first light.

Then he stands and stretches his tall, rangy frame. Not solid, but muscular. A few kilos lighter than in his rugby days, he's in good condition. Fit and athletic.

Dawn is spreading orange on the horizon as he parts the curtains. He pulls on tracksuit pants, socks, a T-shirt and sweater and leaves his bedroom and goes down the hallway to a stout wooden door. He unlocks it and, once inside the spacious room, uses the keypad to disable the alarm.

This is no bedroom. Instead, cupboards, made of solid rimu timber, and steel cabinets line two walls. The floor is rimu also, polished and gleaming, and facing him is a massive antique desk. What light there is steals in from ceiling portals and windows set high in the outer wall. He spares barely a glance at the familiar display of old weapons, artworks and figurines from all over the world, including a magnificent oil painting of a sailing ship, and a massive globe on a stand.

Chase goes straight to the nearest cupboard and unlocks it. He takes out a long narrow object shrouded in a soft cloth. He unwraps it carefully to reveal a sword in a finely-chased scabbard. The cloth he ties around his waist. Carefully he relocks the cupboard and repeats the procedure with the next, from which he removes a long flat box. When he leaves the room he resets the alarm and locks the door.

He carries box and sword through to a covered porch. The old farmhouse is a rambling building from a time when stone and timber were relatively cheap, and large families were common. This door is also locked. As far as he knows, there have never been any robberies in the district, but to lose anything cannot be contemplated. He pulls on some running shoes and a jacket hanging by the door under the porch, and walks towards the barn.

Two dogs immediately fall in on each side of him, one a middle-aged female border collie called Vixen. Border collies are renowned for their intelligence. Vixen walks so close his track pants brush her side. Chase puts both the items he is carrying in one hand so he can put the other on her head, she pushing back against his hand in affection. The other dog is a young Huntaway male by the name of Bandit, large and muscular and full of woof. After getting his pat he bounds in front, the epitome of happiness. Over-excited and racing ahead, he almost crashes back into Chase and Vixen as they walk to the barn. Unfazed, they indulge

Bandit with frequent pauses to prevent collisions.

Once inside the barn, Chase puts his cargo into a carrying tray on the back of a four-wheel Honda motorbike, swings into the seat and, starting the motor, pulls out into the morning. The night chill lingers on the air. Relaxed and smiling, he accelerates through the gears while the dogs yip as they race ahead.

He doesn't rush, content to follow the track at a steady pace as it winds up the hill, the thudding of the four-stroke engine the only thing disturbing the peace. Chase doesn't have to think where he's going and there's no need to hurry. The dogs lope along beside and ahead of him, sniffing occasionally, and easily keeping up.

The hard-packed track climbs up and around a long low hill nestled between two others. Soon after it changes to a steeper climb, they cross a ridge at the exact moment the sun breaks through, creating a magnificent scene of light on a countryside that flows away from them.

This is the raised stretch of central North Island that geologists refer to as the volcanic plateau. During numerous eruptions, including that which formed the great expanse of Lake Taupo, debris settled over a vast area, coating it with dense layers of volcanic ash; pumice, a 'stone' that can float on water; and the black volcanic glass called obsidian.

The Robinson farm is centrally located within the volcanic plateau, six hundred and twenty acres set against a scenic backdrop of dense native bush and edged by a trout-filled river and crossed by streams. Chase continues motoring slowly up the slope knowing that the vantage point that lies ahead will never disappoint him. As he reaches the crest he kills the engine, and the sudden silence is like a dramatic prelude to the wonder before him.

The mist in the hollows catches the burgeoning rays of light that outline rolling hills and rock pinnacles, shaded and shadowed with the colours and shapes of the bush. Then it wreathes above the river, clinging to its banks; hiding and teasingly revealing the view, seemingly deadening the sound of the water.

And in the foreground is the paddock of his dream. No stock, and the grass vividly green and gleaming with dew. The dogs drop beside him, their panting the only sound as he gazes across the land. His own slice of paradise.

The quiet overtakes him and, as so often before, his mind wanders back to that day two years ago when the call came through to his office in Auckland telling him his parents had been killed in a car crash. He had been shocked above the normal trauma of sudden death. He had dreamed of the accident many times. Twice he had phoned a warning to be careful on the roads, a warning lightly dismissed by his mother and father.

Premonitions are something he has got used to, though their accuracy and clarity is always disturbing.

Chase sits on the bike, its motor ticking as it cools in the morning air. So many times he has dreamed of being where he is now, and approached by something he does not understand. He knows it is drawing nearer. In his dream he is never frightened, because there is nothing to be frightened of. Does he truly believe this dream is also an inevitability? But he comes here most mornings and nothing has ever happened.

Chase steps off the bike and takes off his jacket. He lifts the sword from the tray and slides the scabbard through the cloth tied around his waist. He kneels on the ground, as if to salute the panoramic vista before him, and begins to control his breathing.

When calm and focused, he unsheathes the sword in one fluid movement and, rising, rapidly executes a flawless series of thrusts and strikes, both defensive and attacking. The sword is a Japanese katana, beautifully balanced and keenly lethal, its blade whirring as it slices air. As he completes each formal pattern, he kneels again and resheaths. Again he breathes deeply and slowly before he does the next, the sequences increasing in length and complexity. Twenty minutes later he kneels for the last time and rests, controlling his heartbeat.

When Chase replaces the sword and belt inside the carry tray, he opens the flat box. Inside are the components of a hunting bow. A recurve: sleek and black, of obvious quality, handmade, bought in the USA. Whenever he considers its simple and elegant design he is as thrilled as the first time he saw it. No mechanical parts, yet so accurate and so deadly. With the ease of long practice, Chase quickly assembles the bow, attaching the limbs to the riser and, once strung, testing the string is centred and ready. He selects an arrow and nocks it. He looks over the bike, and, sure enough, the dogs are lying in their usual place safely away from the flight and noise of the arrow.

Standing balanced and side on to his target, he draws the arrow back to his cheek and cocks his left wrist slightly. At sixty-five pounds there is considerable weight to draw, but Chase doesn't seem to notice. He controls his breathing, takes a breath and, focused completely on the centre of the target, lets loose. The arrow sizzles through the air and smacks into a blue, hand-sized mark painted on a large hay-filled bale eighty-five paces away. Even though the arrow has only a simple practice head, it hits with a satisfying thud.

Chase checks the dogs again. Vixen senses his look and returns the glance in case she is needed. Then she gazes out at the view, pretending the noise of the arrow flight doesn't bother her.

One arrow after another, he hits the target with little variation. Once there are too many arrows so close that the fletching could be damaged, Chase walks to the target, dogs snuffling around him, and retrieves them. After a few sets he moves further back to around one hundred and fifty paces and starts shooting again. The arrows arch more, but invariably strike the mark.

Sometimes he is amazed he can still do this. He has owned a bow since he was eight years old and Robin Hood was his hero. Occasionally he visits archery clubs, but no one else is as consistently accurate. They pressure him to compete at nationals, but Chase has no interest in that. Now his stomach rumbles, reminding him he hasn't had breakfast. He disassembles the bow and packs it away with the arrows.

When done, he sits between the dogs, contemplating the view. Vixen puts her head on his lap, sighing, and he strokes her velvety ears. His mind again strays back to earlier times. With his parents gone and as their only child, he inherited the farm. Chase returned to his childhood haunts and carried on farming until he could decide what to do with it. The farm was a perfect home in which to grow up, but once school was over he had been seized with a desire to explore new places.

With a marketing degree behind him, Chase moved into the business world. He was bright and good with people, and successfully worked his way up the corporate chain. At a surprisingly early age he was head of sales and marketing for a large (by New Zealand standards) company. Then he was snapped up by a global giant – sucked into the heady world of big business, involved in changes of direction and in the major negotiations that required.

In some ways it was ideal, and the money was good. But in the end his job had cost him relationships, his innocence and, to a certain extent, his grip on reality. Once self-awareness prompted him to recognize this, he handed in his notice and started his own marketing company, Holocene Marketing. His concept was to pick promising products and assist them to grow in the global market-place. Deeply satisfying at first, and with far less pressure, but still something was missing. Probably the products were less inspiring than he had thought.

When his parents died, Chase was surprised at how readily he left the day to day business in his partner's hands and returned to the farm. In the beginning there were non-stop phone calls and emails, but gradually they lessened. The business was secure enough to need only his minimal participation.

He spent two years 'in recovery'. Getting fit was a priority, through hard work and physical exercise; getting back into the martial arts he'd abandoned too long ago, especially with sword and bow. Recently, he had decided to take on a farm manager, who would be moving in, with his family, in a week. That way Chase could keep the farm, which would continue to make a little money, and he could go back to Holocene Marketing.

The idea is less than thrilling, but he needs to move on, get back into something more challenging. So despite the dreams and knowing how much he will miss the farm and the dogs, Chase is now ready to start over.

The rising sun has pushed away the last mist, sending apricot tendrils into hollows and ravines. Chase thinks about breakfast. Then the scene that had played itself out so often lately in his dreams begins to unfold. The build-up of pressure. In unison, the dogs turn their heads. The huntaway growls softly. Vixen and Bandit both move closer to Chase.

Is there a noise they hear that he can't?

He gets up and mounts the bike, the dogs at his heels. Something big seems to pass overhead, but there is nothing there. A nothing that makes him lower his head. A breeze from 'nothing' that pushes him forward on the bike. The dogs yelp and crouch low. Is there a sound? He listens hard. Only the air moving.

His gaze follows the silence of 'nothing' down to the river edge and the empty paddock.

Chase waits no longer. He starts the bike and swings it around, heading back down the track and around to the paddock, to where nothing has stopped, expectant.

Chapter 1

THE DOGS FOLLOWED behind instead of racing ahead or loping alongside as they usually did. When Chase reached the paddock gate he leaned over and unhitched the latch, rolling ahead and using the bars on the front of the bike to push the gate open. He drove slowly into the paddock. There was definitely nothing there. The dogs had stopped at the gate and lain down, Bandit with his hackles up, Vixen looking back towards the house.

Chase stopped and killed the engine. The silence was absolute, the morning chorus of cicadas noticeably absent. Chase's eyes were drawn to the middle of the paddock, even though there was nothing there.

He jumped when someone spoke to him, clearly though not loudly.

"Chase Robinson, please do not be alarmed or afraid. We wish simply to talk to you."

He could still see nothing and despite the reassuring words his heart began to pound. He kept his thumb resting on the electric start and waited. Approximately two metres above the ground of a paddock bathed in sunlight, a dark opening appeared. A doorway filled by a shape. A ramp slid noiselessly from the base of the opening to the ground and the shape, whatever it was, slowly descended, closely followed by another.

Chase remained seated on his bike, heart still thudding. Without taking his eyes off the scene he lifted his left hand to his right arm and pinched hard. Nope; definitely awake.

Soon it was obvious that the two shapes were machines

hovering slightly above ground level, each carrying a container of some kind. A short distance from the base of the ramp, the first machine stopped and the box it was holding extended in all directions and became a table, plain in design and with chairs folded on top. The machine unloaded them, positioning four on the side nearest the ramp and one opposite. The second machine placed several drinking vessels and plates on the table then hovered motionless behind the chairs while its partner went up the ramp and disappeared.

More figures appeared out of the darkness, four in total, of varying sizes and shapes, but definitely, if not humanoid, animal-like. As they walked slowly down the ramp, Chase managed to tear his gaze away for a second, to confirm he was still in his paddock and not dreaming.

Each of the creatures had a head on its shoulders, two arms, and walked on its hind legs. There the resemblance to *Homo sapiens* stopped. The first of them was taller than the others; half again as tall as Chase, and wore a long coat in material that resembled leather. The complexion of its long pointed face was light tan, darker around what he could see of its head. The creature walked with a sway.

The second of the visitors was broader and shorter than the first, and only came up to Chase's chest. Dressed in a dark one-piece outfit with a silver buckle at the waist, it too had a narrow, triangular face, though grey and scaly.

The last two were of similar height, probably standing almost eye-level with Chase. The one-piece outfit of the third was blue, and form fitting. The creature itself was thin and moved fluidly. The face was feline, slightly furred, with eyes that were large and liquid.

The last was ape like, but dressed in what could be

described as almost human styled pants and a shirt, though what could be seen of its body was covered in brown hair. When it reached the table it stopped, long arms relaxed, a hand resting on the ground.

Chase was still sitting on the bike, unable to take his eyes off them. The same voice spoke again in its strange accent, sounding closer to him than the creatures were.

"If you feel you can, please come over to us, Chase." A pause. "This must be frightening for you. Let me assure you again, we simply wish to speak with you."

Chase didn't know how common it was to wonder how you'd react, what you'd say, if you ever met an alien. He had. Now all prepared speeches went out of his mind. Not wanting to embarrass the human race, which apparently he was now representing, he dismounted and walked towards the table. He found it hard to be natural, and he was self-conscious and stiff-legged, as if he had the undivided attention of a large crowd.

He stopped just short of the single chair. He now had a much clearer view of the four creatures. He stared at them in turn, probably rudely, and realized, all of a sudden, they were staring at him with equal interest.

The first, whose feet were shod in rounded boots, resembled a small horse, or kangaroo or some such animal.

The second was like a lizard, or perhaps a crocodile, though less sinister. The eyes that blinked under hooded eyelids were on the side of its face, and when it opened its mouth it revealed small sharp teeth. If it was attempting a smile, it hadn't worked.

The third was halfway between a cat and an otter, and graceful enough in movement to make Chase wonder if it was female. Despite its dress, the creature still came over as predatory.

The fourth was ape-like, with long powerful arms, and was hunched over in a manner that didn't suit his outfit.

Chase, staring at this last visitor, was startled when it turned to the others and spoke.

"I told you he'd be impressed with my fashion style."

The comment broke the tension slightly, and evoked a chuckle from the 'lizard', a slow blink from the 'otter', and a shake of the head from the 'horse'.

"So much for the first contact," the horse said, again with an odd accent.

Chase smiled and the cat purred. "At least he doesn't seem to be offended," it said.

The horse creature gestured to the chair.

"Please, take a seat, Chase Robinson. Would you like a drink or food?"

Like an actor unsure of the plot, Chase took the two steps to the chair, which turned out to be wide, stable and comfortable.

"No, thanks," was all he could manage.

When one and two seated themselves slightly on the angle, Chase realized they must have tails! He wanted to pinch himself again. Sitting alone with the four of them opposite, what this meeting most resembled was a job interview.

He used his breathing techniques to calm himself, and put on his best interviewee manner. He couldn't keep his eyes from darting from one to the other. The otter noticed, and a smile spread across 'her' face.

"Sorry." Chase was embarrassed. "I can't stop staring."

"That's all right," she said. "Soon the different will be the normal."

"We should introduce ourselves," stated the horse. "That will help." He bowed at Chase. "I am Delt."

"Riian," said the lizard.

"Cayrol," purred the otter.

"Gargen."

The ape placed the back of his fist against his forehead in salute.

There was an expectant pause.

"I am Chase." He dipped his head politely, and used a single name as they did. "But you already know that."

"Greetings, Chase," said Delt. "And again I'd like to assure you we mean no harm to you or your world. We are here to offer you an opportunity."

Because of his accent, Chase had to listen closely to what Delt was saying, which made him realize this was hardly different from corporate meetings he had attended globally. You just had to be careful. Mistakes can be made when others are not using their first language.

There was a pause and then Cayrol, the otter, said, "Is there anything you want to ask?"

He did. So many questions. Where to begin?

"We can be patient," she added. "Please excuse our language."

"Your language is excellent."

He was staring again. Not a good idea. Chase composed himself.

"Er ... How is it that I can understand you?"

Gargen, the ape, emitted a hoarse laugh.

"Told you he would be practical!"

A nod from Riian, and again the slow blink from Cayrol. The others looked at Riian, the lizard, indicating to Chase he was 'the tech guy'.

"It is advanced medicine," Riian began. "An implant next to the vocal system links to the part of the brain that deals with language. Briefly, the brain transmits the implant directions to the vocal cords. Implants have been around centuries – marvellous devices. They have definitely reduced the number of wars …"

A polite cough from Delt.

"Ah, yes. Keep to the point."

Riian had obviously been well instructed.

"And how are you able to breathe here?"

"A similar technology with an implant next to the lungs that assists with gaseous exchange. The implant needed for this atmosphere is fairly basic, as your planet is not too dissimilar to our own planets. Now if we were on a sulphur-based planet …"

He stopped himself, avoiding either cough or blink.

"And how is your craft invisible?"

"It is now a simple enough matter for us to make the external molecule coat bond with the environment, undetectable to vision and sensors from primitive radar to sophisticated detecting devices. Only the very latest Federation detectors can find us. The surface bonds and therefore light passes around the craft so it appears you can see through it. Another battle development, I'm afraid …"

Cayrol's tail twitched. This had a faster effect than Delt's cough. Again Riian stopped.

"I can give you information on any of this later, if you wish …"

"Thank you."

Chase was beginning to like the guy. He grinned.

"Okay, the big question now …"

"How did we get here?"

"Yes, the speed of light problem …"

Riian looked past Cayrol at Gargen, who nodded.

"I understand you read extensively, Chase, and that you understand basic astrophysics?"

He didn't wait for Chase's confirmation.

"So you will know that your species has got to the point in understanding that seemingly nothing travels faster than the speed of light. You accept the big bang theory, but cannot yet explain how so much matter got so far in the first nanosecond – the inflationary phase – from the singularity of the big bang?"

"Yes."

Chase, despite himself, leant forward, listening intently.

Riian glanced at Delt, but did not wait for his approval.

"Briefly, Chase, the speed of light barrier only applies to molecules and atoms. In other words, to large particles. In a singularity and at subatomic particle level, the speed of light is slow."

He was in full flow now.

"So we create a naked singularity. A naked singularity is a singularity not surrounded by a black hole. The ship is that singularity. Every part of it and its occupants was broken down into fundamental particles and their antimatter pairs; that is, particles that cannot be subdivided. This is called an *event*. These particles are then moved to wherever we can *event jump* them. There is some amazing physics and how to disseminate …"

Delt interrupted.

"Thank you, Riian. That will be enough for now."

The lizard gave a slight bow.

Chase stared at the aliens as he gathered himself together. "Yes, thank you, Riian," he said. Already he was planning to spend time with Riian …

The band of inter-galactic travellers remained focused on Chase. He would think about all this later.

"Before we get to 'why me' and other matters equally unimportant, I guess the primary question is why do you not reveal yourselves to others on my planet? Is it the 'widespread panic' scenario?"

"That would be a part of it." Gargen settled himself more comfortably. Obviously he was now taking over this part of the education process. "But not the major part." He raised an eyebrow. "You might not like what follows."

Chase shrugged. He had had suspicions of his own.

"It is a matter of biology." Gargen regarded him thoughtfully. "Creatures evolve through competition. Natural selection, I believe you call it. Only the most successful get to pass on their genes."

He seemed to come to a decision.

"For a long time this meant the strongest or fastest survived. Then eventually a jump was made to a more intelligent and self-aware creature. Society developed, but still competition continued, albeit in a different form. Competition now was for communicative ability, which put money and power above strength and size. This could be worse in that it has brought out the true evil in some creatures. You have seen it many times on Earth."

Chase nodded and Gargen continued.

"There was for a long time a split in defining the 'success' of the species. Rich and poor is not how to describe it. Greed versus non-greed can be truer. Intelligence or ability simply intensified the effect, both positive and negative."

He waited until Chase nodded again.

"This is a generalization, but money and therefore power takes over. Imagine the universe with a great intelligence allied to that form of self-serving greed, that potential for evil let loose."

Gargen took time out to think how to put what he needed to say next.

"So until a species is deemed mature enough it is restricted to its home planet. If we can manage it."

He was assessing Chase's reaction.

"One measure of maturity is how well the species cares for individuals, and another for the home planet itself."

He saw the realization.

"Sorry, Chase. There are many civilizations in this category."

Chase grinned wryly. "I get it. We're deemed too evil yet to be let out to play?"

Gargen raised his hands in supplication, while the others made soothing noises.

"Please do not be offended if I do not express this well. Perhaps my language is not accurate."

"Oh, your language is accurate enough, and I am not offended. What you say is correct."

Chase looked towards the stream. He felt like a parent told his child has misbehaved. The open door of the spaceship, the fact he was seeing through it, brought him back to the moment.

"But how can you control this, Delt? How are you enlightened and organized enough to decide correctly who is not worthy?"

"It is complicated, but basically there is an elected body that oversees different planets as selected …"

He frowned, searching for the correct term.

"None of your words matches exactly, but probably *Wardens* is the closest." He thought about that and nodded. "Yes, that word will do. Wardens. We have representatives on or near each planet to monitor and evaluate its citizens. The Wardens have the power to apprehend any craft that approaches and to put a stop to plans that will interfere with a planet's development, especially when it comes to technology."

"So is that why you are here? And is this visit on an approved basis?"

The aliens remained silent, stealing glances at each other.

"I'll take that as a no, then," said Chase.

Delt was quick to jump in.

"This is where it gets complicated, Chase. We need to make you understand and we seek to gain your trust."

Chase frowned. This wasn't how a preliminary conversation with creatures from another planet should go. He decided to give himself an edge.

"I'm listening, Delt, but should you assume that a morally inferior species can be trusted?"

"Please do not mistake us, Chase. This is about a species in its entirety, not individuals. We can only portray things as they are."

An odd phrase. Chase stored that thought. He sensed the quartet were struggling, but with what?

"Chase Robinson, it is true we are not here with Council approval."

Delt was obviously uncomfortable with that.

"However, we do believe we are here for good moral reasons."

Chase raised a questioning eyebrow.

"We need your assistance in securing certain goals and we promise we will not put you into any uncompromising position."

Chase was glad to hear it.

"We need your skills to help us negotiate with a race similar to yours" continued Delt.

Chase couldn't help grinning.

"Immature?"

Delt winced, while Riian averted his gaze and Gargen frowned. Cayrol watched the others with her intense feline gaze.

"I did argue we should be careful about describing the current tenure of the species," said Gargen.

Delt glared at Gargen.

Chase continued. "But you're asking an immature creature to negotiate with other immature creatures? Why?"

Riian and Cayrol seemed to wait for Delt's answer with equal interest. Gargen was checking his fingernails. Delt seemed to be thinking.

"I told you he would be sensitive to that approach," commented Cayrol. "His profile indicated as much."

"Profile? What profile?"

"I am sorry, Chase Robinson. Please let me give you all the information before I make a complete mess of things," ventured Delt.

The expression on Cayrol's face indicated he already had.

Chase wanted something answered first: "I get the impression I'm not a random choice."

"You are correct," answered Delt. "You were selected for many reasons, a few of which you will not yet be aware of."

Before he could question that, Cayrol jumped in again.

"As Delt is trying to explain, the Wardens stop any ship from going to an uninitiated planet. As to how we bypassed the Wardens, the design of the Startrader – that's the name of our ship – and I am her pilot – is advanced. Though the universes have had star travel for some time, event jumping, as we call it, is not officially permitted. Startrader is the first ship able to go where we have no event summary. We can go to wherever the on-board computer predicts a chosen destination to be. The Wardens dislike event jumping because they cannot track a ship until it arrives, and only then if they are watching."

By now Chase's brain was reeling. Delt took over again.

"One reason you were chosen, why we need you, is that, as you come from an uninitiated planet, you will not be found by scan on another uninitiated planet." He grinned. "As we most certainly would be."

Chase wanted to get things straight.

"So event jumping is not general practice?"

"No," Delt clarified. "Only controlled event jumping has been allowed. We took a risk in coming here."

"How long before they find you?"

"In just over five of your hours a probe will come round to your solar system and could possibly detect us," said Riian.

So many questions buzzed in Chase's brain. Some to ask later. Some to ask now.

"So what is the good moral reason you are here then?"

Chase scanned the 'panel'.

Delt cleared his throat. "We need your ability to negotiate terms and deals to help a planet avoid potential disaster. We know of a planet with a humanoid species similar to your own ..."

"Disturbingly similar," murmured Gargen.

"Yes, indeed, though perhaps not as advanced. Its sun is erratic and, although not old, is due for imminent collapse." Delt spoke slowly. "When it does, all life will likely cease within that solar system. The Federation of Galaxies could intervene and stabilize the sun, but chooses not to as it is a natural event."

"That's how narrow-minded the Federation has become," said Cayrol bitterly.

"Again, yes," sighed Delt.

This was clearly a common topic.

Delt continued. "That planet, Tapar, has what perhaps will be its saviour, an extremely rare substance. A substance not easily synthesized and with extremely valuable properties, including its application in the process of event jumping. It is called *cramlimite*. If we can get hold of some cramlimite, we can use it to barter for Tapar's survival with powerful members of the Federation."

He sighed again.

"Not the noblest means of achieving our aim, but we have exhausted all other options.

Silence, except for the cicadas, which had resumed their singing. His visitors waited expectantly for Chase's response.

"So what exactly is it that you want me to do?" he prompted Delt.

"We want to take you to Tapar and then assess what time we have at our disposal before the Federation scans the planet. You would meet the locals and negotiate with them to mine a quantity of cramlimite. Bring it back to the ship and we can then use it to explain to the Federation why Tapar should be saved."

"Why can you not do this yourselves?"

"Because the only seam near the surface is on the edge of a large town," replied Riian. "Besides that, our equipment, or we, needless to say, would almost certainly attract the attention of the Wardens."

Delt broke the long silence that followed.

"So what do you think?"

"We shall not try appealing to your better nature, or flatter you by saying how exactly suited you are to the task," added Gargen. "We know we must leave you to make your own decision."

No pressure then. Chase remained silent. Helping another species was not the issue, but his instinct told him he was not being told everything. Yet somehow he knew this was something he had been waiting for. He got up.

"I need time to think. I will return in three hours and give you my answer."

The aliens took this as a signal to stand. Gargen spoke for them all.

"Thank you, Chase Robinson. We will wait for you here."

They bowed formally and Chase was turning away when he was struck by a sudden thought.

"Exactly how 'not as advanced' as us?"

The others allowed Riian to answer.

"Oh, about your year 1400 AD."

Chapter 2

CHASE WALKED BACK to the bike, started it up and turned to drive out through the gate. As he began the ascent, the dogs reappeared, chastened and fretful. He glanced back over his shoulder as he crested the hill. There was nothing in the paddock now to suggest any presence.

Was there? Or would he suddenly wake up again?

By the time he got back to the house he knew he would go. How often do you get to travel in a space ship? He grinned and went straight to the phone.

Yes, the couple taking over the farm operation could start a week early. They were waiting anyhow. No problem.

Next Chase phoned the business to report he wouldn't be turning up as planned. Did he imagine his partner's relief?

He arranged with his neighbours to feed the dogs and cat and keep a watchful eye on the farm for the day or two it would take the new manager to arrive. He was grateful to live in the country, where a helping hand is always there.

Finally, he contacted his closest friend. He had an opportunity to work overseas, he told him, and had to depart immediately.

"Would you pass the word around?"

The friend was perplexed, but consented. He knew Chase would confide in him if he was in any trouble.

"Take care," was all he said.

"You too."

A rumble from Chase's stomach reminded him how hungry he was. He prepared muesli, made toast and coffee, and added a packet of ginger nut biscuits, the dogs' favourite. He settled on the wide veranda in his favourite chair. The dogs loped up the steps to join him, eternally hopeful. Toast first, while it was still hot, and then the muesli and sips of coffee as Chase tried to get a grip on what had happened.

The experience was almost too big to handle. Chase knew he had decided to go, but had still to examine his motives. Vixen sidled a little closer. Oh, right! Chase broke a ginger nut in half and offered it to the dogs, who took the morsels delicately. Yes, even Bandit. He would miss them.

Back inside he packed a rucksack – only the essentials. How do you dress to fit in with aliens? Two or three changes of clothing. Shoes. Would his camera be allowed? Unlikely!

He tidied the house, showered and shaved. Good things to do before travelling … Chase regarded the katana and bow thoughtfully. Then he slid the sheathed sword through the outside straps of his rucksack, and put a soft leather quiver with as many arrows as would fit with the bow in the carrying box along with a sword sharpening stone.

He set the alarm and locked his office. His neighbour's mobile phone would be triggered if someone set it off. He took his keys out to the dog kennels and hung them on a hidden hook in Bandit's kennel. Bandit wouldn't tell anyone and they'd be safe there.

He gave the dogs a good pat. Vixen was suspicious, sensing something was up. He got their food and fed them, and, despite it not being normal dinner time, they quickly emptied their bowls. He then threw a large bone in each kennel and when the dogs went in each, he flipped the latches.

Finally, Chase secured the house, hiding the spare keys where the new farm manager had been told they would be. With one last look around, he shouldered his pack and picked up the bow box. He started walking back up the track to where the alien spacecraft was parked.

Vixen watched him go, forgoing her bone. A whimper came from her; a whimper he never heard.

*

The visitors were waiting. The doorway opened as he entered the paddock. Chase walked up the ramp, stopping at the entrance. The faces inside expressed alien relief.

"Please," Delt urged. "Come in."

Chase stepped into the spacecraft, which was warm and dry, and stopped to look around. He was in an antechamber, clean and sterile; cream-coloured throughout. There was an internal door with heavy seals on the opposite wall, five or six steps away. It was almost twice Chase's height.

"Welcome on board, Chase Robinson. This must be so strange to you. Please, be relaxed."

"First, allow me to introduce you to the onboard computer," said Riian. He looked at Chase. "K4, this is Chase Robinson. Chase, this is K4."

Chase frowned and turned his head at the sound of the voice he had first heard outside, a voice that was neither male nor female.

"Greetings, Chase. Again, welcome on board. My name is shortened to K4 and I am the ship's computer. Basically I run the ship."

The aliens exchanged glances and Cayrol, the pilot, rolled her eyes.

"Er, hello, K4. Pleased to meet you."

Gargen bustled forward.

"This safety area is called 'The Lock'. None of the internal doors can be opened until the exterior doorway is closed and The Lock declared safe. That means no poison gases, microorganisms or any other harmful substance can enter the main area of the ship."

As he spoke the door behind Chase slid shut, sealing them inside. Another step taken and irreversible.

"Your baggage, clothes and you yourself will be decontaminated now, internally and externally. As will we."

A coolness passed briefly through Chase, along with a glow of light.

"Your weapons caused some debate," continued Gargen. "However, they might be appropriate where you are going."

At Chase's raised eyebrow, he added, "We scan any area we enter. We know everything from what's in your bags to the number of animals on the farm."

"Okay. That makes sense," said Chase. "And it's always good to get used to new technology."

The door opposite opened, and Gargen led the way into a corridor.

"Please follow me."

Chase followed, staring in amazement at what was before him. The hall, and the rooms that led off from it, were truly sumptuous. He stopped before an open alcove like a viewing area, beautifully decorated and furnished with reclining chairs. At one side was a bar, managed by a compact robot.

Gargen laughed, and Riian added his own burble of delight at Chase's expression. Delt frowned, but Cayrol slinked up to Chase, smiling.

"It always amuses us," she purred, "an immature race's typical portrayal of spacecraft as minimalistic, stark and bare. Why would we not prefer luxury? The weight doesn't matter and rooms are only restricted by the size of the craft. That is dictated by how far you want to walk around a ship and where you can park."

Chase chuckled. She was right.

"Nice!"

"This is a viewing room," Delt added. "The seats are adaptable for any body shape and you can choose personal or shared visual display. It's as if you are in that vision, either alone or with others sharing being seen. This is where we got together to study your planet – and you."

They continued through the ship, awaiting Chase's reactions. In most rooms it was difficult to work out their primary purpose. Some had soft floors with covers that served as bedding – and low tables for eating. One room in particular resembled a rock formation with a cave. Another was decorated as – what? A rainforest?

Chase glanced at the lizard, Riian, whose lips twitched as he nodded.

Another stretched out like a never-ending savannah without walls. Would that be for Delt or Cayrol?

The retinue halted before a luxurious room with deep carpets and a four-poster bed.

"K4 prepared this for you," said Delt. "Is it to your liking, Chase?"

How could it not be? A room like this would please a prince.

"The room is perfect, thank you."

Not exactly his taste, but it would certainly do. Delt

relaxed.

"You can leave your bag here if you wish."

Chase placed his things on the ornately carved coffee table and, after a quick look around, rejoined his hosts.

"How big is this ship?" he asked. "It's like being in the Tardis."

They looked at each other in confusion. K4 helped.

"Earth science fiction story; time craft with larger internal dimensions than external."

"Of course, you have not seen the Startrader without cloaking," said Riian. "Our ship is circular, 212 metres in diameter, 48 metres in height."

"Wow!"

They came to a larger room that at first didn't seem to have any walls or a complete floor and that overlooked the paddock and stream. In the middle was a module with a touch screen on top.

"This is my room," said K4. "The control or drive room for want of a better description. Though the ship can be controlled anywhere, this is where we feel the ship to be directed from."

Chase was still studying the 'no walls' aspect. It was worse than walking on glass.

"Perhaps we should consider take-off now, if you are ready, Chase," said Cayrol. "The time to next scan by the Wardens is getting close."

Chase nodded. He was incredibly nervous.

"Seating semicircle."

Cayrol was in charge now. An appropriate 'chair' came up behind as specified, facing the open space.

"How are you with heights?" asked Gargen.

"Okay, generally."

Suddenly not so sure. Why did Chase think he was about to be taken on the rollercoaster ride of a lifetime?

"We don't need to make this uncomfortable," said Gargen. "Floor, please."

The floor immediately solidified to a curve that ended where the wall should be, leaving the front screen clear.

"The 'Trader can be controlled by voice only. K4 can take us anywhere using the dissemination process we described. We tell K4 where we want to be, and the 'Trader is jumped there. Time is immaterial."

Chase knew he was supposed to say something. "Okay."

"Best to show you," said Cayrol. "K4, five hundred metres up."

No sensation. The view outside blurred and immediately the 'wall' was 500 metres above where they had been. The landscape rolled away into bush with mountains in the background.

"Around view, please."

Now the walls seemed to disappear and Chase had a panoramic view of his farm and the surrounding land. The farmhouse was so close, so familiar – but from an unfamiliar angle. Chase was fervently grateful the floor was still beneath him.

"Time and distance are immaterial?" he ventured.

"Yes, mainly so."

"Can I have a go?"

"You can, but first K4 needs to know exactly where it is you have in mind and to ascertain nothing is there already. Checking the safety of the ship, you understand. We cannot do what we want to do if there is any risk involved," Cayrol explained. "And sometimes K4 has to move us out of danger."

"Okay."

Chase considered.

"Waitemata Harbour, Auckland city; level with top of the Sky Tower, northeast, one thousand metres. Please, K4."

Immediately they were presented with the view overlooking the Viaduct on Auckland's waterfront, with the Sky Tower and the marina to the fore, cars flowing over the Harbour Bridge towards the North Shore. Behind them was the volcanic island of Rangitoto.

Chase spoke again.

"Uluru, Ayers Rock, one thousand metres due east, five hundred metres altitude."

The scene changed again to where the blazing Australian desert baked the ground around the great red monolith, while walkers the size of ants trudged the tracks.

They indulged him further with the Statue of Liberty in the early evening in New York, the statue lit up against the darkening sky. The Coliseum in Rome was also illuminated and still being photographed at midnight.

"Can we go off planet now?"

His request was low pitched. Cayrol gave the command.

"Earth's moon, one thousand kilometres from equator, dark side, just short of sunrise."

And they were there. The moon filled their view, craters and rocks clearly visible. Then a glow and the sun coming out from the edge of the moon. Automatic dampeners protected them from the unrestricted glare of the sun.

Chase gasped in awe.

"Saturn," Cayrol instructed the ship, "near rings, five hundred thousand kilometres, sun preceding edge."

Now they were above the rings, the sun exposing more and more detail of the huge particles that seemed to flow below, with Saturn in the background, its swirling surface filling the view.

They silently regarded Chase, respecting his emotional response.

Finally, he was able to speak. "Is it possible to view another inhabited planet?"

Cayrol gave the directions. The surface of this planet was mainly green foliage evenly punctuated by structures, some with humanoids on them, while various herbivores roamed the landscape.

"My home planet," explained Cayrol. "Like other species, we made initial errors. Our society now is organized and equitable. We build many of our homes and workspaces underground. Other native species are preserved and protected, as you can observe."

"Thank you, Cayrol. Must be something to show someone your home planet."

Cayrol nodded.

"Am I the first of my species to see other inhabited planets?"

"I believe so," said K4, "though you are not yet recorded as being the first."

Chase digested this, half-smiling.

"So now what?"

Delt resumed his administrator role.

"We need to discuss our plans and progress them. K4, meeting circle, please."

The external view dimmed as the chairs rearranged in a circle.

"Where would you like to start, Chase?"

"The big picture, Delt. Where are we with this threat from Tapar's sun?"

K4 replied on Delt's behalf.

"Such matters are not entirely certain; they can speed up or slow down. Our calculations are that life on Tapar will be destroyed soon, probably between twelve to eighteen months from now."

They all considered this.

"K4, what do we know of this species like mine?"

"Typical pre-industrial sapient species that has developed the wheel, iron, weapons and horticulture. Sophisticated cultural activities and religious beliefs. Where you will be going, there is a royal or feudal system. Periodic wars, but no major players at present, so relatively calm. The town you are negotiating with is large, really a city, on a river plain and is walled; its castle has long been the guardian of the mountain pass beside the river. The townspeople are traders and used to travellers, so you will not be out of place. We have some further information and detail available – no large amount – for you to look at."

Gargen added, "As they are medieval, no doubt they'll need iron to make steel tools and weapons. In the hold we have two tonnes of base iron in ingots for you to barter with. I have a sample you can show them."

"How do I mine the … the …?"

"Cramlimite. We will provide you with a locator that finds and grades the cramlimite before you mine it. The device resembles a medieval tool so it will not be a problem. You will need to negotiate the mining as part of the deal."

He added, "We had period clothing and accessories made for you."

"Thank you." Chase smiled approvingly at such efficiency.

"Do you wish to take your … your weapons?" (The word was obviously repugnant to Delt.) "They are unlike those the natives use, but you will be a foreigner there."

"Yes. Better to have them. How soon do we start?"

"We have one local day before the Wardens' scanner is out of range to detect us," said K4.

"We have little time to prepare you then," said Riian.

"When does scanning resume?" Chase asked K4.

"We do not have direct access to that information. All I can do is scan and leave before they return. Recent cycles were in the proximity of every six to seven days, like Earth."

"So I will be alone with no way of contacting you?"

"Sorry, Chase, that is so," said Delt. "A communicator would be sensed by the Warden probe. Your cramlimite detector will not be, and we can be back in an instant at our meeting point."

"Which is?"

K4 bought up a plan on the viewing wall, which showed a mountain ridge, a river, the large walled town, a castle and a forest. He indicated a location in a clearing about five kilometres from the town.

"We will drop you there," said Delt. "This area shown on the foothills near the river is where the cramlimite is. There's a fault line on it and a stream running through."

Chase studied the area Delt indicated, frowning.

"So if it all turns to custard, I get to the drop-off point and wait for you?"

There was some confusion amongst his listeners, until K4 explained.

"Another colloquialism. But yes, a reasonable assertion."

Chase continued to stare at the screen while they busied themselves with organizing food. A plate was put near him and a drink.

"Try this," said Cayrol.

The plate was laden with what passed for a bread roll, tomato, egg, carrot sticks and cold meat. He went for safety and tried the carrot. Yes, it *was* a carrot.

"Synthesized, of course," Cayrol confirmed, "but hopefully taste and nutrition are identical."

Chase nodded and went back to studying the plan on the screen. As he consumed his own food, he surreptitiously noted what his companions were eating. Delt, clearly a herbivore, was munching from a large bowl of grasses. Riian, the lizard, was eating something in lumps like white tofu, while Cayrol consumed raw meat, finely diced. Gargen was content with a selection of fruit and shoots.

The convention seemed to be to politely disregard what another was eating, with Cayrol definitely the odd one out.

A thought occurred to Chase.

"So who owns this ship and how does that work for you all?"

Delt stopped chewing; the others kept their eyes on their food.

"This ship was part of a developmental organization's research that we contributed to. Technically it still belongs to that organization, the Zalos Corporation, which is owned equally by us all and others."

"So ...?"

"They know we have it and arguably it could be for research, and as they are unable to communicate with us they have not been able to request its return. This does not sound good, but we feel our cause is justified."

"So what would happen if we're stopped by the Wardens?"

"We would be made to justify ourselves in front of a Warden council and our developmental organization over the use of Startrader."

"And me?"

"Returned to your planet as no one would believe your story anyhow."

"And this is what happens to me even if we are not stopped?"

"We would like to think Zalos Corporation can offer something of interest to you," said Gargen, "if that is what you wish."

"Even though I come from an immature society?"

Delt either missed or chose to ignore the jibe.

"Yes, it has happened before."

Chase's brain was now in full business mode.

"Okay, if I am to do this, I need an equal share in whatever valuables I gather, and membership of the Zalos Corporation. I do not want to go through all this without a say in the next corporate step."

Silently they consulted each other.

"I think that's fair," said Riian, and Gargen and Cayrol nodded in confirmation.

Delt was a little ruffled, but compliant.

"Let K4 record, in our presence, that Chase Robinson has equal shares to whatever valuables we obtain, and equal membership in the Zalos Corporation."

K4 said, "All in agreement say yes."

A chorus of assent.

"All not in agreement say no."

Silence.

"Welcome to the Zalos Corporation, Chase Robinson."

That had gone easier than Chase expected. Now, time to get to work.

"We have a day to get ready," he began …

Chapter 3

CHASE STOOD WAITING for the inside door to shut and the outside door to open.

"Don't abandon me here, K4."

"Acknowledged," said K4, surprising Chase. He hadn't realized he'd said it loud enough to be heard.

Chase stepped through the doorway and onto the ramp. He took a moment to survey the landscape – grassy fields and trees; uncannily similar to home. He could be back on Earth. Before stepping off the ramp he looked down at his feet. Better get this right: *One small step for a man …*

He was dressed now in fibre trousers, a linen shirt and a plain leather jacket, with matching boots. His sword hung in a scabbard from his belt and his bow was slung over one shoulder, with a quiver of arrows – as many as he could cram in – across his back. A leather satchel was looped over the other shoulder.

Now he really felt like Robin Hood! Mentally he reviewed what he needed and what he had to do. The cramlimite locator was safely tucked away in a wooden box you could fit in the palm of your hand. The box was carved and had direction arrows and an indicator concealed within the design. An iron ingot weighed down his bag.

He had spent his last hours on Startrader learning all he could about the planet, especially this region, and the locals. The impression he had formed was that Tapar was oddly like late medieval Europe.

Delt spoke behind him.

"Good luck, Chase Robinson."

The others added good wishes, and he thanked them gravely and bowed in farewell before descending the ramp and stepping onto another planet. He tilted his head, conscious of the tiny implant under the skin on his neck. The procedure to insert the language tool had been quick and painless. Cayrol applied a salve, and within hours the incision had healed completely. Perhaps he should keep it permanently; he might finally be able to understand Vixen and Bandit.

Chase knew the cart track he was following led to another and then directly to the town. He was determined to keep his mind on the job ahead, but was constantly distracted by the fact of being on another planet. A flock of yellow birds flew past him, chittering. The colours, smells, plants, trees and birds – all similar to Earth, but with slight differences, immediately noticeable to a country boy like Chase.

The mountain range was close. As Chase's track ran parallel to the foothills, it could have been anywhere in New Zealand – except for the types of trees.

Chase kept the map in his mind as he went on. There was movement through the trees and he stopped motionless. The trees formed a barrier from which he observed creatures who revealed themselves as bovine in shape, with long and powerful haunches. Shorter than his own domestic Friesians, they were brown with a copper-green hue to head and shoulders, and all had udders. So definitely female and mammal. Chase watched, fascinated, until he realized there was a bull moving amongst the herd. Time to go!

The trees were thinning out. As he walked, he was trailed by a swarm of miniature butterflies. A flying bug buzzed his head. Could he remember which insects on Tapar were safe and which likely to cause problems?

*

A scream came across a clearing and Chase turned quickly, his hand on his sword. A running figure that, as soon as he was spotted, angled towards him.

Alarmed, Chase swung his bag down from his shoulder and brought his bow around to his left hand. As the figure neared he could tell, though it was dressed like a man, that it was definitely female. The girl glanced back over her shoulder and at that exact moment what looked like a boar cannoned out of the trees. She shrieked again and ran harder, faster.

She was close enough now for him to see her face, and the auburn hair bouncing in a ponytail behind. Her eyes were wide with fright and she shouted as she ran.

"Help! Help! *Run!*"

The boar – if boar it was – was short-set and powerful, charcoal-grey in colour, with formidable tusks curling from under its jaw. Enraged and on the charge, it was closing fast.

Chase drew a solid broadhead from his quiver. Without taking his eyes off the boar he nocked the arrow and, turning to balance himself, drew back. On the broad chest of the boar he visualized the blue spot on his training bale. He drew in a breath and opened his fingers to release the arrow. His view then, almost slow motion, was of the arrow powering off and the girl turning back mid-run as it flashed past her towards the boar.

The arrow flew around one hundred and twenty-five paces to the target, dropping under the beast's jaw and smashing into its chest. Immediately the power went out of it, and the boar first staggered and then crashed face down into the rough grass, sliding along on its side. The legs pumped uselessly at the air and then it stilled.

Chase became aware that the girl had run past him without stopping and that he had another arrow nocked.

He stood taking deep breaths for a minute watching the beast, and then looked around. No one and nothing in sight. He put the arrow back in the quiver. Cautiously he approached the boar, much larger than he had thought, almost the size of a bull, but shorter, with immense cloven hoofs and a snout wider and more pronounced than on an 'Earth pig'. With some difficulty, Chase pulled out the arrow. There was a gush of blood. The beast stank. Chase wiped the arrow on the grass and slid it back with the others.

After one last look he turned and continued back past the place he had fired. No sign of the girl. Chase resumed his journey.

*

As he walked on steadily he began to see signs of habitation: smoke curling from the chimney stack of a house, stock mostly like the 'cows' he had already encountered, and smaller animals, some with hair to the ground, others with fur banded in horizontal stripes of black and blue.

The road was little more than a cart track, but level enough for easy pacing. Now there were more people about: two men loading firewood on a cart, a young lad herding stock. There were fields of crops neatly fenced, and gates that led into gardens planted with rows of vegetables, tended generally by old men or women. All wore clothes not unlike his own.

One or two glanced back at him, with only mild interest. When he passed a group of children playing on the road they looked no different from ordinary human boys and girls. Chase didn't know whether to be disappointed or relieved that he could blend in unobtrusively.

Then he reached the town wall, solidly built from the rough rock that came from the ridge. There were patches of moss and lichen on it, but smooth enough with no visible gaps. Impossible to climb. A castle, functional rather than picturesque, made the eastern edge of the wall. A keep could be seen inside the walls with two towers on the ends of its outermost wall, which was some fifty paces back, and overlooked the northern external town wall.

The walkway to the castle entrance crossed a deep ditch. Guards were on duty at the gate, men in uniforms with leather chest amour, swords at their belts and long halberds; two-handed pole weapons that combined a spearhead with a battle-axe in their hands. A man dressed in an elaborate uniform broke from addressing them and approached Chase as he neared the gate. He stopped a pace or two in front of Chase, tucked his ornate helmet under his left arm and placed his right fist over his heart.

"Greetings, stranger. I am Fruel. You are welcome and expected in our town. Your name, please?"

Chase bowed as politely as the man.

"Thank you, Fruel. I am Chase Robinson."

"Welcome, Chase Robinson."

He pronounced the name carefully.

"I am here to escort you into the castle. Please accompany me."

Chase nodded and obeyed, though he remained wary. Expected? And was this how they normally welcomed strangers?

Fruel led the way without further conversation. Chase had no sense of animosity; Fruel's formality was professional. Chase had always been good at reading people, an essential skill in business negotiations, and was confident he was not being misled.

The men walked into the town, where the two keep towers overlooked the wall, and on into a major square behind which was the wall of the castle with parapets. Chase was not an expert, but the castle appeared sturdy and well-designed. If the wall was breached, the castle and keep could still hold, and enemies inside the walls would be vulnerable to attack from above.

Around the square were houses and shops, two taverns, stables, a foundry and military quarters. Banners and hanging baskets of flowers lent a festive air, and the town dwellers were busy and jovial. Seemingly a celebration was in preparation as trestles, radiating out from the taverns, almost covered the entire square. Obviously crowds were anticipated.

Fruel guided Chase through the main entrance, into the castle interior, wide and open. Inside was a single large room, like a museum with exhibits; everything from manikins wearing leather armour to ploughs, stands with quilts on display, a loom, and all sorts of weapons. Through the far door was a smaller room, hung with tapestries. There were rows of seats down each side. Fruel exchanged salutes with two guards dressed almost as elaborately as he.

He turned to Chase.

"Please wait here, Chase Robinson, while I inform the King of your arrival."

He departed, and Chase was suddenly apprehensive. What? The King! There had been nothing in K4's information about protocol and neither had he anticipated a meeting with a monarch. Things were happening way too fast.

Chase was conscious of being under scrutiny from the two guards. Though they were not aggressive, they were alert. Weighing him up. He pretended to study a hunting scene on the nearest tapestry. The men depicted rode what appeared to be oversized goats, and were chasing a boar like the one Chase had killed. Two men came through a side door talking earnestly, and Chase had a quick glimpse of a corridor before they closed the door. They went out through another door and into another corridor.

Fruel returned.

"The King will see you now."

"Excuse me," said Chase quickly. "Before we go in, how do I address the King?"

Fruel smiled; clearly gratified that Chase wanted to be correct.

"*Sire* is our usual form of address," he said, "but in our State Sire is used as an honour, not just for royalty" and beckoned Chase to follow him through the guarded door.

The setting was again unexpected. The chamber was imposing and the walls decorated with countless paintings, many of them portraits. But there was no throne, no regal display.

Four guards stepped out from the left wall and grouped themselves around a semi-circular couch. Tables, chairs and other smaller couches faced this main couch. As Fruel and Chase drew near, the guards closed rank, eyeing Chase's bow and sword. Chase calmed his nerves with slow, deep breaths.

The crowd around the couch parted and revealed a central figure, a tall and wiry man in plain clothes of high quality. The King. He stood, as did an elegant woman in a long dress rich with embroidery, her upswept hair encircled by a band of gold. Two young women stood on the Queen's far side. One was the girl from the paddock, still dressed in her boy's outfit, whispering to the other, who was similarly attired to the Queen. This second girl's hair was unbound and redder than the first. Both girls were in their early to mid-twenties – older than Chase's first assessment. They were enough like the Queen for him to identify them as Princesses …

Uh oh!

He became aware that while he was studying the girls, the King was studying him. The courtiers, too, were silently focused on the tall stranger in their midst.

Fruel halted and gestured to Chase. He bowed to the royals and Chase followed suit.

"Sire, I present Chase Robinson. Chase Robinson, his Majesty King Sulliman and her Majesty Queen Rebekka."

Both the royals tilted their heads in acknowledgement. Not being sure what to do, Chase gave a small bow to them individually. The King chuckled.

"Nicely formal, Fruel, but we owe this man a debt of thanks. Let us not cause him any discomfort."

He stepped forward and approached Chase. Despite the amiability of the King, the guards and Fruel remained watchful. The King put out his hand and Chase stepped forward and extended his own for a firm handshake, with a grip around each other's wrist. The King, a handspan shorter than his visitor gazed directly into Chase's eyes.

Chase had an immediate sense that he was in the presence of a man both intelligent and capable.

"Welcome to Staal, Chase Robinson."

"Thank you, Sire. I am pleased to be here."

The King nodded, approving the straightforward reply.

"I understand you have already met a daughter of mine," he said, with a chuckle.

"For an extremely brief moment, Sire."

A round of laughter reverberated through the chamber and Chase risked another glimpse at the girls. The auburn-haired girl grimaced in embarrassment, while her sister hugged her and giggled.

"Indeed," said the King. "She tells me she enraged a bull boar and ran past you in full flight."

Chase nodded again.

"She also told me you killed it with a single bowshot from at least one hundred and thirty paces."

The King was serious now, and his eyes fixed again on Chase's.

"I was lucky, Sire, and I doubt it was that far."

The Queen whispered audibly, "And modest, too, husband."

"I don't rely too much on luck, Chase Robinson. But I forget myself. Please allow me to introduce my children. My son Raul."

A man in his late twenties, the image of his father, stepped forward to grasp Chase's hand as his father had done, and like his father, looked Chase in the eye.

"His wife, the Princess Laura."

A petite, dark-haired girl curtsied and again Chase bowed.

"My daughter, Princess Sonja."

The flame-haired woman, now identified as the older of the two girls, smiled and curtsied. As Chase bowed in return, he realized how beautiful she was. Similar in look to her sister, with a paler complexion and sparkling green eyes. Intelligent, observant and clearly enjoying the situation, Sonja was as graceful and elegant as her mother.

"The Princess Carolie."

She strode up to Chase. She was equally appealing, her eyes blue and her skin creamy. The tips of her ears showed through her auburn hair, damp curls of which clung to her wide forehead. Her mouth was curved in a mischievous smile. Still flushed and dishevelled from her run, the Princess Carolie moved like a dancer.

She held out her hand, male style, earning a "Tsk! Tsk!" from her mother. Fruel was shocked, but the King merely shook his head and smiled. Chase didn't hesitate. Etiquette or not, he took her hand and grasped it. She, too, had her father's habit of the direct gaze and Chase's heart began to race. For a few seconds both of them forgot to let go, then Chase resolved the moment, courteously withdrawing his hand and bowing.

"I am honoured I was there to help, Princess. I am not sure it would have caught you anyhow. You run extremely fast."

Some chuckles around the group and Carolie smiled, but before she could speak her brother intervened.

"No, it would definitely have caught her, Chase Robinson. Bull boars do not stop and are killers. And if you put an arrow in the beast, without killing it, as my sister did, that would have enraged it further. My father is correct. We are indeed indebted to you."

Carolie was glaring at Raul, annoyed to be embarrassed

more and cut out of the conversation, and Chase shifted uncomfortably. Sonja stepped in to act as mediator, obviously an accustomed role.

"We are holding our summer festival over the next two days. My sister was wont to supply a boar for the feast, and surprisingly missed."

Sonja spoke in a low tone for a woman, her voice warm and comforting. Carolie's voice, by contrast, was husky and musical.

"The beast was enormous. The biggest I have seen off the mountains this many a year."

Raul raised his eyebrows.

"Then perhaps we should collect it for roasting," he said to his father, who nodded. Raul turned to Chase.

"Your kill to claim, but might we use it for our celebrations?"

Chase nodded. "Of course."

Not sure that it was his to give … Raul gestured to a guard who, nodded, bowed and departed.

The King then introduced the other townsfolk present. Four of them were guildmasters, and had obviously been discussing the menu. One represented the Bakers' Guild, another the brewers, the third the meat farmers, and the fourth the agriculturalists.

The King said, "I need to decide how to thank you for your timely intervention, Chase Robinson. However, we are busy with arrangements for today's festivities. May I ask you to excuse me?"

Chase bowed again. He was getting the hang of it.

"Sire."

Fruel and Raul bowed to the King and stepped back with Chase. The guildmasters huddled back around the

King. Queen Rebekka excused herself briefly to her husband and joined Chase.

He saw where the girls had inherited their height and beauty. She gestured to a couch and settled beside him.

"So where do you hail from, Chase Robinson?"

Perhaps later he could request that this gracious lady call him Chase. He followed the story line laid down in the ship.

"I am from a country on the other side of the south sea."

He was not a man who relished lying, but his story was accepted at face value. The Queen regarded him intently as her daughters moved closer.

"And what fortune brings you to us, Chase Robinson?"

"I am a trader. I am here to make a deal, if I can, with the appropriate person, about acquiring a local resource."

She arched delicate eyebrows. He added hastily, "Nothing serious or large scale; stone from your local mountains."

"My husband would be the man to talk to in the first instance."

She glanced over to where the King was deep in conversation with the guildmasters and others around an oval table.

"Your business must wait. Today is extremely busy for us all."

"I should take my leave, ma'am."

"No, no. I did not mean for you to go. You have made this day a double celebration instead of a tragedy."

Sonja clasped her sister's hand more tightly.

"We mean to be excellent hosts," the Queen continued. "Do you have lodgings in our town?"

"No, my lady." He borrowed the term from so many

books and movies. "Fruel met me at the gate."

She seemed to be evaluating him.

"Then you must stay in our guest quarters until we find somewhere more suitable for you."

"Thank you. I am grateful."

Chase inclined his head. The Queen beckoned, and Fruel materialized. Was he the Royal Chamberlain, too?

"Will you escort Chase Robinson to our guest quarters and ascertain whether he has all he needs?" the Queen instructed. She turned again to Chase, smiling.

"Now if you will excuse me. Come, daughters, we have much to do."

The Princesses took a last look at Chase before following their mother out of the room.

"Chase Robinson, if you will follow me," said Fruel.

Strangely exhausted, Chase was glad to obey.

Chapter 4

HIS ROOM was as he would have imagined, unlike most of the castle that Chase had been shown so far. He was enclosed by stone walls, and the floor and ceiling were of solid wood. Massive beams supported the ceiling and the bed was solid, with a thick mattress stuffed with down. On a sturdy table a ceramic bowl had been set, the matching pitcher filled with hot water for washing, and a huckaback towel draped over the chair. The room was lit by fat candles by the bed and on the table. All was tidy and clean.

In the corridor, Fruel had discreetly indicated a separate room furnished with a plank bench with a hole cut in and another pitcher of water beside. A toilet!

Fruel, friendly and relaxed now rather than formal, asked him if there was anything else he required. There was not. Chase's polite behaviour at court had obviously put him in Fruel's good books.

"You're invited to dinner this evening in the town square," Fruel added. "You're to be guest of honour."

At which Chase frowned, worried. He did not want attention.

Fruel studied Chase carefully, misinterpreting his frown.

"Er … I know you have been travelling. Perhaps you did not pack formal attire?"

Chase murmured agreement.

"If you so desire I will have something sent to you for tonight."

"I would be grateful."

Chase had no wish to appear under-dressed if he was to

be the centre of attention, and Fruel was only too happy to be of service to a man who had saved the Princess Carolie. He departed.

Alone and unobserved, Chase chuckled aloud. He was in a real castle, the guest of a King and Queen! He imagined the talk he could present at the next Chamber of Commerce meeting. So far international business had not included reception by royalty. Things had moved fast. Already he had found who to talk to about the cramlimite, and the King seemed a reasonable man.

Chase unstrung his bow and hung it on one of the row of hooks on the wall with the quiver beside it on another. In the town square below, stalls had been set up, and queues were forming outside the taverns, He decided to go for a stroll. He had always liked markets.

He decided his bag and other possessions were safe enough in his room. Should he hide the cramlimite detector? No, the box was innocent enough and Chase suspected that if anything were to be stolen from him, the King and Queen would not be happy.

He did note how things were placed before he left, however, so he could tell if anything had been moved.

Outside in the square he blinked in the sunlight. He considered his best idea would be to walk around the town in a circular route and hopefully end up where he had started. The crowds were building up, and Chase realized many of them must be from the surrounding villages and farms, dressed up to celebrate.

The stalls sold a variety of goods: dress materials and ready-made clothing, trinkets, cheap jewellery and carvings, other practical items like bowls, brooms and scrubbing brushes, and workmen's tools. There was good stitched leatherwork, including harnesses and saddles. Sweets and fruits and steaming bowls of food made him realize how hungry he was. Buskers and jesters and acrobats performed for coins thrown into the hats in front of them, and like stallholders everywhere the sellers loudly hawked their wares.

Chase was disconcerted by the constant and curious stares. One obvious reason, besides the fact he was a stranger, was his height. He realized now that the King was above average height and that Chase stood over a handspan higher than the men he had seen so far. Damn. He was also carrying his sword and few others did besides the guards. A tall man with a sword. No wonder he was attracting attention. Best to keep moving. Especially as he was being followed by two men who didn't bother to hide the fact. He stopped to inspect some rings while he thought about it, towering over the nervous stallholder, when one of the men stepped forward.

"I am under instruction to purchase anything you desire, my lord." He clinked coins in a bag. "May I do that now?"

My lord? Chase was taken aback. So they were guards. Minders, not spies or robbers.

"Oh, no, thank you. I'm just looking."

The man nodded and stepped away. Chase turned away and the stallholder was obviously relieved, despite losing a sale.

As Chase sauntered on, he realized he was enjoying himself. He was an actor in a costume drama, except it was real, it was actually happening. And not on Earth, not with his own species. He strolled past a bar where – no surprise – most of the patrons were male. Mostly workers from the fields by the look of them, and drinking beer, presumably, from steins. A few were already drunk …

He wouldn't mind a drink himself; to sample the local brew. His minders had already anticipated him.

"Our local ale is excellent, my lord. Will you try a mug?"

"Only if you both join me."

The men glanced at each other, grinning.

"Only if you insist."

"Then I insist."

The man who had first spoken to him went off to order a round, while Chase and the other found the corner of a bar leaner.

"Chase."

He held out his hand. The guard hesitated only momentarily before he gripped Chase's wrist.

"Went."

"You've got a good job today."

"Yeah. I'm not usually this lucky."

The two men sized each other up. Went was burly and bearded, with a friendly manner.

"So are you a full-time guard?"

He might as well learn a little here.

"No, my lord."

"Chase, please."

"Ah – Chase. I'm a part-timer. We only have around twenty-five full-timers and the rest of us do different hours depending on our levels."

"Levels?"

"Yes. I'm on Level Two, one week in every a month. Level Three is one week every two months and Level Four is on call."

The other guard returned and deposited three steins in

front of them.

"Chase."

Again Chase held out his hand. Again the pause before the man grasped wrists.

"Raymol."

"Raymol is full-time. Level One."

They all drank.

"Not bad," said Chase. The men grinned and nodded. "Good, actually."

Went resumed the conversation. Chase couldn't help noticing Raymol was uneasy with the subject.

"So where are you from, Chase?"

Chase repeated the story he'd told the King. He wasn't worried about revealing he was after rock; it would have to come out in due course.

"What kind of rock?"

"A special rock. I've been told it can be found near here."

"Special how?"

"We add it to make metals we find useful."

"Oh. So are you a lord?" Went asked.

"I don't think so, Went."

"But you have a sword and that bow. You speak like a lord."

"Do I? That's how we all speak where I come from."

The men relaxed, and Raymol leaned forward.

"I hear that you dropped a bull boar with one arrow from one hundred and fifty paces."

Chase laughed out loud. Chinese whispers!

"A lucky shot and probably no more than one hundred paces."

"That's still great going," said Went. "Who made your

bow, Chase?"

"A famous bow maker in my home town."

"How far can you shoot?"

"I'm reasonably accurate up to about one hundred and fifty paces."

"Gods. So you did make that shot!"

"Probably not."

He laughed again and the two men joined in. Chase noticed they were being watched.

"So you take turns at being guards? Not a bad idea. What are your duties?"

"Mainly historical," Raymol replied, "from when the provinces warred. We keep the peace and settle disputes. We patrol the countryside to deter bandits and we guard the mountain passes."

"Mountain passes ... Who are you guarding them from?"

"Mainly the Varden on the other side of the ranges. They used to raid us whenever they wanted, take what they could. A little over two hundred years ago the King's ancestors united us and trained the guards to repel the raids. We built the castle and the town. Things have been good and we prosper, but we still have to see them off every so often."

"Ah, that's why you have reserves ... Levels on rotation."

"That's right. We have around one thousand Levels across the State."

Chase drained his own stein. He spoke carefully, not wanting to offend the men.

"Your King seems a reasonable man. The castle isn't ostentatious ..."

Both men frowned.

"Er – is plain and simple."

"We're a plain and simple people. That's why we thought you were a lord."

Went gathered up all three steins in one hand and held out the other to Raymol for coins. He headed for the bar.

"Hardworking, too," continued Chase.

"Yes, indeed. King Sulliman and Queen Rebekka are our royalty, but act along with the Town Council, which the King heads. All of them have other functions besides their formal duties; mainly to do with trading with other states. Gardal couldn't afford any other kind of royal family."

"Gardal is the state?"

"Yes. So how does your state work, Chase?"

"As a democracy. Leaders get selected by regions on majority vote and we pay them to represent us. They belong to parties – groups of like-minded thinkers and doers, so they act in conjunction with each other and the party ideologies."

"Sounds complex and costly," commented Raymol.

"Oh, it is," Chase grinned. "And probably not perfect, but what system is?"

"What we have seems to work, and I am not sure we would adapt easily to any other system."

"Then you should stay with what you've got."

"I'll drink to that."

"Me, too," said Went, returning with the refills. "Whatever it is."

The ale was strong and Chase still hadn't eaten, so he called a halt after two, despite Went's best efforts to persuade him otherwise. He headed back to the castle, not wanting to be late for the evening's celebration.

In his room clothes had been laid out on the bed for him. Leather trousers, soft and supple, that fitted him perfectly. A cotton shirt with vines embroidered across the shoulders and a vest to match his trousers. A black cloak of some warm and heavy material. A small sword or long dagger in a sheath fitted neatly under his arm. If he had been Robin Hood before, he was Aragorn now. As he had seen few men wearing swords, he hung his own back on the hook.

Before he left the room, he checked his bag. Nothing had been disturbed.

*

As Chase walked out of the castle, Fruel appeared from nowhere and signalled for him to follow, leading him through the crowd to where the King and Queen were in the town square. Several bands were playing different music at different locations.

"Thank you for the outfit, Fruel. How did you get the sizing so exact?"

Fruel tapped his own nose.

"Ah, we all have our talents, my lord."

"True," said Chase, laughing. "I am in your debt."

Fruel was gratified and Chase knew he had made an ally.

Fruel stopped not far from the King and his entourage and waited. Before long the Queen noticed them – Chase was hard to miss – and glided over to relieve Fruel of his responsibility.

"You are having quite an effect on our town," she murmured, linking her arm with his.

"Me?"

His surprise was genuine.

"A tall, handsome stranger walking through town. A

hero who rescued a Princess. You certainly set tongues wagging. So many questions for me to answer!"

She laughed at his concern.

"Don't worry. No one will be able to get to you past my daughters."

She smiled again at his confusion, but said nothing more because they had reached the King. Sulliman held a full stein and wore a fur-lined cloak befitting his status. The outline of a bird of prey was embroidered on it, a bird not unlike a bald eagle. He was talking animatedly, but broke off when he saw Chase.

"Ah, you got him, my dear. Well done."

He surveyed Chase's finery.

"Fruel?" he enquired.

Chase nodded and pursed his lips. The King smiled with understanding.

"He certainly has his uses. Welcome again, Chase Robinson. I am sorry I had to end our meeting earlier. Any other day but today I could have welcomed you in the manner you deserve. Tell me now. How may I reward you?"

"Sire, I was lucky to be in the right place at the right time and to stop the beast. I am only grateful I was there and it turned out well for all of us. I require no reward."

The King said nothing, subjecting Chase to a close scrutiny. The Queen, too, was silent and observant beside him. Finally King Sulliman spoke again.

"I believe you, Chase Robinson You are sincere. It seems you are an honourable man."

His eyes crinkled with his ready smile.

"However, in Gardal it is our custom to reward our heroes. Let me give you a lesson in kingship. This is our midsummer festival, one of the events of the year. Our people are happy, and we have the chance to make them happier."

He winked.

"Acknowledging a hero will do that and makes the royals look good too."

Chase turned to the Queen.

"Madam, could my reward be an ale with the King?"

She shook her head, smiling, and the King's laughter boomed out.

"That's not exactly what I had in mind," said his Majesty, "but I'd like that too!"

He clapped Chase on the shoulder and signalled for a refill. When the steins arrived, the two men clinked them together and drank.

"Have you seen your kill?" asked Sulliman.

"Kill? Oh, you mean the boar."

"Here."

The King steered Chase through the crowd, who parted to let them through, until they came to a roast the size of a small bull turning slowly on a spit.

"Your kill, Chase Robinson. My men say you shot it at one hundred and seventy paces."

"No way!"

Chase laughed, too, but as he stared at the roast, he wondered what would have happened if he had missed. He hadn't, and he put the thought aside.

"That makes the meat even more special, doesn't it?" said the King, leaning towards Chase. "They'll all be eager for a slice of the hero's bull boar."

They watched while they sipped their beer. Two men turned the spit together, one at each end, while another basted it with liquid. A fourth man tended the fire, keeping the flames on the outer edge, the glowing hot embers under the meat. When the flames dropped, the embers were raked under and more wood added on the edges.

Prince Raul joined them, transferring his stein to his left hand so he could offer the right hand to Chase.

"Did you have a pleasant afternoon wandering around our town?" he asked.

"I certainly did, thank you. So many stalls, and the town looking great."

"Be sure to tell my sisters. I believe they had much to do with that."

The King interrupted.

"Time to make my speech. Follow me, gentlemen."

He led them to a raised platform not far from the roast. King Sulliman faced the crowd with his Queen and their son beside him. The Princesses were there too, enchanting apparitions in full-length gowns with elaborate stitching of grapes and fruit. Sonja's emerald green highlighted the rich colour of her hair and Carolie's blue silk darkened her eyes to sapphire. Laura, standing beside Raul, was in a burgundy satin that set off her fine features and dark complexion.

Chase couldn't help staring at the King's daughters, who calmly looked him up and down and curtsied. A number of town dignitaries stepped up on the platform and ranged themselves behind the King.

And Fruel materialized by Chase in his usual fashion.

A signal, and the bands stopped playing. The crowd was quiet, if not silent.

King Sulliman was clearly accustomed to public speaking. He started by welcoming them all, and then listed the state's accomplishments over the last year: the good crops, the steady rise in stock numbers, a new bakery, a clothing manufactory, and so on. The crowd cheered every item he listed.

He wound up by complimenting the brewery on this year's ale, which got the loudest cheer. He then thanked the guards at all Levels. Without them, he said, Gardal would not be the safe, prosperous state it was today. He asked the crowd to drink to the guards and they cheerfully obeyed.

He invited a couple of the town councillors to speak briefly on their own work, and singled out various individuals for thanks and awards. These were handed out by the Queen and the councillors – to apprentices who had finished training, guards or civil servants who had earned promotions; others who had excelled. The presentations were quick and efficient so as to retain the crowd's attention.

As he neared the end King Sulliman stepped forward again.

"Tonight," he said, "I have a special award to announce, something that doesn't happen often. A very special award for a very special act that happened only this morning."

Chase wanted to slink away, but Fruel grasped his arm.

The King described the scene. A Princess being chased by the largest bull boar seen in the State of Gardal for many a year. The bowman who dropped it in its tracks from one hundred and eighty paces with a single shot through the heart. A bowman who wanted no reward other than ale with the King! The crowd cheered and whistled.

"Chase Robinson," King Sulliman ordered. "Please come up on the platform."

Chase, red-faced, did so to a repeat of the cheers and

whistles. The Royal Family grinned at his discomfort and the King pinned a medal on his cloak, grasped his hand, and allowed Chase to make his escape off the stage.

With the formal part of the evening wound up the King and his retinue left the stage, which was quickly taken over by a band.

Husband and wife were smiling.

"I think that went well, my dear," said the King. "Don't you?"

She squeezed his hand.

"I do."

All the others congratulated Chase, not allowing his embarrassment to fade. The Princesses attempted to remain dignified, but their giggling ruined the façade. Raul and Laura seemed to enjoy the moment. A number of the councillors looked at Chase with interest as they grasped his wrist in congratulation.

Chase turned the medal to inspect it more closely. A bird of prey, a replica of the design on King Sulliman's cloak.

"Thank you, Sire," he said over the crowd.

The King raised the stein that had materialized in his hand and nodded his reply.

"Now, everyone." The Queen was obviously a practiced organizer. "We all have mingling and congratulating to do."

She sorted them into teams: the King and Fruel, herself and the baker, Carolie and the plump woman who seemed to be in charge of the alehouses and hotels, Sonja and Laura with a guildmaster each, and Raul and Chase.

"Try to keep moving and try to congratulate everyone who got an award. The alehouses will get merry fast," – she smiled apologetically at the alehouse lady – "so get to them first."

She eyed Raul and the King, who immediately assumed an air of innocence.

"You don't have to drink to everyone. Chase, don't let Raul lead you astray."

Chase couldn't help chuckling as they split up obediently.

"I hope this won't be too arduous for you," said Raul.

"I'll be fine, glad to do my part." He glanced at Raul. "Bit embarrassing though!"

"Ah, well. My father knows how to keep our people happy and working together. I have spent my entire life learning from him."

"Then you will be a good King, too."

Now it was Raul's turn to colour up. He recovered with a grin.

"Shall we make a wager on how far your shot gets by the end of the night?"

He drank while Chase laughed.

"I reckon it will be two hundred and twenty to two hundred and thirty paces," said Raul after some thought.

"You're on. I don't think it will get past two hundred."

They clinked steins to seal the deal.

"Like taking candy from a baby," chuckled Raul.

A friendship had begun.

Chapter 5

THE NIGHT WENT WELL and Chase was soon accustomed to accepting compliments, evaluating responses and being, for now, the focus of all eyes. Raul and he developed a good working relationship, politely refusing drinks, saying enough without getting caught up with any guests too long. Raul would briefly describe the next in line, if they should be congratulated for awards and when to move on, especially when steins were low.

Then a steward appeared.

"Dinner is ready, my lords."

Raul and Chase followed him to the high table – and were very ready to do so. By now Chase was ravenous, but a little apprehensive when he was directed to a seat beside the King, whose Queen sat on his Majesty's other side. He did pause long enough to indicate Raul should take the offered place, but Raul laughed and pushed him down, turning to his wife and settling her first before sitting next to Chase.

The Princesses were seated opposite him. Sonja raised her glass of wine and Carolie smiled.

"How has your day been going?" she asked.

"Interesting." Chase was deliberately cryptic. "May I say what good work you did to make the town so festive?"

That made both women smile.

The guests were served with a true medieval feast. Wild boar and other meats; roasted root vegetables that compared well with those grown in Chase's own garden; bowls of fruit and baked custards and pastries. He tried not to gobble it down too fast, and to enjoy the family conversations going on around him. He soon forgot their titles, savouring the relaxed and jovial mood, enjoying his novel situation.

The Princesses had him under a non-stop question attack, from which he was rescued in turn by Sulliman, Rebekka, Raul and Laura. The two young women were witty and smart, and conversation was easy and natural between them. Chase was hard-put to work out which he liked more, Sonja or Carolie. Not that it mattered …

Then Raul turned to him and said, "Time for me to collect."

He beckoned to a steward serving drinks.

"Tell me, Rupit, how far away from Chase Robinson was the bull boar when he shot it?"

"Why, Sire," the man replied, "I heard that it was two hundred and thirty paces, but I am told he is a modest man, so it was probably …

The table erupted into howls of laughter, and Chase shook his head slowly.

"Unbelievable! Okay, Raul, what do I owe you?"

"An open bet with my son?" exclaimed Sulliman "I thought you were smarter than that!"

"Apparently not," said Chase sadly, to more laughter.

The next few hours were some of the best of Chase's life. He was at ease with this family, and the Princesses were captivating. Both could make his heart race and that was a worry. He had to remember he was only here to save these people.

*

The morning after was bright and clear; too bright and clear for Chase, whose head ached from the ale. He forced himself to get up for the day's training, stringing his bow and tying on his sword. Down at the stables he asked if he could borrow a sack and some hay to stuff it with.

"I will be putting holes in the sack. Is that all right?"

The two grooms shrugged and grinned.

"Only if we can watch."

Chase walked out through the gates and across the nearest field. Under the trees at the far side he started his training, kneeling in meditation before he went through his patterns until the beer was sweated from his system. Then he set up the sack, bulging with hay, and tied it to a branch to go through his sets of eighty-five and one hundred and fifty paces. He was aware first of the children watching, and by the time he was ready to use the bow a sizable crowd had collected. He needed the practice so he continued, trying to ignore the Ohs and Ahs, and the applause at the end.

Self-consciously, he stalked back towards the castle, with a swarm of kids around him. Some asked questions and when Chase replied they all drew nearer. He saw Raul coming towards him across the field. When the Prince neared, he told the children, "Go on now! You can watch again tomorrow."

"Good morning, Chase. My father would like to see you now."

Though the day before had gone well, Chase still felt as if he'd been summoned by the principal. The two men walked back together.

"How's the head?" Chase enquired.

"I can still hear the drums from those bands," confessed Raul. "Yours?"

"Everything was too bright this morning, better after

sweating some of it out though …"

They both chuckled.

"Good night though."

"It certainly was." Raul pointed at Chase's sword and bow. "I've never seen weapons like those before."

"I'll show them to you when we're out of public view."

He saw a flutter of colour on the castle wall. Carolie and Sonja were watching.

Chase and Raul walked into the King's meeting chamber, the guards opening each door as they approached. The King and others were at a table set with food.

"Morning, gentlemen. Have you had breakfast?"

"I might risk it," Raul said, and Chase shook his head.

"Not yet, Sire."

The steward left the room and the King indicated adjacent seats.

"Chase," began the King, "this man beside me is Amstraad, the chief stonemason."

Chase and Amstraad exchanged handshakes. The stonemason's hands were as rough as the stone he worked with, and his body was stocky and powerful.

"Amstraad keeps our walls strong, and the castle and housing stonework in good order. We use mainly stone in Staal."

Naming the town was unusual. Chase had noticed they usually preferred to talk of 'the State'. The King laid down his fork.

"Now, yesterday when the Queen asked you what your purpose was here, you told us you wanted to trade stone from our mountains."

"Yes, Sire. You have some stone, next to a stream, which

comes down from the ranges nearby, that I'd like to trade for. Our metallurgists say it would be useful to them, and we suggest we could exchange some for iron for your smithy."

"How much of this rock do you want?"

Well-prepared by K4 on the Startrader, Chase replied promptly.

"Two cartloads would be sufficient."

"Our smithy would need to see a sample of the iron."

"I have it in my bag, in my room, Sire. Do you wish to examine it?"

The conversation was interrupted as the steward returned, laden with a tray of food. He set it down before Raul and Chase.

"No, no. Breakfast first. If you could take it down to Meadl, our head smithy. Raul, will you introduce them?"

"Yes, Father."

"And Meadl will tell me of its value."

The King and Amstraad exchanged a shrewd glance before Sulliman pushed his plate away.

"And how do you propose to mine this rock and transport it?"

"That would have to be part of the arrangement, Sire."

The King turned to the stonemason, respecting his status.

"That would depend on you, Amstraad. Are you able to help with this?"

Amstraad stroked his beard while he pondered.

"I could have three or four men available in a few days if it was made worth my while," said Amstraad pointedly.

"I could make sure the smithy has extra iron for making tools."

Amstraad nodded. Both men knew a deal was being brokered.

"Good," said the King. "We will talk of this more later."

"With your leave, Sire."

Amstraad departed and the King turned his attention to Chase and Raul as they tackled their food.

"Chase, I understand you practiced with your weapons this morning."

News travelled fast here.

"Yes, Sire. I had to clear my body of some of the ale I drank last night."

The King laughed.

"You had an audience, I am told."

"I did. I have promised to show my sword and bow to Raul, Sire. Would you like to see them, too?"

"I would."

Putting aside his knife and fork, Chase demonstrated the recurve bow. Simple, so it could have come from their own time, but the material it was made from was lacquered. Chase covered that as best he could by describing it as a special type of paint from his homeland. Both Sulliman and Raul had a go at drawing the bow.

"Chase," said Raul as he handed it back, "you must be stronger than you look."

They laughed, and Raul gave Chase a friendly pat on the back and turned to the King, his eyebrow raised expectantly. Both men nodded. Sulliman spoke first.

"Chase, we have no great bow marksmen at the moment in the state. Could I impose on you to do some training of a few men while you're here?"

Clearly the King had a need to ask, and thought he could – he did it so readily. Chase bowed.

"I would be happy to, Sire. There should be time before Amstraad's men are available."

King Sulliman half-smiled, as if acknowledging that Amstraad would keep them waiting. Usual business practice, after all.

Now Chase drew out the katana. Both men marvelled at its grace and the keen sharpness of the blade.

"Would it stand up to a broadsword?" Raul murmured.

Chase merely shrugged, even knowing that it would. The less attention they paid to it the better.

*

After breakfast, he picked up the bag with the iron ingot and headed out with Raul to the foundry. Chase shook hands with Meadl the smith, a bald man with arms that bulged unnaturally with muscles.

When Chase pulled out the ingot, his eyes lit up. Chase smiled inwardly. 'Advantage me,' he thought.

Meadl took him on a tour of the foundry, which could have been a working museum back home. He thanked Meadl, and made no effort to reclaim the ingot. Chase knew he'd have had to prise it from Meadl's fingers. Unlikely he would succeed.

"We'll go to the guards' quarters now," said Raul. "Guard Major Boste is away for a few days. He's on duty with a patrol at the mountain pass barracks."

He told the corporal that Chase was a bowman from another state.

"The King asked if he'd like to meet your marksmen and compare notes."

Raul was as tactful as his father. The guards were enthused with the idea and began to make tentative arrangements. They tried to persuade Chase to compete in

70

the afternoon's archery contest, but he firmly declined.

Their errands completed, Chase and Raul wandered through the town, where the festivities continued. Various competitions were in progress: boxing and wrestling, weights and spear-throwing. And the archery competition.

Chase tried to keep in the background, but it was obvious the fame of his shot at the bull boar and the morning's shooting preceded him. Seemingly, it put off the competitors, because most shot badly and even the winning shots were unimpressive.

They continued on their way, and were shortly intercepted by Carolie and Sonja, who announced they were taking Chase on a tour of the clothing and material manufacturers. Raul's eyes sparkled with mischief, and he declined any attempt at rescue, excusing himself as the girls led Chase away.

If Chase had been able to concentrate, he might have found the details of the clothing and fabric manufacture interesting. But the women stood too close, gazed at him too intently, as the masters of each type of product explained and expounded. A few facts filtered through. Mainly they produced linen from the flax that grew so abundantly in the swampy areas on the plain where the river slowed.

Every sort of use had been made of the material: clothing, bed linen, and other household items, much of it decorated with elaborate stitching. The dressmakers and embroiderers smiled and nodded as Carolie and Sonja explained processes. None of them stopped or pricked themselves with the flashing needles in their hands.

Then they moved on to the wool products, the spinning and the weaving, and the cutting into clothes and blankets, all richly decorated, too. Then leather goods and even here the work seemed mainly done by women. Chase couldn't help but admire the quality of the work, especially the vests and waistcoats, and the outdoor jackets and coats. Sonja explained that Gardal traded most of the linen and leather goods with other states.

By the time the tour was over it was close to dinner time and the ladies suggested Chase meet them in the dining hall after they'd all changed. He went back to his room where he found hot water waiting in a ceramic bowl, with a rough huckaback flannel. He decided on a full strip-down wash, musing on the smells he had noticed when dealing with others, particularly the workers and guards. People didn't wash themselves or their clothes as much as on 21st century Earth, or at least where Chase lived. Already he was getting used to it.

Where was the Startrader? What would he do if they never came back for him? If they had an accident or were waylaid by the Wardens. He was tense as he dried himself. No, that was silly. They wanted the cramlimite; of course they would be waiting.

Fruel had put out another soft linen shirt for him. He would have to pay the man back somehow!

Down in the dining hall Raul waited with his father.

"So, Chase." The King was grinning. "How was your afternoon? I heard you went on a tour with the girls."

"Yes, Sire. Your son sold me out."

He raised an eyebrow at Raul, who snorted with laughter.

"Actually," Chase continued, "I am impressed. Good products of high quality. Must be to Gardal's trading advantage, I should think."

The King nodded.

"Yes. No one else has our quantity of linen and we do exceedingly well with the leather goods, too."

Queen Rebekka walked in with her daughters, the women chatting lightly together. As they approached, the men bowed and Chase followed suit, the girls smiling back as they assessed his garb and style. Dinner was a quieter occasion than the previous night, but the talk flowed easily with the women describing their purchases and the Queen questioning Chase on what he had seen that day.

The King leaned forward.

"Meadl the smith has been to see me. We'll talk tomorrow, Chase. Dinner is not the right time to do business. What are your plans for tomorrow?"

"Raul has organized a get-together with the guards and others – and I compliment him on his tact, Sire! We'll be 'comparing notes' on the use of the bow. And I'd like to check out where the rock that I'm after is, if I may."

"The guards suggested morning, before the wind gets up," said Raul.

"So we could walk up to the rock in the afternoon?"

"Walk? Don't you have prenner where you come from?"

"Prenner?" repeated Chase, realizing the saddles he had seen that day weren't for horses.

"Oh, this should be fun." Raul's smile was intentionally evil.

"Now, now," said the Queen, "you be careful with our guest."

"Oh, Mother ..."

She gave him a mother's look. Chase guessed he was in for a surprise tomorrow.

Chapter 6

CHASE WOKE EARLY from an unusual dream of men travelling in the mountains, each displaying a red stripe across their breastplate armour. A dream that troubled him.

*

When he met with Raul as agreed, both men had bows; Raul's shorter, but sturdy. In the paddock they collected the bags of hay, prepared and waiting. On the far side a group of twenty five to thirty men, mainly guards, stood ready, while children watched nearby.

Chase spent a good few hours with the men.

"I was taught to shoot a certain way," he began. "It might not be the best way for everyone, but it works for me and I'm happy to show you how I do it. Okay?"

A murmur of agreement and he stepped forward and took his stance, shooting a clutch of arrows accurately into a palm-sized target on a bale eighty-five paces away. The men were suitably impressed; none had done any near as well in the competition.

They set up other bales and took turns shooting, with Chase watching them keenly and giving advice. A couple of men improved almost immediately and began to help the others. When they finished all had aching arms, but marksmanship was notably better.

They crowded around Raul and Chase afterwards, requesting practice every morning. Chase needed to continue in his good relations with the locals and readily agreed.

"Will you need more arrows, lord?" one man asked.

"Yes, and, please, it's Chase."

Two of them asked to examine his bow.

"We want to try and make something similar."

Chase laughed. "Good luck with that!"

Raul touched his elbow.

"Time for lunch."

"I'm more than ready." Chase turned to the men. "Tomorrow then? Same time, same place."

After lunch, Raul took Chase down to the stable 'to meet the prenner'. The sight of them reminded him that, yes, he was on another planet. Prenner were the size of thoroughbred horses, but most closely resembled goats, probably mountain-bred, with nimble feet and powerful rumps. The prenner eyed him with suspicion; perhaps he smelt different to their usual riders.

Chase had grown up on a farm in a hilly part of the volcanic plateau. He knew how to ride horses and excelled at it, with a relaxed style and good balance. Once the grooms had saddled up the prenner and helped him mount, he was soon riding comfortably around, slightly to Raul's annoyance.

Chase had the cramlimite detector in his bag slung over his shoulder, with a hand pick and a long coil of rope. He wore his sword, and his bow and quiver were slung behind him. They were about to leave when the Princesses rode up on prenner.

"Are you ready?" called Carolie.

Both girls were dressed in leather trousers like the men. Raul made no answer, obviously not expecting them.

Taking the change in his stride, Chase simply said, "I think so. Shall we go?"

The riding party walked the prenner out of the gate and

along the wall. Chase was getting to know his mount and the different manner in which it moved. He was also considering how to use the cramlimite detector without raising suspicion. Best not to let them see it.

Staal was a walled town, well-sized for its time and fortified, with the river running below along its western edge. The town had been thoughtfully located on a glacial mound left by the last ice age, which afforded it protection and ensured that if the river flooded, the town was in no danger.

The walls facing the ranges were solid and built on an outcrop that added height and shielded the town from the prevailing wind. As they trotted past the end of the town wall, Chase studied it closely. The ground sloped away towards the plains and the ranges, and he saw clearly where the river emerged. The secondary stream was a few hundred paces further east, exactly where the map had shown the cramlimite fissure to be.

A sudden burst of laughter came from the Princesses. Apparently their mounts wanted to gallop down the slope, and Carolie and Sonja willingly allowed it, leaning low in the saddle as the beasts quickened their pace. Raul sped after them and Chase's mount wasn't to be left behind. Chase gripped with his thighs and kept his back straight, his hands low and his heels down.

The prenner's gait was totally unlike a horse's. In fact, it ran more like a rabbit with front legs picking a stable footing and back legs pumping together. The rocking motion was weird, but Chase soon got into the rhythm of it. He urged the prenner forward and soon closed on the others. These things were at least as fast as a horse.

They raced along a track that led straight to the range

with the river on their left. Raul and his sisters frequently glanced back to ensure Chase was still with them, with some surprise that he was. The prenner didn't seem to be built for endurance and began to slow. The four riders reined them in to a puffing walk and rode side by side.

"You kept up well," said Raul, a bit miffed. "I thought you had not ridden a prenner before?"

"We have something as large but different where I come from," Chase replied. "The gait is different, but once you learn balance you never forget."

"Do you come from somewhere a very long distance from here, Chase Robinson?"

The enquiry came from Carolie.

"Please, it's just Chase. A very long distance," he confirmed.

If only they knew how long. He decided to change the subject.

"From what I understand the rock I am after is in a fissure where the stream comes out."

He pointed. The valley and stream were closer now, the ground littered with rocks. Chase kept the conversation casual as they rode up to the ridge.

"How long have you and Laura been married, Raul?"

"Almost two years ..."

He was interrupted by Sonja and Carolie, who chorused "Babies, babies, babies! We want babies."

They dissolved into giggles, and Raul reddened. Sisters can be so mean.

"You're lucky," said Chase. "She's an extremely nice girl."

"Yes, she is; and the only daughter of the man who owns the largest bakery in Staal!"

"What?" Chase couldn't help smiling. "And she's so slim."

"I know. And they make the most wonderful cakes and fruit breads!"

"A really good catch then."

Raul nodded, laughing.

The ranges loomed over them and they turned right down a track running parallel to the mountains. A swarm of blue birds rose before them, but caused no reaction in the prenner. Chase watched their graceful flight and then turned, immediately realizing the girls had been watching him.

"Are *you* married, Chase?" asked Sonja.

"No."

The girls exchanged glances, but said nothing.

Raul raised an eyebrow.

"No one good enough?"

Chase considered this.

"No. Mainly because I'm working and travelling so much."

They rode on in silence, Chase absorbing the different sights and sounds of Tapar. Eventually they reached the rocks that bounded the stream rushing into the valley. Close up, they weren't rocks but boulders, many as big as cars or houses. Chase had in his mind where the fissure was; it would take a climb. He dismounted, and the others followed suit, tying the prenner to a low-branched tree.

Raul produced some round balls from his pocket and, flat-handed, fed one to each prenner.

"They're sweet-toothed beasts," he said to Chase. "These will keep them occupied for some time."

The prenner sucked happily as he spoke.

"I think the fissure is up there."

Chase indicated a broken outcrop on the other side of the stream, which was fast but shallow. He crossed it rock to rock, followed closely by Carolie, Raul and Sonja, who handled themselves with ease. He headed up the valley, eager to locate what was needed. The sensors must be good to identify a particular type of rock among the mass of boulders. Where was Startrader now?

With the others still behind him, Chase was able to take out the cramlimite detector and activate it. He pushed on two indistinct marks together as instructed and the device lit up. Seven parallel rows of five minuscule blue lights radiated from one edge of the box with a single light beneath. The rows would indicate direction if you pointed the detector straight at the cramlimite, and the number of lights showed how close you were. Four lights already. Good. He was close. If he turned the detector away, the far lights dropped in number.

The single light was a purity test; if that lit up, the cramlimite was good enough. Right now it was off. Chase kept climbing, checking direction carefully and making sure the detector wasn't seen. When he came to the base of a smooth steep slope, he pocketed the detector and waited for the others. If possible, he wanted to test the rock alone.

"It is up there." He indicated the slope. "How about I climb it and drop the rope so we can get up easier?"

The others nodded agreement and Chase started the climb. Carefully. No hospital here …

At the top and safely out of sight he used the detector again. He was close now. Chase walked along a bank with overhanging trees and a cliff face behind and above. The detector guided him to a crack in the cliff face less than a pace in width. The rock here was black and crumbly, metallic in appearance. The centre light flashed. Yes!

He went back to where the others waited below, faces tilted upwards.

"Found it!" he called.

He tied the rope around a convenient rock, testing its hold, and dropped the coil over. He gripped the rope tightly and yelled down.

"Anyone coming up?"

Someone already was – Carolie. No real surprise there! He helped her over the last few steps. Then a less confident Sonja, and lastly Raul, with a bag on his back.

"So let's see this precious rock of yours," he said.

Chase showed them where it was, and used the pick to fill his bag with samples. Raul watched, while the girls rested nearby. He examined the opening again. The seam of rock was clear, but there wasn't much in view. He could only hope they'd get enough. A chilling thought, when the future of this planet and its inhabitants depended upon it. He buckled the bag.

"Got what you want?"

"I think so."

"Good."

Raul opened his own bag to reveal breads and pastries and a bottle of wine.

"You've got your samples, and I brought along some from Laura's father."

"Well done," said Chase "Finally a use for you."

Raul's jaw dropped, and the girls burst out laughing. He took a playful swipe at Chase, and began to spread the goodies out on a flat boulder. The food was entirely delicious, and they took turns at swigging from the bottle.

"No class, brother!" Sonja shook her head. "You should have brought cups."

Content to bask in the sun, relieved that Chase had found what he was after, brother and sisters relaxed. Chase worried secretly about the amount of cramlimite present.

The conversation turned practical. How would Amstraad get the rock out? Raul was confident there would be no problem. His men were used to splitting rocks and could lower it down in baskets on pulleys.

"What are your plans once you have the rock, Chase?"

Sonja looked at him intently as she asked the question.

"We will cart it to where it will be picked up," he replied, "and I will return with the iron."

"I don't mean that business." She waved a dismissive hand. "I mean afterwards."

He realized all three of them were waiting for his reply.

"What we need this rock for is important. I need it to finish or try to finish what I have to do."

He paused.

"I haven't planned beyond that."

"What is so important, Chase?" said Raul.

Not being able to tell the truth was extremely difficult, but he knew he could not.

"I cannot tell you. I promised not to on my word of honour."

Chase hoped that would work for them.

He went on, "I can only assure you that it will not harm you at all. It will, in fact, be important for your future."

Had he said too much? Carolie regarded him, frowning.

"You are clearly from far away." She paused, and Raul and Sonja nodded at her to go on. "And you have some mystery about you. We can only trust you and hope that you are, as you appear to be, an honest man."

Chase was humbled by her words and answered solemnly, "I can assure you that I am. I am in your debt for what your family and town has done for me since I arrived, and I promise that whatever I do will be always for your good."

A long pause between the siblings before Sonja responded for all three.

"Then we trust you, Chase Robinson, and will help you all we can."

Chase was choked up, and couldn't speak. Here, picnicking on another planet, he knew he had found good friends.

Chapter 7

IN THE MORNING Chase awoke, disturbed again by the dream of men marching in armour in the mountains. He must consult with Raul and find out how to describe what he had seen without appearing like a warlock or a shaman.

*

After breakfast, the two men went off together to practice. Chase addressed the guards, who were waiting in the paddock.

"A good bowman – we say archer – from where I live once said there is no point firing two hundred arrows badly in practice. Better instead to do twenty perfectly. Today we will start with the best twenty each of you can do."

Chase made sure to give pointers to each man, and some shots were repeated two or three times. He also went through his sword practice, a little to the amusement of the guards.

At the end Raul approached him, grinning.

"We do swordplay practice in the guard barracks if you want to learn how to use that thing or borrow a real sword."

"Why not?" Chase was serious. "I'm showing you how to use a bow better. You can show me how to use a sword better."

Raul stared at him. "Seriously?

Chase laughed. "Seriously. Shall I drop by later?'

"Surely."

Back at the castle they met with the King.

"I've talked to Meadl who is happy with the quality of

the iron bar," said Sulliman.

Chase barely suppressed a smile. Who wouldn't be?

"Amstraad has confirmed that he can have four men available starting tomorrow," – he paused – "depending on what you're offering us."

Ah, so the trade begins.

"The difficulty we have is knowing how much of the rock we can get. It is in a narrow fissure and there may not be the amount we need."

"How much is enough?" asked the King.

"A cartload would have to be enough. Now, what I can offer …"

Chase considered the weight of ingots on Startrader.

"Equal the weight in ingots for what we get of rock, Sire. You decide how to share that between Meadl and Amstraad. Also the use of a cart for transport at the end. And some in exchange for cash now. I've incurred some debts."

This was a bargain and both men knew it. The King didn't pause long before putting out his hand.

"Deal?"

Chase shook his wrist, local style.

"Deal."

Things were progressing nicely.

*

At lunch, Chase made a point of praising their picnic goodies.

"Would you like to visit the bakeries this afternoon?" asked Laura.

Raul waved his hand warningly.

"Stop eating lunch now, Chase. Save yourself!"

He was introduced formally to Laura's mother and

father, a pleasant, hard-working couple, surprisingly shy but immensely proud of their daughter. Especially that she had married into the Royal Family. Both insisted on personally escorting the party through the bakery.

If this had been a working museum back home, it would have been hugely successful. The smells were seductive, and Chase got to taste an astonishing array of mouth-watering delights.

"How do you sweeten things?" Chase asked.

"We use cane grown in the south," Laura replied.

"Ah, sugar," said Chase and they all looked at him in amazement, not expecting him to know their sweetener.

"And this paste?"

"Made from nuts."

Before they departed, wrist clasps and hugs were exchanged, and a basket of sweet and savoury pastries handed over. This Chase and Raul decided to donate to the guards to preserve their own waistlines – a popular decision among the soldiers. In the gymnasium they donned protective gear for head, arms and chest, and selected practice staves.

Raul assumed Chase was in need of training.

"We will begin by practicing defensive blocks," he told him. "I will attack and you block, like this."

He demonstrated the outside V-blocks.

The two men moved a few paces apart. On signal, Raul moved in fast and struck hard at Chase's shoulder. Chase blocked and moved away and forward. He could have hit Raul, but didn't. They repeated the move a few more times before Raul said, "Are you ready for real?"

Chase nodded.

Raul attacked fast, but Chase deflected easily and

smacked Raul on the shoulder. He winced and rolled the joint.

"Right, then," he said and attacked again.

It was too easy for Chase. He continually evaded Raul and hit him frequently. He was fast, his footwork was good, and he had a longer reach. He had also decided that Raul was a little too cocky. Raul, frustrated, began to over-extend. Chase blocked and stepped past to swat down Raul's stave, bringing his own up to Raul's throat. Raul stood still.

"Thanks for the training, my friend. We should do this more often to improve. You are a good teacher!"

A round of chuckles and outright guffaws came from behind them. Raul and Chase turned. Half the guards were grouped in the doorway. When they saw the scowl on Raul's face, they exited rapidly. Raul stared down his nose at Chase, and Chase gave him an apologetic grin. Suddenly Raul laughed too.

"I agree, all except the bit about the good teacher! Maybe you can show me that practice thing you do in the mornings?"

Comrades again, they walked out. Raul rubbed his shoulder.

"Did you have to hit so bloody hard?"

*

That night at dinner there was much laughter at Raul's expense, noticeably from his wife and sisters. Showing his bruises earned him no sympathy, only additional giggles.

"A trader with exceptional weapon skills," observed the King. "You are a surprising man, Chase Robinson."

"No, Sire. And I do regret if I embarrassed your son before the guards." Chase turned to Raul. "That would never be my intention."

His obvious sincerity brought the laughter to an end. Raul was genuinely surprised.

"Oh, you did not embarrass me, my friend. I did that myself. They saw how swiftly you moved and how well you moved." He chuckled "I am as good as any of them. None of them wanted to be me!"

He reached out his hand and Chase shook it heartily. Yes, he had friends, and before he retired that night the King handed him a pouch heavy with coins.

"Down payment on the iron," said Sulliman.

"Thank you, Sire."

Chase was delighted. He had money!

*

That night the dream recurred and again he had forgotten to ask for advice. He made a promise.

Today!

His business deal came first. Amstraad awaited him downstairs, and Chase showed him a sample of the cramlimite he had taken.

"Doesn't look that special to me," the stonemason commented.

"I agree. Still, if that's what they want ..."

He shrugged and Amstraad nodded.

As he was going to miss breakfast, Chase begged a bag of food from the kitchen. He rejoined Amstraad and his work crew outside, all of them mounted on prenner, except for one man, who rode in a cart loaded with equipment and pulled by two more of the beasts.

Another prenner was waiting for Chase in the stables, saddled up. Chase added his own bag, and off they went. He was introduced to the other men, who seemed excited about being out of the town as well as about the project.

"I left a rope there as a marker," said Chase, and described the fissure. Amstraad barely looked at him, though he listened carefully enough.

"Might be hard to get this stuff out," he grumbled. "The surrounding rock might be too hard."

Chase didn't reply, simply nodded. From what the King had said, if anyone could get it, it would be Amstraad. Imagine if he knew how important it was!

They kept pace with the slow plod of the cart. Chase had a chance to think. He needed to get to Startrader to obtain the iron, be updated on the situation. Perhaps if he went back by himself, he could go by …

The sun flashed white for a second or two, making them shield their eyes, and then settled. The prenner skittered and the men paused, holding their mounts and looking at each other. Though Chase knew it must be the sun on its dangerous course, still he asked.

"What was that?"

"Don't know," said Amstraad, ahead. "Sun does that sometimes?"

"How often?"

"Once a luna. Used to be once a year."

They carried on, clearly uneasy. This confirmation of the Startrader crew's story was a small comfort but only made Chase more determined to succeed in his quest. He wanted to hear what Amstraad would think of the seam of rock.

It seemed to take forever to climb to where the cramlimite surfaced.

"This fissure might be a problem," Amstraad admitted, looking down inside it. "But we *can* break away the surrounding stone on this side to get access to some of your rock."

He hunkered down and started drawing diagrams on the ground. Chase watched for a while, but soon realized he wasn't needed and that it could be days before they were done. So he thanked Amstraad and departed.

He wanted to meet up with Startrader. He soon got his bearings and followed farm races and narrow tracks to the edge of the forest. In such good weather, the trek was enjoyable and he was riding an oversized goat on an alien planet …

When he eventually found the clearing he reined in the prenner and remained on its back, willing the door of the spacecraft to open. It didn't. He rode slowly across the clearing, expecting to touch an unseen barrier. He didn't. Startrader wasn't there.

Okay. So they could be in orbit waiting for him. He slid off the prenner, gave her a sweet and tethered her to a tree stump. He ate his bread and cheese, drank from his water bag. He lay down on the grass, head resting on his clasped hands, and watched a yellow spider-like creature spin a web. Little things were what reminded him most that he wasn't on Earth. Perhaps their sensors would tell them he was there and they'd come.

An hour or so later he had lost patience and was still alone. Should he leave a message? He had brought nothing to write on or with. And how would they know to look for it?

The sensible conclusion he came to, as he remounted his prenner, was that a Warden scanner was in the neighbourhood and Startrader forced to be elsewhere. What if they couldn't come back, ever? The sun strike earlier was still clear in his mind.

*

Raul declined further sword practice when Chase returned. Too sore apparently. He volunteered some of the guards instead.

"In the hope one of them gets you!" he said with feeling.

Chase smiled and took stance against the first man. The guards were experienced fighters and though initially he handled them easily in turn, as Chase tired he backpedalled more often, using space to avoid strikes and injury. He didn't escape altogether, ending up with some welts. Good training, he told them as he thanked them and left. They started comparing bruises.

*

Amstraad returned late and reported to Chase. They'd managed to breach the wall some, but had to proceed cautiously so as not to lose the cramlimite, or 'rock' as he called it.

"Thank you, Amstraad. May I buy you an ale?"

Amstraad considered this for a second.

"One, perhaps. I need to get home."

Over the ale, he went into detail of how he planned to weasel out the rock.

"It's like a narrow tube coming up to the surface. What we get in the fissure will be the majority, and the rest not worth the effort to dig out."

"Hopefully we'll end up with enough."

"We shall, if we're careful."

Amstraad peered at Chase over the froth in his stein.

"I understand you're a marksman with the bow."

"Depends what you mean by marksman."

Amstraad continued as if Chase hadn't spoken.

"I also understand you're good at training others in

this."

"I'm not sure about that either."

Where was Amstraad going with this?

"I have a son who is twelve and is good with the bow. Could you make him better?"

Amstraad's plea was sincere. Chase couldn't refuse it.

"We do training sessions in the morning before the wind gets up. Get him to come to me and I'll show him what I can."

Amstraad beamed.

"I am grateful to you, Chase Robinson." He held out his huge paw. "And thank you for the ale. I must be home."

Chase pondered on the exchange as he finished his ale. Seems that human nature applied here, too. And he knew that Amstraad would do his best to get all the cramlimite he could.

He set down his empty tankard and got up to go when a barmaid glided up to him, swinging her hips.

"Would you like anything else, my lord?"

"No, thank you. I must be going."

She did little to hide her disappointment, confirming his theory that 'humanoid' nature was much the same as human behaviour back home. A gaggle of barmaids gathered around the bold girl as he went out the door.

At dinner, Chase brought up the subject of sun strikes. The rulers confirmed the timing the stonecutters had described. He could hear K4's voice: 'Less than eighteen months.' The burden of responsibility was suddenly heavy on Chase's shoulders. He sank into abstraction, until Raul nudged him and he became aware he was under regard.

"Sorry," he stammered. "What did you say?"

"I was asking how it went today with Amstraad," said

Sulliman, smiling.

"He's a good man and will get all that he can."

The King nodded. "You're a good judge of character."

"Of males, anyhow," said Carolie. "He completely missed the advances of a young hussy at the Bull Boar this afternoon."

The women were laughing openly. His mouth fell open.

"How did you know that?"

They only laughed louder and refused to say.

When dinner was finished, Chase asked if the King and Raul could spare him a minute in private. The rest of them left.

"What's on your mind, Chase?" he asked.

Chase hesitated, took a deep breath and plunged in.

"I will have to explain myself and I hope I do it properly."

His listeners exchanged glances.

"I don't know what your culture thinks about people who know things before they happen," he began. "I don't want you to think I'm weird or a demon."

He paused.

"Go on," said the King. "We try to accept most things."

Not entirely comforting.

"When I was a child I had dreams before waking of things that came true. I still do."

Chase drew in a breath, watching them carefully.

"I dreamt of my parents' deaths beforehand, for example, and other things that were important to me."

"What have you dreamed now, Chase?" asked Raul.

Perceptive of him. Chase took another deep breath.

"These past few mornings I have awoken from the same dream of armed men coming through the mountains, each with a red stripe on his breastplate, and carrying weapons."

Raul and Sulliman froze suddenly, but it was Raul who spoke.

"Varden."

The King turned to Chase, his eyes narrowing.

"And what else do you know, Chase Robinson?"

His sharp tone surprised Chase.

"Nothing at all, Sire. The dream is simple and short … Do you think they *are* coming here?"

The King was all serious ruler now.

"Based on a dream? No."

He was thinking hard, and when he spoke, it was mostly to himself.

"The Keep will hold them off."

"Father, Boste returns tomorrow."

King Sulliman nodded, then excused himself and left.

"Did I do the right thing, Raul?"

"What, warn us or worry us?" Raul replied. Then, at Chase's expression, "I hope you are not right, but if you are, we are forewarned."

The King surprised the senior guard by ordering the gates shut and locked that night, and the sentries on the wall doubled.

Chapter 8

TWO DAYS WALK UPHILL or a full day's walk downhill, the pass from Staal is the perfect site to block an army. And that's what the townsfolk of Staal did, over 120 years ago. They built a keep on the floor of a narrow gully. Impossibly steep cliffs on each side and walls as high as rock can build it, the Keep stood guardian, the only pass across the ranges. The alternative was two weeks' ride on the plains through foreign states in both directions. Otherwise you had literally to go through the Keep, which had a stout door at each end, controlled by the guards.

Yes, there were regular raids by the Varden; roving bands who could only get around the Keep at high cost, and never enough to be anything other than a warning of the consequences of failing to guard the pass.

The ten-man patrol under their leader Major Boste exited the Keep in single file, replaced by a relief patrol. Twenty men could hold the Keep easily and a patrol was stationed there for fourteen days, with a new patrol arriving every week.

The spy in the recently-arrived patrol waited until the agreed time. He walked up to the two guards on the uphill gate.

"Smoke?"

He drew out a pouch from his jacket.

"Thanks."

The first guard stepped in front of the other and reached out. The traitor's knife went straight through his heart. For a few puzzled seconds he remained upright, providing cover for the enemy to kill the second guard. He risked a glimpse behind, stepped over the bodies and opened first one gate and then the other. The gates were narrow and solid, high enough to allow entry to a rider on a prenner. He signalled to the men hidden as close as they dared and they jumped up and raced towards the gate.

Calmly the traitor pushed a heavy wedge under the edge of both gates, now fully open, kicking them hard with his booted foot.

A shout rose from within the Keep. He had been seen. He drew his sword out and waited to defend the gates from the guards inside until his countrymen could reach him. He was killed, but the wedges held fast long enough for the struggling guards to be set upon by the Varden.

A desperate battle ensued, but the outcome was inevitable. Many hundreds against twenty was no contest. A few survivors managed to lock themselves high in the Keep. The Varden ignored them for now. The road was wide open before them and led directly to Staal.

*

The waking dream had changed. Chase dressed hurriedly and went down to the dining hall. Raul was there with his bow.

"I've never been great with this thing, but I think I'm getting better ..."

He broke off. He had seen Chase's face.

"What's wrong?"

"I think they've taken a small castle in the mountains," Chase said quietly.

Raul rose.

"I'll talk to Father. See you later."

He left. Outside, Chase noted the extra activity on the

walls and around the gates, which could be shut at a moment's notice. He took bow practice again. A boy, unmistakably Amstraad's son, waited apprehensively.

"Your name?"

"Ah, Ferrer, Sire."

"Well, Ferrer, your father said you were keen on the bow and asked me to give you a few pointers."

"Ah, yes, if it pleases you, Sire."

The boy was nervous; now might not be the best time to test his ability.

"Ferrer, I want you to join that group of men and we'll do some training together. Later, you can show me what you're capable of."

"Sire."

He turned and ran to the waiting men. One of them broke from the group as Chase walked up. In his arms he held a bundle of arrows wrapped in material and tied with a leather belt.

"Wow."

They were something special. Chase selected an arrow and balanced it in his hand. The length and weight was exactly the same as his own arrows. And it was iron-tipped. A medieval broad head!

"Amazing," Chase said. "Well done."

"Thank you, Sire."

The man relaxed.

"Once I got going it was hard to stop. They're slightly heavier, and much longer than our arrows, Sire. This is a thank you for your training from the King, Sire."

Chase cradled the arrows in his left arm. How many? Enough, hopefully.

"Thank you. And you are ...?"

Chase held out his hand.

"Baesel, Sire."

The man wiped his hand on his tunic before wrist-clasping Chase. The dream had taken hold and Chase had an important question in mind.

"How many arrows do we have in the armoury, Baesel?"

The man thought hard.

"At least two thousand, I would say." He grinned. "When I get bored I make arrows."

"You're an extremely useful man to have around, Baesel, and thank you again."

Chase walked over to the trainees and carefully put down the arrows.

"First, shooting accuracy as usual, and then we'll attempt a little repetitive quick-fire practice. Watch."

He stood in balance and eyed the target. He reached his right arm over his right shoulder and pulled an arrow from the quiver, smoothly nocked, aimed and fired. The arrow hadn't hit the target before Chase had another in his hand and was nocking, eyes steady on the target. Six arrows in the palm-shaped marker in short order impressed them all. They clapped with enthusiasm.

"Okay, but speed cannot come at the expense of accuracy. You must hit a target, or else the target could kill you …"

Picking up how serious he was, they quietened.

"… and nothing is worse than wasting any of Baesel's fine arrows!"

Baesel was embarrassed, but pleased, adding his own chuckles to theirs.

He spent individual time with them all, and especially

Ferrer. The boy was so nervous that he shot wildly, and the shame worsened his aim. Chase had to talk him through the idea of breath control and being calm. He got off some good shots then.

"Well done, Ferrer." Chase's praise was warm. "Your father's right. You do have potential."

*

In the early afternoon, Chase rode out to see how Amstraad was getting on. He and his men had taken some cramlimite that was obvious from the fissure, carefully, so it wouldn't fall down the crack and be lost. A few baskets were full to the brim with it. Then they had broken away the wall on one side of the fissure and were working upwards, attempting to retrieve any cramlimite that might be out of sight. That didn't look too promising.

He had a private word with Amstraad.

"I spent some time with Ferrer this morning. He's a nervous young man."

"Gets that from me. Sorry. We're better with stone than with people." He grinned. "Especially lords."

Chase grinned back, acknowledging how much of his own bravado was a cover-up.

"You'll be glad to know, he does have potential. Once he was calm he made some fine shots and, more importantly, he knows how to listen. Hopefully, he will relax with me and that will help."

"Thank you," Amstraad said simply.

"No problem. You've got a good lad there. I'll see you tonight or tomorrow."

He exchanged farewells with them and swung himself down the rope. Then he rode to the clearing again. Still no Startrader. His concern was lessened by the pleasures of the ride. He was beginning to appreciate these prenner.

*

The Varden came stealthily to the end of the valley and saw before them the town of Staal. Their leader climbed to a ledge and surveyed the area from his hidden platform. A cart with three men on and a single rider on a prenner came along the nearby track and turned towards the town. The Varden let them go. They needed to stay hidden until the attack.

He climbed back down and signalled for the sentries to be in position. The other soldiers were ordered to rest and eat. They would cross over to the town later in the dark of night. Plans had been decided. Now all they had to do was carry them out.

*

The Staal gates were diligently guarded and extra men lined the walls on alert. Chase was apprehensive about what the King would think or say if nothing came of his dreams? Still, better that than not say anything and allow the worst to happen.

Fruel approached him.

"Sire, his Majesty is with Guard Major Boste in the meeting room. He would like you to attend upon him."

Boste was a lean and muscular man, not unlike Chase in build, but a fist shorter. As Chase approached he heard what Boste was saying.

"We left the Keep early, Sire, and there was no sign of Varden. What has caused this concern?"

The King evaded this question by introducing Chase.

"This is Chase Robinson, Boste. He is here trading rock for iron. We should get some good weapons from the deal." He added, "He is also a marksman with the bow and has

99

been training some of our men in the mornings."

Boste shook hands with Chase, but eyed him warily. Chase decided to put the man at ease if he could.

"Not training as such, Sire. You have good security and discipline with the guards in Staal, Sire. A fine group of men." He turned to Boste. "We're sharing different techniques, that's all."

Boste nodded slightly, and grunted guardedly. He resumed his conversation with the King.

"Again, Sire. Why do you anticipate trouble?"

Sulliman understood the situation he had created with Boste and didn't hesitate to put it right.

"A traveller came through saying the Varden were on the move, so as you were not here we upped the guards. At the least, it will be good practice."

He was deliberately offhanded, and Chase wondered if he regretted his actions.

Boste frowned. "No movement has been reported to me."

"So humour me, will you, my old friend? For a few days only."

Boste bowed.

"Of course, Sire."

He spoke with little enthusiasm.

"If you will excuse me, I have men and family to attend to."

He nodded to Chase and left.

The King and Chase shared an unspoken communication. Then Sulliman asked, "How is Amstraad doing?"

"His best, Sire, but it's tricky, with not much of the rock showing. A few baskets so far."

"Oh, well. We can only wait and see."

The King was clearly distracted and obviously relieved when the Queen entered. Chase bowed and she smiled.

"Come on, you two. Dinner is waiting."

The evening was an unusually quiet affair with the King, Raul and Chase in sombre mood and the ladies sensitive to it.

*

The Varden leader was surprised and disappointed. He had been assured that the town gates, though guarded, were usually open in summer, even at night. Yet here they were, closed, and there were men on the walls.

So be it. From where he lay he motioned the laddermen forward, to be followed by the bowmen. Keeping low, they crept as close as possible and on his signal started running towards the wall at its lowest point near the gate and keep.

Chapter 9

CHASE'S DREAM, now nightly, was slightly different. Men with a red stripe still, marching through the mountains, and there seemed to be more of them …

*

He was woken by the ringing of alarm bells. Hurriedly he dressed, pulling on last his boots and a leather jacket. He strapped on his sword belt and sheathed his blade. Swinging a packed quiver and bow over his shoulder, Chase gathered up the spare arrows and, heart thumping, ran down and into the square.

In the lantern light the King stood tall, surrounded by guards and the townsmen and women. Soldiers on the wall fired arrows amid the clamour. The King stayed calm and issued instructions. When he saw Chase he called out, "This isn't your fight."

Chase called back, "I doubt they know that, Sire."

King Sulliman nodded. After a few moments he said, "We could use your bow on the wall."

Chase ran for the stairs and picked himself a space between two men and dropped the extra arrows against the inner wall. He risked a glimpse over the parapets. Flaming arrows were arching over the walls, probably not intended to burn the town, but mainly to add to the confusion.

The Varden men were trying to set the siege ladders. Chase could see six in various stages of erection, focused on the lowest part of the wall near the gates. The laddermen wore helmets with a broad brim designed to repel arrows. The ladders were topped with chains, which they were trying to loop around the parapets. The Staal defenders were shooting back at them, but were being successfully targeted by Varden archers. Some of the Staal defenders already lay dead, on the ledge or on the ground behind.

Two chains were thrown over almost simultaneously. Immediately the Staal defenders, desperate, rushed forward to break the chains, but the Varden bowmen protecting the laddermen had done their job too well. The attack force was ascending the ladders in their hundreds. The Staal men ducked up and down, firing wildly. Chase shouted along the line.

"Don't waste your shots. Remember, these are Baesel arrows!"

He was rewarded when a ragged cheer rose from the bowmen and the shooting slowed. Now they took turns to fire at attackers racing up the ladders. Chase pulled an arrow out and sighted. He flinched involuntarily as a Varden arrow from below bounced off the parapet.

Chase had shot at deer, pigs and goats and even a bull boar. Never at a human being. He didn't want to do this, but the expression on the first man's face gave him no choice. He let go. The arrow smacked the man square in the chest, slicing through his leather armour, and sent him crashing into those below. A cheer went up and several archers grinned approval. Chase felt vaguely sick, but shot two more and gave encouraging shouts before moving along the line where the attackers were closing in on the top of the wall.

A Varden warrior reached the parapet and Chase let loose. The arrow hit him under the arm and he toppled over backwards.

"Come on, come on!" Chase shouted at the men. "Take a

breath before you let loose and hit the target. Get them! Get them! Good shot!"

Boste was now at the top of the steps. He saw the shot and gave Chase a measured look before shouting instructions to send swordsmen spreading out along the line. Chase risked a quick look over the parapet, dodging as an arrow whistled past.

He needed to take out their bowmen so the guards could shoot more easily from the top of the wall. A Varden archer was aiming upwards at an angle, only Chase's standard eighty-five to ninety paces off. Chase took careful aim and sent the arrow into his chest. Shooting downhill made the arrow drop slightly on its flight, but didn't slow its speed.

After a few more hits the enemy bowmen realized their peril and backed off into the early morning gloom, making them less effective and allowing the defenders to take safer shots. Chase continued to hunt and aim at the Varden bowmen.

In a moment's pause between shots, he recognized the person beside him. Ferrer! He grabbed the boy by the shoulder.

"What are you doing here?"

Stupid question.

"Fighting, Sire. I think I got one!"

He pulled the boy away and bent close to his ear.

"Ferrer, I have something more important for you to do. Soon we're going to run out of arrows. Find Baesel and get him to send more up. They must keep arrows up here. Stay and help him."

"Sire, I know where he is."

Ferrer took off at a run.

Despite better shooting, despite their losses, the ladders were on the walls and attackers were making it to the parapets. Chase had only an instant to decide which man to shoot first – whoever was the most immediate threat.

Then they breached the castle defences. A man pushed a defending swordsman over backwards and, swinging his sword wildly but with intent, chopped down the nearest bowman. Immediately another attacker climbed over the wall behind him.

Instead of using their bows, a number dropped them and drew swords. Now it was no longer defence, but a mêlée; the attackers had a foothold on the wall. Bowmen further away couldn't shoot at them because of defenders in front. The attackers reached the summit of another ladder and Varden started climbing over from that one too, swinging wildly.

It was all happening too fast. The defenders were driven back by fierce fighting from attackers, highly trained, well-armoured and prepared to take losses. Finally a brief impasse halted the Varden when the Staal defenders brought out the halberds; the two-handed pole weapons.

Still the attackers had the advantage on the stairs, slowly driving the defenders, with Chase behind them, back to the bottom of two sets of stairs where another impasse resulted. Bodies lay where they had fallen, on each side of the stairs. Wounded Staal were dragged away while injured Varden were instantly dispatched. The noise was deafening.

Chase found the King nearby, Raul beside him, both with sword in hand. Boste joined them, his own weapon bloody.

"It appears they're content with holding where they are," observed Raul.

"Yes," confirmed Boste. "They're getting men on the wall before making the next assault."

He was right; men were streaming over the wall. Boste regarded them thoughtfully.

"If our arrows flew far enough we could break them from up there …"

"… and attack from all four points: the two stairs and along the wall. They aren't trying to climb the other ladders now they have breached."

The King had immediately grasped Boste's intent, pointing to the upper ledge and base of the stairs. Both turned to Chase.

"Is that too far?"

The King indicated a platform on the closest tower above.

"Soon find out."

Chase headed off at a run, carrying his bow and stack of arrows up the stairs to the towers. There was a narrow platform on the tower, above the wall height, with a roof and sturdy wooden poles. Chase leaned over the edge, looking into the confusion. Men were dying on both sides as they tried to attack or defend. The stairs were eighty to ninety paces away, the wall at least one hundred and thirty paces. No, it wouldn't be easy.

He lined up on a giant of a man who seemed to be directing the attack. He let loose the arrow, but the man moved sideways at that moment and the arrow hit the man behind him. The burly man looked up and pointed at Chase and bellowed a command.

Shields were immediately raised in front of him and two Varden nearby produced bows and fired. Chase jumped behind a pole as the arrows thudded into the platform.

Chase shot one bowman as he nocked another arrow and traded arrows with the second. Chase's arrow sliced the Varden's arm, while the Varden's arrow fell short.

The leader was protected now with shields so Chase settled to the task of picking off the Varden, concentrating on where the battle raged fiercest. At the base of the stairs the attackers surged forward. Chase took out the soldier in the middle front, making them lose structure and more men before they re-formed.

Across the right end of the wall several Staal men had been separated from its protection, with the Varden closing in. He ran so he was as close as he could get. He saw a Staal man run through with a sword and as he fell; saw that it was Went, one of his minders on the first day. Enraged he fired several shots into the Varden. Given space, the Staal men charged and were able to rejoin the others. Briefly they saluted their saviour, and Chase recognized both Fruel and the blacksmith, Meadl.

Chase continued to shoot at the battle edges, giving advantage to the Staal men. He noticed that the Varden numbers were not increasing any more – no more of climbing the ladders, all the remaining Varden were on the wall. The element of surprise they had relied on had failed and the toll so far was high. Chase kept firing arrows, though he was tiring now. He cleared his mind to be free of what he was doing, to concentrate solely on targets.

The intense concentration almost cost him his life. He leaned forward as he fired and it was the perfect opportunity for two Varden bowmen Chase hadn't seen. Both fired and two arrows struck him glancing blows. One creased his forehead on the hairline; the other tore through his jacket, slicing his chest under his arm.

With deadly accuracy he retaliated. He put an arrow through the one bowman's arm, and immediately put an arrow through the other's neck, hiding behind his countryman as he fumbled to get an arrow on the string.

Up on the wall the Varden realized they were losing men and surged down the stairs, driving back the Staal. Chase unleashed half a dozen shots into the leading Varden and halted the charge. As the Staal drove them back, he saw Boste among them. Bodies in the way, and the Staal use of pikemen, kept the Varden from charging and losses were still running high. Would they surrender if they lost their leader? Chase started to look for him again, still shooting. He was getting low on arrows …

Ah! There he was in the centre of a group of well-armoured men, still protected by shields. Suddenly they charged at the bottom edge of the stairs and broke through, but instead of fighting they ran, some dozen of them, towards the keep. Chase shot one, but they burst past the ring and out of sight. Where were they going? To the women? Some Staal men followed.

Chase decided to go after them. The Queen and her daughters were in there. He hit the bottom of the stairs running. Raul was there too; he had just come off the battle line. Chase shouted.

"Raul, the women!"

He drew his sword, knowing he had a comrade behind him.

They rounded the corner and nearly fell over a mound of bodies. The Varden had set a trap and killed a number of the Staal men chasing them, though some Varden were down also. There were still half a dozen Varden at stand there, defending their position at the doors to the inner castle. Raul and Chase joined the fight and soon had the Varden on their heels.

One of the Varden lunged at Chase and he parried the thrust and sliced through the man's arm. He then ran him through the chest. Being close was a lot harder than killing a man with an arrow, and Chase couldn't take his eyes off the man, standing over him. Fortunately another two Varden fell and then the Staal had numbers superiority and drove them away from the entrance.

Snapping out of his daze Chase yelled, "Come on!"

He and Raul broke away, past the skirmish and into the castle, leaving the Staal men to deal with the surviving Varden. They ran into the hall and heard fighting down the passage to the left. Two guards lay dead, beside two dead Varden. They had been protecting the room the women were in.

The two men burst in on a scene of clashing steel, screaming women and yelling Varden. The women had barricaded themselves behind upturned tables and two Varden were struggling to get to them as Carolie, Sonja and the Queen among others swung swords with varying degrees of skill from behind the barrier. It had bought them precious seconds. Carolie met a swinging sword with a good block.

On Chase and Raul's entry, the Varden turned. One was the massively built leader Chase had identified, and the other was dressed in fine armour. They attacked.

Chase took on the leader. He was a fighter used to overpowering his opponents with strength and he scythed at Chase, coming fast. Chase blocked and moved past the man to make him stop and have to turn and be forced to advance again.

The man obviously knew other Staal would be coming to the rescue. He needed to kill these men and take the women hostage before that could happen. He didn't have time for a long fight. That might have caused his error. He lunged forward. Chase evaded him and sliced though his left shoulder, his non-sword side.

The man bellowed and his arm went limp, blood pouring from the wound. He charged, but Chase was ready. He deflected the broadsword to open the man up, and sliced him down the front, from collarbone to hip, through his leather chest armour. Blood gushed out in a torrent and he fell.

Chapter 10

THE OTHER VARDEN had cornered Raul. With repeated blows he had smashed Raul's sword down and held his sword to his throat and laughed maliciously.

"Die!" he shouted at Raul, and swung back, arm raised to strike.

Laura screamed.

Chase got to him running and drove the hardened point of the katana through the laces on the back of the Varden's leather armour. The blade went through his body easily until only partly stopped by the chest armour. One sharp intake of breath and the man's sword dropped from his hand as he slowly collapsed, dragging Chase's sword down with him.

Chase lifted his hands and pulled out the katana. Raul pushed himself away from the wall and the two men stood in silence for a second, before stepping forward into a brotherly embrace. Raul spoke first.

"You saved me."

Chase found he could say nothing. The women could and they surged towards the men, saying their names, half-crying, half-laughing, and hugging both men hard. Laura was kissing Raul's face over and over, her own face wet as she pressed it against him. Sonja and Carolie had flung themselves into Chase's arms and were sobbing against his chest.

He held the katana flat against his body, helpless against their onslaught. The Queen stepped forward and held Chase's face in her hands. She was speaking and he could make no sense of the words. The other women in the room held each other and cried.

At last Chase came to himself.

"The battle."

Raul broke free from his wife and retrieved his sword, prepared to fight though he seemed to have a problem holding the sword. There was a sound of running feet in the hall and the men stepped in front, bracing themselves with raised swords. But it was Staal guards, and as the leader saw the Queen and the Princesses were safe, he let out a breath with relief.

"It's over, Sire," he announced to Raul. "The Varden have surrendered."

*

Raul and Chase were eventually allowed outside after Laura had insisted on tearing a strip off her dress to bind Raul's hand, and Sonja and Carolie had padded handkerchiefs together for Chase. He held it against his forehead to stem the blood flow from the arrow nick. His chest wound stung, but was not serious and he said nothing about it.

In the outer keep, where the ambush had taken place, the sight of bodies and the smell of blood, overwhelmed him. Chase barely made it to the garden before he threw up again and again. Like a match replay he recalled the face of every man he had killed.

Raul's hand was on his back when he finally stopped vomiting.

"So, Chase, you're not as tough as you think you are."

"I never said I was tough!" Chase wiped his face. They looked at each other. "Let's go."

The surviving Varden, some sixty or so, were in the

square in ranks, on their knees, hands being tied behind and eyes downcast. The King was there with his guards and some of the townsmen. When he saw Raul and Chase approach, his face lit up and he stepped forward to embrace his son.

He obviously knew what had happened inside.

"So, we still have true heroes in our land. We owe you both our womenfolk, our most precious possessions."

"Father, the true hero is Chase," stated Raul. "He saved not only them, but me."

"No, Sire," said Chase firmly. "We could not have done it without both of us."

The King held out his hand, and Chase grasped it with his own. The next instant the King had drawn Chase to him and held him close.

"I owe you more than I have, Chase Robinson."

Chase freed himself and put his hands on the King's shoulders. He looked him in the eye.

"No, Sire, you owe me nothing."

After a moment of calculation the King said "Raul, can you take charge here? I must see my wife is safe for myself."

The King departed, guards with him, as did a few others with similar concerns. Chase turned to Raul.

"Why did they go for the women?"

"I don't know. To demoralize us, maybe. Or are we missing something?"

He focused his attention on matters to hand. There was much to do, and he fired off instructions. The fires were being damped down and there were many injured and dying, both Staal and Varden. An infirmary was set up in the 'museum' and women came in from around the town, nurses and midwives. The stable hands and grooms were fixing broken bones and sewing cuts under the supervision of the town doctor, who was also doing what little he could for the dying.

The Staal bodies were lined up next to the wall for identification and listing. A careful search was made of the external area before the Varden bodies were taken outside the gates and dumped unceremoniously against the outer walls. Varden bodies thrown down from the upper walls landed sickeningly on the corpses below.

To Chase it was a surreal world of screams and moans, of helping others, of broken families crying over broken bodies and the motionless dead. So much sadness. So much confusion. Why had the Varden attacked Staal?

His arm was grasped and Chase turned to find himself face to face with a bloody Boste. The Major gripped Chase's hand.

"Do you know what you did for us today, stranger?"

Chase frowned, momentarily perplexed.

"You saved our town. You saved many lives." Boste peered into Chase's face. "Including my own. Thank you, stranger."

Chase, too perplexed to argue, shook his head. Boste turned to leave, but this time Chase caught *his* arm.

"I would feel happier if we removed the ladders from the wall and kept the gates ready to be locked with watchers on the wall."

Boste stopped.

"I should have thought of that. Can you attend to it for me, please? I need to see to my men and my family."

"I will."

Boste headed off again, full of purpose. Chase retrieved

his bow from the tower then headed for the gate. The guards were obviously trying to figure out what to do next.

"Guard Major Boste has asked us to secure the town," said Chase. "We need two men solely on the gates ready to shut them if needed. We need lookouts on the walls above to make that call. Can the rest of you go out and take down the Varden ladders and bring them inside?"

Grateful for direction the guards got moving. Chase went outside with several of them to bring down the ladders. The men had to climb the ladders to the parapets and unhook the chains that held them to the wall. Working together, they carried them all inside.

None of the men, including Chase, could help periodically checking across the plains to the mountain pass. A thought occurred to him. With the last ladder secured, he rounded up another team of men.

"We are going to need arrows. Find as many as you can, inside and out. Pull them from bodies, even the broken arrows, and get them to Baesel."

His last instruction was to ensure the guards were on rotation.

Once done, Chase sought out Raul again. He was in the meeting room with the King, a conclave of the town councillors, and the military, including Boste.

The Guard Major saw Chase approach.

"All under control?"

"The gates are guarded and a watch set. The ladders are inside."

"Good. Thank you."

Conversation had ceased while they conferred, but now the King rapped on the table.

"Back to other urgent matters," he said.

"We need to bring in more Levels," said Boste, "in case we get another wave of Varden."

There was silence as they digested what this meant.

"Do you fight on prenner?" Chase asked.

Boste took up his thought immediately.

"Yes. The Varden have to be on foot to come down the pass … Sire?"

The King nodded.

"Agreed."

He beckoned to a senior guard.

"Send messengers. All Levels around the State who own prenner to meet armed at Middle Ford before first light, then to Staal."

The man left.

"Next?" said the King.

"Food."

Laura's father jumped in, the bakers' guildmaster.

"Nobody has eaten all day, Sire. We can produce a volume in the bakery, but it won't be enough."

Chase realized the battle had taken longer than he thought; into mid-afternoon. Somehow food was unappealing at the moment.

"We need to get everyone to bring food out into the streets," said a councillor.

"Get the town criers to circulate that," the King ordered. "Anything the bakers can assist with will be reimbursed."

"There is no need for reimbursement, Sire." The baker was set and determined. "Imagine if we had lost."

"Master Baker, also offer to the prisoners, please," said the King.

The baker, surprised, opened his mouth, then closed it again and nodded and left with the councillor.

"What next?"

The King was untiring.

"The dead," said Raul. "We must start burial. It is summer and we don't need disease."

The King sighed. He looked out the window.

"Where did the day go?" he murmured. He knew. They all knew. "Tomorrow?"

"I will check with the doctor, but that should be fine. I will arrange burial parties – and help from the guards too?"

Boste nodded. Another councillor spoke.

"Medical. There are many wounded. We should get help from around the State."

"Good idea," said the King. "See to it."

That councillor left.

The King waited. Nobody spoke. When he was sure they weren't going to, Chase cleared his throat.

"The Varden. Clearly they have taken the pass. We don't know if they will attack again. We need to assume they will. We need to maintain a solid defence and consider how we can retake the Keep."

There was a deep silence as they all contemplated difficulties and possibilities.

"Quite right," said Boste. "On the first, I will organize the guards and townsmen if you, Chase Robinson, can get the bowmen together and make sure they have enough arrows?"

"Certainly, Major. I have already instructed guards to retrieve any arrows they can and take them to Baesel. On that, Sire, may I recommend Baesel for an award? Without his arrows, we would have been lost."

"Agreed," said the King. "Many others need rewarding, too. When we are safe we can do that."

Boste stood and pressed his clenched fist against his chest.

"Sire, in case anything happens to me, I want it formally recorded that, in my opinion, the Lord Robinson saved our town today. My King, he also saved my life specifically and many others with his actions and that bow of his."

Chase was stunned. The Lord Robinson? He felt himself colouring. Around the table heads were nodding.

"Duly noted." The King was equally formal. "Thank you, Guard Major Boste."

Boste bowed and left. The others tried to follow him, but the King raised a hand.

"Raul, Chase, wait please."

The others filed out. The three men were alone.

The King sized them up and started slowly.

"Well done so far, gentlemen, but I fear we have a way to go. Boste is an experienced soldier, but I need you two to lead with me."

He concentrated his gaze on Chase.

"I realize you are not one of us," he said, "and you've already done so much for Staal, but the men will be strengthened if you're out there. They talk of you."

This was too much for Chase.

"Ask Raul how I ruined your garden earlier … Sire, I am no hero …"

The King would have none of that and put a hand up to stop Chase.

"That is the best sort, believe me. This is now about the men raised to a point where they cannot only do battle again, but believe strongly that they will win."

Chase was reminded yet again of what a leader the King was, how well he understood his people.

"He's right," Raul added. "You know that, Chase. Father, the Varden may not return."

"Oh, I believe they will."

The King paused and began counting on his fingers.

"One – they have the Keep. Two – they know we are weakened. And three – the two men you killed in the ladies' chamber today? One was the King's right-hand man, and the second was his son, Prince Karib."

Chase blanched.

Nobody spoke and the King continued.

"I also believe we were saved by your dreams, Chase." He raised a questioning eyebrow. "Had any more?"

"This morning, and the same … Only more men, if I think about it."

"Under the circumstances, I believe that is the next wave. How many men were in the attack today? Four hundred?"

Chase and Raul nodded.

"Then reason four – it would take more men to hold the town and state than they attacked with today, especially with their losses. More Varden are coming, and soon. We need to plan how to retake the Keep afterwards …"

He paused and the young men knew why.

"If there *is* an afterwards."

Chapter 11

WHEN HE AND CHASE were outside again, Raul took a deep breath. By now it was late afternoon and the prisoners were seated, not kneeling, with bound hands and feet, and flanked by guards.

The town criers shouted instruction and the stewards were handing out food. Some approached the guards with food for them and for the prisoners.

"I'd better go and make sure there is no problem with that," said Raul, and he headed over.

There was a tug on his sleeve. Chase looked down to see Ferrer looking up at him like a puppy with his new-found master.

"You okay, Ferrer?"

The boy nodded, bashful and eager.

"Yes, my lord. Please, can I help you?"

"Yes, you can. Go and find some of the bowmen. Tell them to spread the word to get together by the second stairs as soon as they can. Also, do you know where Baesel works?"

"In a store behind the barracks, my lord."

"Thanks."

Ferrer saluted smartly and set of at a run. Despite himself, Chase grinned as he turned towards the barracks.

Baesel was at his usual occupation, making arrows. A young lad was sorting through the stack of broken and bloody arrows on the floor, checking heads and flights and sorting them into three groups: broken, missing bits, and reusable.

Chase walked around him and over to Baesel. He put out his hand and spoke formally.

"I believe the State owes you and your team a vote of thanks. Having that many arrows on hand probably saved our town today."

The three elderly men at another bench stood up taller with pride. Baesel shook Chase's hand and mumbled, "Thank you, my lord, but it is the men who fire them ..."

"No, Master Fletcher. Men with bows are useless without arrows."

Chase looked around the workroom with interest. One of the men was sorting a pile of willow-like branches, long and thin like dowelling, in a tub of brine,. He removed one and cut into the wood, following a template on the bench.

The second man was nicking tracks where the flight feathers or fletch would be inserted and a groove for the bow string, and at the other end a groove for the arrowhead.

The third was inserting the flight feathers and arrowheads and wrapping narrow twine around the feather and arrowhead base, securing them with tar. They were then left to dry, the shafts tightening on the fletch and heads. Baesel was using a foot pump to drive a stone wheel to make the arrowheads from flint stacked beside him. He paused to speak to Chase.

"These men taught me everything I know, and now we're teaching the boys. We were lucky its summer and we had just brought back a cartload of straitvine from the swamps."

"And we're lucky to have you all working for us."

Chase indicated the growing bundles of finished arrows.

"How many arrows do we have at the moment?"

"Several hundred new arrows, my lord, and Jacib over there is going through the used arrows, but I need to check them."

"We need as many as you can get to us immediately." Chase nodded at the pile of reusable arrows. "Is that about a thousand?"

"You are expecting another attack, my lord?"

Baesel's voice shook, and the elderly men stopped what they were doing.

"We must assume that, Baesel. Do you have any arrows for me?"

"Yes, my lord. We made yours first."

He showed Chase forty or fifty arrows. The boy called out.

"I have some here, too, Master Baesel."

He pointed proudly to his own pile, which was at least double. Had he really fired that many?

"Thank you, Jacib," said Baesel. "I'll need to check those. Load up with these first, Sire."

Chase filled his quiver. *Sire*? Then he remembered Fruel's comment when he first arrived about the word Sire, just an honorary title...

"When you've checked them, get Ferrer to bring them to me. How do you want to distribute arrows to the archers?"

"How many archers are left?"

Left ...

"Not sure, Baesel. I'm meeting with them now."

"Send Ferrer to tell me and then send the archers, but not all at once, please!"

On the way to the stairs, Chase walked past the hospital where Carolie and Sonja were assisting. It didn't look good in there. Sonja held a man down while a cut was stitched.

Carolie was cleaning another's wound with alcohol and he was screaming.

When he joined the archers, many of them were still eating. Ferrer approached him as he was counting.

"Ferrer, tell Baesel we have thirty-four archers."

Nowhere near as many archers as before the first battle. Not enough …

The men rose respectfully as he approached them.

He gestured for them to be at ease.

"Congratulations, men, you did yourselves proud today. We repelled a determined enemy!"

There were cheers and backslaps, though some faces were strained and haunted.

"We need to be ready in case they try again."

He sensed the anxiety. A man put up his hand.

"Do you think there will be more, Sire?"

Part of Chase's mind realised they were now addressing him as 'Sire', but instead of arguing he simply answered the question.

"I don't know, but we must and will be ready if they try again. We'll be on the alert and finish them off quicker this time."

The men grinned at each other.

"With all that practice this morning you will be better shots. With the experience you have from this morning you will be more careful with your shots. With our victory today you will know we can do it again."

When they cheered this time, it was with conviction.

A group of women standing nearby and carrying bows had listened to Chase's speech. Ignoring a few derisive comments, their leader, a brawny flaxen-haired woman, stepped forward and stuck out her chin.

"My lord, we would like to help. We are as good shots as the men and will not let you down."

One of the bowmen snorted, but Chase saw nothing except the women's determined expressions. What was the culture around women fighting? The Queen and the Princesses were not unfamiliar with weapons. His call, perhaps?

"Very well. Welcome."

They all let out a held-in breath. The men shuffled and shrugged, but said nothing.

"Right. To work! First I am going to pick Levels as group leaders, and divide you into six groups. We need balance in the groups, none stronger, none weaker than the others. Then you will go in turn to Baesel and get your arrows. After, some drills …"

Ferrer appeared at his elbow. Chase counted the women and then leant down.

"Tell Baesel we now have forty-one archers."

The boy's shoulders drooped, but he turned obediently.

The drills were carried out with quiet determination.

Later Chase met with Boste and they exchanged news.

"How will we break the chains on the attacker's ladders?" Chase asked.

"Heavy chisels and mallets are being taken up onto the walls already."

They fell into further discussion and it was getting dark when Chase walked into the dining room. Without speaking the Princesses got up and walked over to wrap their arms around him. He held them close for a few seconds. The King and Queen exchanged glances, and Raul was smiling tiredly.

A little embarrassed Chase sat down. Before he could

eat a woman appeared beside him with a bowl of water.

"For your hands, Sire," she said.

As he washed, she set about cleaning and wrapping Chase's head wound. Finally she was finished and he thanked her as she cleared up and left.

Carolie set a bowl of food before him and Sonja poured him a fruit drink. He was indeed starving and extremely thirsty. He downed two mugs and then attacked the hot food with relish.

Still with food in front of him, the King opened up the discussion.

"We don't usually talk about important things at dinner, but I fear we must tonight."

Without waiting for any reply he continued, "In turn, can all of you give me an update?"

Raul reported first.

"The prisoners are in a storeroom under guard. The arrangements for burial are underway." He looked at his mother.

"The guilds have got together and are managing the town food supply," said the Queen.

The Princesses talked about the injured, and Chase repeated the update from Boste and how his archers now included bow-women, which seemed to amuse the ladies. The King raised an eyebrow, but made no comment.

When he resumed it was to speak about morale among the townsfolk.

"I hear you made a good speech to the bowmen ... and women."

Chase smiled. Nothing went unnoticed in this town. The King continued.

"The town is in shock, saddened by our losses, and

tired. If the Varden attack again soon, would we be ready?"

No one answered. Finally Chase said, "Yes, Sire. The fighting men and women will be better than we were today."

"They must be; there may be far more of them …"

The rest of dinner was a sombre affair. It was getting late. Chase did one last walk around. Baesel was still working hard and handed Chase a bundle of arrows. Chase patted him on the shoulder.

"Thanks, Baesel. Hopefully I will not need them." He managed an unconvincing grin. "Get some rest."

Exhausted, Chase went to bed. He was woken again by the alarm bells ringing.

*

The Varden gathered their numbers, about two thousand men, at the exit of the pass. Their leader was the older Prince. Unlike his brother, he had nothing to prove, and had already realized, as the Varden flag was not flying on the castle battlements, that his brother had failed and could well be dead. In the dark, he spoke to his men from on top of a massive boulder.

"Your countrymen have been defeated. Your brothers are dead. This is not just about taking the town; this is a battle for revenge. We will make them pay."

As before they crossed the plain before full dawn. This time they were expected, the guards on the alert, and the alarm was raised earlier.

*

Chase felt a sense of déjà vu as the bells clamoured. He pulled on trousers and boots and grabbed his weapons. He ran down the flight of stairs and met Raul coming from the other. The men embraced briefly, right hands gripped at the base of the thumb.

"Good luck."

"Shoot straight."

Outside and running, he found Ferrer beside him.

"Do you need me, my lord?"

"Yes, Ferrer. Stay near me."

The Staal had responded quickly to the alarm and most of the archers were at the stairway, the steps still dark with blood, and facing Chase.

"Which groups have all members here?" he asked the leaders present.

"Group One, my lord."

"Group Two, my lord."

"Group Five, my lord."

"Okay. As we drilled. Groups One, Two and Five into positions one, two and three. The remainder by the wall minding the arrow stocks and be ready to replace. Wait for my signal to replace."

The twenty-one men and women took to the stairs carrying bows and quivers. Chase followed them.

The view from the wall was intimidating. The Varden had realized they had been seen in the first light and were not far away, jogging by the river towards them. In the faint light of dawn, it could be seen how hugely their numbers had increased from the day before.

What would they think when they saw the bodies of the Varden dead?

Chase's heart thudded. Not that many days ago he had been on his farm on Earth, planning to go back to work. Now he was on another planet unknown light years away, armed and ready on a castle wall, with a real chance he'd be killed in a medieval battle …

He breathed in slow and deep, trying to appear calm. People were watching him. His archer groups were evenly positioned along the low section of the wall. If the Varden didn't concentrate their attack on that section he would slide the defence along. If they went for a broad attack he would plug the gaps with Groups Three, Four and Six. He looked down at them. They were watching him, and Ferrer was too.

Men with pikes and swords were spreading out along the wall behind the archers, ready to repel ladders. Others grasped chisels and mallets to break chains if necessary. On the edge of the square a few men and women were ready with water to put out fires. The King and Raul, dressed for battle, spoke rapidly together.

When they looked up, the King acknowledged Chase with a clenched fist salute that Chase returned, nodding. Then the Varden were on them.

"Hold," shouted Chase to the archers. "Wait until you are sure of your shot."

Chase watched the Varden archers run up and start firing, followed by the laddermen. He lined up on the closest. The Varden was not aware of the range of Chase's bow and Chase actually saw the surprise on his face as the arrow knocked him onto his back, feathers protruding from his chest.

Chase switched off his emotions, shutting out the cheers around him. He could sight his targets easily in the early morning sun and he walked along the line and back to pick them off. The laddermen pressed forward to be met with arrows as they neared the wall, the defenders' shots more accurate this time. The enemy suffered heavy losses before any ladder was close enough to be threatening. The noise of shouts and screams on both sides increased.

These attackers were different men from yesterday's. The Varden archers didn't back off; others stepped up and took their place and it was the same with the laddermen. Chase was firing continuously, and his arm was aching from yesterday's efforts. The Varden archers had some success and several Staal archers were hit. Chase considered bringing up more archers, but decided to wait.

After sustaining heavy losses, a couple of Varden ladders made it to the wall and men sprinted up to secure the chains. This time, however, Boste had pikemen push the ladders away at an angle. One slid sideways and the men fell off while the other ladder dropped to the ground. A pikeman took an arrow for his efforts.

The battle was cruel and bloody with the Varden finally getting ladders on the walls, though unchained, and making height bit by bit. They protected themselves with shields, but the angle the Staal bowmen had along the wall meant they still had shots, though they themselves were exposed and took losses. Amongst the carnage below a Varden managed to throw a chain over. On the other side of the parapet a Staal farrier with a chisel and mallet began smashing the links. No Varden got on the wall before the chain was broken and the ladder pushed over, but more Staal were hit.

Chase signalled Group Three to come forward, which they did immediately, filling the gaps. The Varden were experienced warriors and fearless. Their bowmen started climbing the ladders to fire closer at the Staal archers, trying to protect the laddermen.

Chase shot a man on the ladder down from him and felt a burn on his right shoulder as he turned. An arrow had narrowly missed him, slicing through his vest and grazing his skin. He rounded on the shooter and found the man reloading mid-ladder with another beside him taking aim. Chase ducked behind a parapet and the arrow smacked into it. They were hunting him. Clearly he had been identified as a problem.

The archers beside him saw that too, and dispatched both Varden. Where was the instruction to get him coming from? Chase looked out onto the field and saw a group of Varden behind a red-striped wooden barrier held by two soldiers. The leader was obvious among them, dressed in elaborate armour, directing as the others pointed and runners rotated.

Chase unslung his quiver and found what he needed, one of his original arrows from Earth. He took position and gauged the wind. The man might just be in range. At the least he could return the favour and give him a scare.

He was taking his stance when the archer beside him screamed and clutched at an arrow protruding from his chest just under his throat, falling at Chase's feet. The face betrayed that it was no man, but one of the women archers. Chase forced down his anger and took stance again and readied himself. He could see the man from the waist up. Clearly they didn't realize they were in his range. Chase judged the distance, and imagined himself on the hill at home. This shot was not that much further and he had the advantage of height.

He drew back and held his breath, finger tips light on the string. He moved them slightly and the arrow was released. Chase followed the flight from down the bow as if he were the arrow as it arched. He knew it was close. The point dipped and smacked into the leader's stomach and

Chase thought he could hear the sound as it pierced the leather.

The man looked down at the protruding arrow and then up at Chase. He fell to his knees, his men grabbing him and pulling him down behind the wooden wall. Staal on the wall had seen the shot and shouted without stopping their work. Nor did the Varden stop. They came in mass, a full assault. Everyone it seemed was determined to mount the ladders; but they had lost their structure and a crowd was building below as they struggled to get the ladders up and make the ascent. The loss of their leader seemed to have affected the balance of the attack and it stalled.

Chase signalled for Groups Four and Five to join them, praying they wouldn't overcrowd. They brought arrows with them, including a number for Chase. Where did they get those? He fired again and again. Ferrer and Baesel …

The ladders were up, but not chained. The bodies below and the men holding them were enough to stop them being pushed over. The pikemen stabbed the Varden trying to get onto the wall and they fell onto those below. Arrows flew from above and below. By now the noise was almost unendurable.

Finally a few Varden made it on to the top of the ladders. After yesterday the Staal knew the importance of keeping the Varden off the wall. In the frantic slashing and stabbing, bodies hindered the Staal defenders and a Varden managed to climb the parapet and leap down into the Staal fronting him. All three toppled over backwards onto the ground below, a few seconds' breach that allowed two or three more Varden to make the wall and attack with swords and daggers while the defenders fought back with pikes and swords. The Varden managed to form a cordon and two more leapt on to the wall.

Boste ordered a charge and the Staal crashed into the Varden. A scrum of death ensued. The resulting pile-up backed up to the ladder, which stopped more Varden getting onto the wall. A Varden stood on the ladder and lifted his sword and Chase shot him over backwards.

A thunderous rumbling rose over the din around them and those who could, looked out over the plain. A wave of men riding prenner charged into sight and smashed and hacked across the back ranks of the Varden, scything through.

The carnage in the field was immediate, but not on the wall. For what seemed an age, but was probably only seconds, everyone stopped and stared. Then the action resumed. The Varden on the ladders acknowledged they were trapped and started back down. The Staal on the wall rushed forward to take a final swing at chosen opponents, and the archers kept on shooting, not to miss any chance. The cheers and yells of triumph echoed around the walls.

On the field the next wave of prenner sliced through the Varden, but that first element of surprise had been lost. Prenner went down as the Varden slashed at the riders' and prenner's legs. The speed of the prenner and the press of numbers contributed to the chaos. When the next charge was launched, a number of Varden panicked and started running for the pass. That started a torrent, and the first wave had rounded now and came at pace along the main body of Varden that had begun to stream away from the wall.

Several more prenner went down, tripped by living men and bodies, but generally they were sure footed and solid enough to bounce men off their chests. Then it became a rout. The prenner circled and scythed through again, and although a few Varden formed blocks with shields, as the numbers around them depleted, they realized they would soon be isolated. That's when they ran.

Now it became a massacre, as Varden in flight tried to defend themselves against men on prenner and were cut down. Chase stood on the wall, bow hanging from his hand, and watched in a strange mixture of horror and relief.

The Staal crowded behind him, still cheering, slapping each other on the back, embracing. His thoughts flew to the Princesses. He wanted to know, absolutely, they were all right, though in his heart he knew they were.

A hand on his shoulder – Boste, seemingly unscathed. He held out his other hand and Chase took it, leaning his bow against the parapet. The men stood there, grasping each other by the shoulder, their hands firmly clasped.

As he let go, Chase said quietly, "You are quite a soldier."

"And you are quite a man. I could not be more grateful that you are here at this time."

"Hail, our warriors!" a familiar voice called behind them, and both men turned to face the King and Prince Raul. The Staal men and women stopped watching the retreating Varden and fixed their eyes on the significant encounter unfolding before them.

"Guards Major Boste, this moment will be written in our history and your family will live in its glory for generations."

The King and Raul stepped forward and formally embraced the gallant soldier.

When they released Boste, he saluted them.

"Chase Robinson," the King continued, "we do not know where our hero – our saviour – came from, but this State will forever be in your debt."

Another formal embrace with father and then son. When Raul stepped back there was blood on his sleeve from the wound on Chase's upper arm.

"And you need to get that looked at." He turned to the King. "Father, now he's ruining my clothes as well as your garden."

Laughter from the crowd; at this moment they would laugh at anything.

Raul stood back. "Glad to see you were lucky again," was all he said.

"Glad we got through," Chase replied.

Out on the plains Staal on prenner were chasing Varden, killing the fleeing stragglers as the massacre rolled away from them. An idea began to take shape in Chase's mind.

The King went forward and shouted to the crowd below.

"Victory is ours today. We are safe again."

A massive cheer rose around the castle, rolling on and on.

Chapter 12

THE QUEEN AND THE PRINCESSES met the King, Raul and Chase in the courtyard among many other reunions. They had been in the group tasked with ferrying the injured and the dead from the wall, the wounded to the hospital, the dead – Staal and Varden – to join yesterday's corpses.

The Queen hugged her husband and her son, and the Princesses rushed forward to take hold of Chase and press against him, kissing any part of his face they could reach. With them bundled in his arms, last thoughts were effectively banished from his fogged mind.

The King's brain, however, was still ticking over.

"Boste," he asked, "who will be in charge in the field?"

"Lenar or Sharl, Sire," he replied.

"We should ride out and control the troops. We don't want them chasing the Varden up the pass to fall into an ambush."

"Indeed, Sire."

Raul turned to Boste and Chase.

"Who's coming with me?"

"I should remain here." Boste spoke with regret. "I know I am in charge of our forces, but I cannot leave the Castle if you are not here, Sire. But I am also responsible to protect you."

"What if I went?" Chase said. "I'd like to know how many of the Varden escaped."

Boste only took a moment to say, "I would accept that. Thank you."

Raul and the King exchanged glances and Raul signalled

a guard and ordered mounts to be brought to gate. The women went with them, Sonja and Carolie still clinging to Chase.

"We need to get back to the hospital," the Queen reminded them, and kissed her husband, murmuring words into his ear. The Princesses kissed Chase and turned with their mother, glancing backwards to watch Chase mount his prenner, with their father and brother and twenty or so guards.

The three men rode through the gate with the guards behind. They hadn't gone far when Chase called, "Excuse me, Sire, but may I check something?"

The party slowed and followed Chase to where the wooden painted 'wall' the Varden had brought down through the pass lay abandoned on the ground, with bodies strewn around it. The man Chase had shot, still in his full dress armour, was slightly beyond them. As Chase rode up, his head moved slightly. He was still alive.

Chase gazed silently down at the horror he had caused. The King and Raul rode up beside him. They dismounted, holding their prenner's reins. The man's eyes were fixed on them with hatred.

"I think that's Erran, the Varden King's oldest son," said the King. "Only son now. You killed the younger prince yesterday …"

He frowned, gauging the distance from the wall.

"Did you get him from there?"

Chase nodded. The soldier focused on the King.

"You! I am King Erran now! My father died last winter."

He half-rose and fell back with a gasp of pain. Sulliman made no direct reply.

"That might explain why they attacked us like this," he

stated flatly. "Old King Loomat would not have risked such bloodshed."

The exertion of talking had brought a gush of blood from Erran's mouth. Chase felt sick again.

"At least that means we will be safe from attack for a time," the King continued. "So many men lost; the King and both Princes gone. A battle for the throne will weaken them more …"

He shook his head. "So greed makes evil for us all."

He signalled to the guards.

"You four! Transport King Erran to the hospital and see what can be done for him."

He didn't sound too hopeful.

The guards set to, and the King's troop remounted and carried on towards the pass, the prenner's gait rising to a gallop and all in close convoy.

"What a shot, Chase!" Raul called. "Just how far can you shoot that thing?"

"I was lucky, being on the wall and with no wind. That's about my limit."

"The legend of Chase Robinson grows!" called out his father riding beside. "Killed the enemy King – by the time we get back it will be from three hundred paces."

Chase winced; still appalled by the damage his bow had wrought. The King read his expression correctly.

"He was a bloodthirsty bastard, Chase; he would have killed us all. You did the world a favour!"

That helped, but not much.

They came across many dead, and in an open area a literal pile up of Varden bodies. They had obviously tried to make a stand but, by then, the Staal cavalry were efficient and ruthless. For Chase, the nightmare went on.

At the base of the pass, fighting continued with the Varden desperately defending their comrades who were scrambling up and away. The rocks and boulders limited the ability of the prenner to attack and the Varden took advantage of the impasse to make their escape. When the King rode up to the Staal leaders, he found them debating what to do.

The men hailed each other. A Staal guard wheeled forward to address the King.

"Greetings, Sire. As you see, we have got most of them. Just deciding what to do with this lot."

"Well done to you and your men, Lenar. A famous day in our history."

"Thank you, Sire. I am grateful you were able to hold them out of the castle until we arrived. Would have been very different if you hadn't."

"We're grateful, too. We have heroes to celebrate this day and yesterday. But first, what are your thoughts here?"

"We were in agreement, sire. Looks as though we need to deal with them hand to hand."

"I wonder whether that is necessary, Lenar. There are no more than two or three hundred left from well over two thousand. There could be some benefit in leaving some survivors, and another engagement might not be worth the losses. I will try to talk to them first."

He rode forward a few paces instinctively flanked by Raul, Chase and Lenar. Chase unhooked his bow and held it ready.

"I am King Sulliman," the King declared boldly. "Who is in charge here?"

A man with a manic expression stepped out from behind a boulder, pulling an arrow from his quiver and raising his bow. In a flash Chase had an arrow nocked and was sighting his bow. A bearded soldier appeared beside the Varden archer, grabbed his bow and forced it down. He looked at Chase who slowly lowered the tip of his bow.

The man nodded his thanks to Chase while the archer sank to his knees, sobbing. With a hand on his friend's shoulder, the big man replied.

"You asked who our leader is. That would be me now, King. My name is Combinus."

"Combinus, our States have been at a relative stand-off for some time now. What has provoked these attacks?"

The reply was terse.

"That's not for me to say, Sire. Only our new King and his court can answer that."

The King stared at him, saying nothing. The man continued, knowing his answers could decide if battle recommenced.

"He probably decided you were soft and it was time we took your lands. Clearly he was wrong."

The King nodded and took a minute to think.

"Do we need to continue this or can you be an emissary for future peace with us?"

Combinus gave a wry grin.

"Do I have much choice, Sire?"

"We want the Keep left without damage."

The man was grim.

"I am unable to make that call, Sire. I could be put to death for doing so and there will be someone senior to me at the Keep."

"Give us a moment."

The King signalled the others to move closer.

"Thoughts, gentlemen?"

"We could chase them up the pass," said Lenar, "but it would be ambush at every corner."

Nods of agreement.

"I believe he could not release the Keep to us," Raul added, "and he could have said he would and then not do it. I think the man is honest."

"And it would be worth it, to have an honest man reporting back what we've done with a little gratitude to us," said Chase.

"We are in agreement then."

The King turned his prenner back to Combinus.

"We will not impede your return. Please do your best to make those in charge realize we will destroy all who attack us. However, when you are ready, we will welcome trade."

Combinus saluted fist over heart and bowed. He ordered his men to go up the pass and they watched them file away. Some supported injured comrades, and many Varden kept glancing fearfully over their shoulders, hardly daring to believe they were being let go.

The King introduced Chase to Lenar.

"You are fast with that bow, Chase Robinson," said Lenar, with a grin.

"That's not the half of it," jumped in Raul, laughing.

The King acknowledged their compliments to Chase with a tilt of his head. Then he looked hard at the pass.

"We still have a big problem, gentlemen."

"I have an idea, Sire, but we will need to act soon," said Chase.

"Good. Let's head back to the castle. The women will be worried. But first things first."

He turned his prenner to the surrounding Staal and raised his sword to his men, who roared hurrahs in celebration. After deploying a force to watch the pass they headed back to the town.

When the King and the others got back to Staal they were told that King Erran had not survived transport to the hospital. Nobody commented further.

Sulliman asked the group to meet with him to discuss Chase's plan or any others. Word had passed about the massacre of the Varden, and an impromptu celebration was going on in the square. Something like the midsummer party, but less organized and with them all knowing it was to somehow come to terms with all they had gone through in the last few days: the terror, the effort, the sadness and the eventual relief. They still had the wounded and dying to attend to and the dead to bury. In such circumstances, nobody wanted to go home; they wanted others around them.

Boste joined the group in the meeting room along with the Queen and councillors. King Sulliman waited for the congratulations to die down and turned to Chase.

"You have an idea?"

Chase took a deep breath. Treat it like another sales meeting, he cautioned himself. He almost grinned at the thought.

"Yes, Sire. It's a simple plan, and based on what we know. My thought is that a force of us go up to the Keep, then we choose something short of a dozen or so of us, our best swordsmen, dress them in Varden gear, blood and bandages, and send them to the gate as survivors of the battle. Once let in, they try to hold it until reinforcements get there to help."

In silence the others considered.

"We would have to go now," Chase continued, "so it

will not seem strange we are so far behind. We would have to hope that most of the beaten force from today has continued on past the Keep. There are possibilities around that. And I have questions for whoever knows the Keep the best. But that's the general idea, Sire."

"We?" said the Queen. "Do you intend to go, Chase? You have already done too much for us."

She looked at her husband. Sulliman stared at Chase, but said nothing.

"I agree with you, Mother," said Raul, "but he is probably the best swordsman in Staal."

"Really?" Boste said. "As well as the bow?"

"Yes, he beat all the Level Ones we had here, one after another, several times. I still have bruises from the training staffs!"

Lenar raised his head.

"It is a good plan, and I think the only chance we have to take back the Keep. I will join him if you will allow it, Sire."

"Has anyone else got any ideas?" the King enquired.

Only shaking of heads.

"Then start your planning and let me know when you're going. Chase, Raul, wait a second, please."

When the others filed out, the Queen also remained behind. She didn't look happy.

The King stepped up to Chase.

"I am not one used to uncertainty, or owing so much, but I am now."

He drew in a breath.

"Chase, you have been with us only a short time and already we owe you all that we have, many times over." He raised hands in supplication. "You don't need to argue. We understand you are a humble man, uncomfortable with praise."

He moved closer to Chase and looked him in the eyes.

"We don't understand why you continually risk your life for us. You are not family; you are not from Staal and you haven't been here long."

Half to himself he added, "Perhaps you are just noble …"

Then he spoke firmly.

"You need to understand you have become important to us. We don't want to lose you after all you have done for us."

The King glanced at Raul.

"You have become my son's friend. My wife already thinks of you as a cross between a hero of legend and another son. Me? I guess I feel the same way that both Raul and Rebekka do. I would prefer to call you friend than son though."

He paused, frowning in consideration.

"As for my daughters, I have never seen them like this; both of them closer than they have ever been and now, as if they have finally found their purpose. Anyhow, they would kill me slowly if something happened to you."

After the emotion of the past few days, Chase struggled to speak.

"Sire, it's as if I've known you all my life. I don't have any say over my actions. You are my friends. I know how important this is and I know this is your best chance for success. I will not fail you."

"With me beside you."

Raul stepped forward and placed one hand on Chase's shoulder, another on his father's. The Queen wept quietly.

The decision was made.

The group settled down to work out details. Boste and Raul talked to Chase about the Keep, and the distance to the closest hiding place – unfortunately nearly three hundred paces.

Logistics were the business of Lenar and Sharl – food and weapons and the props the ruse demanded: Varden uniforms and weapons and bloody cloths to wrap around 'wounds'. None difficult to get.

Over a meal ordered by the Queen, the Staal with Chase decided on the attacking party. They picked two men they hoped could copy Varden accents. Raul, especially with his injured hand, was not a good enough swordsman to make the fourteen they decided they would need to hold the door. He tried to pull rank, but they stood firm. Chase placated him by saying he had to lead the support attack. They decided two hundred men would ensure they could recapture and hold the Keep.

The guards went out recruiting volunteers before the soldiery got too drunk. Raul and Chase walked among the townsfolk and guards to cheers and pats on the back. To Raul's amusement, the distance of Chase's shot killing the Varden King had indeed nearly reached three hundred paces. No one noticed they weren't drinking the ale in their hands. They noticed small 'discussion groups'. As each guard delivered their message, men's faces hardened. With an early start essential, they ducked off to bed as soon as they could get away.

Chase found the Princesses sitting on his stairs, waiting for him. Silently they stood as he approached and went into his arms. He held them close as they took it in turns to kiss him. Sonja was weeping and Carolie blinking back the tears. He wasn't going to say, "What's wrong?" He knew.

He held them closer. "I will be okay. I promise."

"How can you be so sure?"

Sonja spoke with such force that Chase was taken aback.

"Did you have one of your premonitions?" Carolie said hopefully.

Oh. So the King must have told them. Or the Queen.

Under the circumstances, if nodding was a lie, then Chase lied. Somehow he did feel, for no logical reason, that he would return. He kissed them both.

"When I get back, we need to talk."

"You promise?"

"I promise. Now go to bed. Please."

In his own room he found a clean shirt and breeches, rolled bandages and ointment for his wounds. Fruel. The man's a legend, thought Chase. He washed, put some of the horrible smelling ointment on his wounds, and climbed gratefully into bed.

Yet despite his exhaustion he found it hard to sleep. So much blood and gore. He could still smell blood. So many deaths. Two Princesses, equally lovely and lovable … How could he hurt either of them?

How had he got into this?

Oh, yes. A space ship. Startrader. He was supposed to be trading iron for rock. How many problems was he going to cause? Finally Chase worried himself to sleep.

Chapter 13

NEAR MORNING, while it was still dark, Fruel put his head around the door. He coughed and when Chase stirred he said, "You will want to eat before departing, Sire."

Sire again?

"Thank you, Fruel, and for the clothes and ointment. I owe you."

"You owe *me, Sire*?" The man standing in the doorway was genuinely offended. "Your arrows saved me and the others with me. We owe you."

"We worked as a team, Fruel. Without all of us we would not have won. We saved each other."

Fruel considered this but Chase could tell he was not convinced by his words.

"Your food is ready, Sire," was all he said.

After breakfast, the hand-picked men met at the stables. Varden clothes were donned and weapons examined. They discussed Chase's bow and agreed it would be a dead give-away. Especially with the shots he had made during the battle. His sword, being covered by a Varden sheath, was deemed acceptable. Chase picked up a Varden bow. Short and powerful; accurate from close up, but with a limited range. He slung it over his shoulder with a quiver. The others seemed happy with that.

The King arrived and quietly went around, wishing them luck.

"Don't take any unnecessary risks," he told them. "We can find other ways to hold the pass."

The men nodded, knowing this to be unlikely. After the

last few days they would be vulnerable. At last they were ready and piled into the waiting wagons, which would take them to the entrance of the pass. They would have to walk and climb enough in the next days.

In a nearby paddock a team of farmers were already deep-ploughing the ground.

"To make the digging of burial holes easier," Raul confirmed. "A mass grave for the Varden. Individual Staal will be buried in the cemetery by the south wall. Glad I'm not doing any of that."

They sat in silence as the wagons creaked towards the pass. Once deposited at the start of the pass, they began the climb at a smooth rather than a fast pace. Chase wondered how far behind the Varden from yesterday they might be. How many Varden would be at the Keep? Perhaps they would pass it by …

There were bodies beside the track and on the banks of the river, left to die because they could travel no further. A few were still alive. Boste tried asking how long they'd been there and got no answer. They left them. What else could they do?

Had what waited for them not been always on his mind, Chase would have enjoyed the trek and views. He had a pack of Varden clothes and food, his sword and bow. Nothing heavy. His boots were only passable though. Fortunately Chase had enough experience of tramping to take plenty of woollen socks to keep his feet dry. *Thanks again, Fruel*. The day was long and tiring; mostly uphill. The men were silent, with what lay ahead on their minds.

That evening they camped on a ledge high above the water. Though it was nearly dark, Chase went to the edge of the track and found a tree fifty odd paces away with a patch of lichen at chest height. He sighted the Varden bow. The arrow hit the tree in the centre, lower than Chase expected. He became aware of Raul beside him.

"I'm not sure it's sporting to shoot a man there," he observed.

"Stop him though, wouldn't it?" Chase was grinning.

Raul winced. "True."

The second shot was only a hand below the lichen, and the third was dead centre.

"Okay," said Chase. "Might need these."

He rescued the arrows from the tree. One head came off so he left it. Only twenty-three left …

After food, the watch was set, and the two with Varden accents practiced their story and likely questions and answers with Lenar and Boste advising. Then they settled in for an uncomfortable night.

Next morning a steady drizzle added to their discomfort. Boste estimated they'd be at the Keep mid-afternoon. They walked on in silence.

When they stopped for a late lunch, Boste confirmed the Keep was not far. They would need to proceed slowly. They sent two men, familiar with the area, ahead as scouts.

"You are in charge now, Chase," said Boste. "It's your game."

"It'd be good to check the Keep for activity before we go in."

"There is a promontory that overlooks the Keep. We can climb to it without being seen."

"Good idea. That'd be a help."

As they got closer, Boste kept them informed. The scouts returned and reported no sign of Varden, and were dispatched again to check a lookout that the Varden could be using if they knew about it. They weren't.

Two other scouts had gone ahead to study the Keep and Lenar, Raul, Boste and Chase climbed up too. From behind the rocks on the edge of a ridge they surveyed the Keep through the drizzle. Blending in with the valley slopes on either side, it worked to plug the pass.

"Does it flood here?" asked Chase.

"Yes, but the water flows away from the Keep; it's on a rise."

"Wow. The perfect block."

"Indeed."

Boste spoke without humour. They knew that that one of their best assets was in the hands of the enemy.

There was activity in the Keep, but nothing on the land immediately preceding it, and not many Varden on the walls. Past the Keep they could see a group were moving single file away from the Keep and on and out of sight. They rejoined the others. Chase was so nervous that his stomach was churning.

"We need to try now," he told them. "Hopefully we are not too far behind and the longer we wait the more unlikely our presence will be."

The fourteen made sure they were in distinctive Varden gear and added rough, blood-stained dressings to imaginary wounds.

"I need to be near the back, with a leg wound so I can stoop," said Chase. "My height might make me recognizable."

They ran through a final check on signals and wished each other luck. Then taking a deep breath, Chase reminded them.

"At our signal, come fast." They nodded. "Let's go."

*

A small band of survivors limped onto the valley floor leading up to the Keep. They were in view for thirty seconds before the guard on the wall reported their presence to those inside.

He waved down to them, and a couple of the strays waved back, seemingly relieved to have made it. They hobbled to the gate, some of them helped by others. When they got to the gate, it remained closed. One of the men looked up and called, "Are you going to let us in or what?"

"Where have you come from? The rest were in hours ago?"

"We were by the river; had to wait until night to get into the pass. Also we weren't moving that fast."

He motioned to the wounded with him. There was a pause, and then another question.

"What company are you from?"

This had been well-rehearsed.

The man looked around as if considering. "Sword Two, mainly. Or what's left of it."

No reply, so he continued.

"We have wounded and we are soaked. Let us in. I think we are the last."

Chase was sure they could hear his heart thumping up on the wall. After what seemed like an age, a door opened. Before they could enter, soldiers emerged. *Oh, we didn't expect that ...* Chase kept his head down. But they were there to help with the injured, and one of them came to take over from Lenar, who Chase was leaning on. Chase tried to appear shorter. Then they were inside.

Chase quickly surveyed the place as he was being led to a medical section in stables near the entrance. Not too many

150

guards. None on the inside wall, and mainly medical personnel around them. He signalled the few deceivers who were still by the doors as two Varden guards were shutting the door. The Staal struck. The two guards went down, but not before one of them screamed. Damn!

Everyone stopped to look. Chase and the Staal knew they had to act now. Chase threw his helper into the medical area and drew his sword.

"Stay down, all of you!" he hissed loudly to the medics. Weaponless, they complied.

Chase scanned the courtyard. At the entrance to the Keep, the Staal had opened both doors and signalled down the valley. The supporting force leapt up and sprinted towards the Keep and the men inside took up defensive positions to keep the doors open. By now what they feared had happened, as two Varden soldiers, alerted by the scream, came out of a doorway above the stairs opposite to investigate. Immediately they shouted, drew their swords, and charged down the stairs at the Staal. A few seconds later they were followed by a stream of others, in various states of undress, pulling swords from scabbards.

The Staal swordsmen had formed a wedge between the wall on one side and a room on the other, defending the open gate. Chase was in centre position. The Varden were panicked by the open doors and charged in close. The first few went down easily.

The others following stumbled into them and each other, and lost momentum and that advantage. As they all tried for the door they got in each other's way and were able to fight in one place only, close to the wall on the left. Chase came at them from the side and wounded several before they spread and tried to take on the Staal individually in the narrow space.

The fight was close and frantic; both sides knowing all their lives were at stake. More Varden were piling out of the room opposite. They had relied on the Varden only having a 'holding' force still at the keep, but the final large group had not left the keep and set off for Varden. However, the corner with the doors behind them was difficult to get to with determined men blocking the way.

One, then two Staal fell. Boste bellowed, "Step back!" The line tightened again. The Staal were being slashed to pieces. Chase, though using his height and sword length, still bled and was stung with pain from wounds on his arms and left thigh.

More Staal went down, including Lenar. Suddenly the line broke and the Varden literally piled on top of them, falling on each other. Chase was under several bodies and time slowed. His memory flicked back to being in a rugby ruck. He held enemy arms so they could not stab him. How long had it been since the signal? Where were the Staal? A Varden rose above him and raised his sword when a blur slashed the Varden blade and then his chest and continued to hack at the men on Chase until eventually he was free.

Instinctively he groped for his katana. The blur turned into the familiar, worried face of Raul, which broke into a grin.

"I may not be as good with a sword, but I'm fast!"

Chase didn't get a chance to reply. Staal charging in through the gate pushed them aside and against the wall. They flooded the courtyard and the Varden were driven back in a murderous battle. Chase and Raul joined in, fighting side by side. Chase realized the wound on his thigh was a problem as he couldn't move his left leg easily. Now he learned what it is like to fight for your life. Everything happened too quickly to be afraid, and pain had to be set aside.

The Varden style was slash and thrust, and he found he was able to avoid or deflect then strike, wounding first and moving in for the kill. This battle was not like the movies. You tripped over bodies and fought against the overwhelming clamour of blade on blade, yells of rage, screams of fear, and the ugly sounds of men dying. You could smell of blood as you fought. Blood on you and on your sword hand. Fortunately Chase's katana could be used double handed and the handle was tightly bound with string, allowing for a firm grip.

Now the Staal were targeted by Varden archers firing down on them from the inner wall. Chase finished his current opponent off, simply by using his longer arm reach to go over the Varden's sword hand and stab him in the throat. He shouted at Raul, "Cover me."

He limped back to where his Varden bow had fallen when Raul saved him. The quiver was still on his back. Chase chose a place to stand and began to line up on the archers. He dropped the closest, and the bowman next to him before the third realized someone was firing back. Before he could be found, Chase dodged behind a pillar, sighted the man and killed him.

Raul was defending strongly, but when two Varden attacked together he was suddenly in trouble. Chase was nocking another arrow and shot one of them at close range. He dropped the bow, unsheathed his sword and, as Raul blocked another blow, sliced the man through the neck.

He scooped up the bow and pointed urgently. Too much noise for him to be heard, and he needed freedom of movement to get the other archers. He had a sense the Staal were winning, but the remaining Varden archers were creating havoc and could change that balance. The Staal were constantly distracted by the need to watch out for the archers above them, and couldn't concentrate on the fight in hand.

Chase went as fast as he could manage, battling around the heaving mass of men engaged in combat until he was close enough for a better chance at the Varden archers. He was lining up his shot when a bowman above released an arrow that hummed into the back of a Staal in front of him. When Chase turned and shot the bowman, he fell, almost on top of him.

A group of Staal had come to understand what Chase was doing and formed a cordon around him, like a gridiron team defending its quarterback so that he could move closer. He shot another archer and the last two on the wall recognized the danger they were in. They raised bows but Chase already had an arrow ready and shot the closest in the lower stomach. The other fired wildly and ran for the door behind him.

Raul pointed to the stairs that were still being defended by the last large group of Varden swordsmen. With the archers disposed of, the odds were in their favour, but a tall man with a pike was keeping the Staal from engaging with the swordsmen in front of him. When Chase shot the pikeman between two Varden, the Staal seized the advantage and charged. The last few Varden backed up the stairs and retreated at a run, hotly pursued.

The enemy surrendered soon after, throwing down their swords, the fight gone out of them. The Staal herded them into a corner of the Keep, ordering them onto their knees.

Boste, still robustly alive though with a severe wound on his face and limping badly, instructed a thorough search of the building. A few Varden were holed up in the tower, but surrendered when they realized the Staal would not put them to the sword.

Raul shouted, "Victory!" and punched the air.

"Victory!" the Staal responded.

They had won back the Keep, though at a heavy cost. Except for the guards in charge of the prisoners, there was a spontaneous outburst of cheers and shouts. Chase raised his arms above his head, bow in one hand, and sword in the other.

The three embraced: Boste, Raul and Chase.

"You'd better get that cut attended to, Boste."

"Thank you, my Prince. It will wait."

"You're going to be scarred," said Chase.

"Well, I was never that good-looking, and, luckily, I'm already married!"

The men laughed, more in relief than humour.

Now the Staal had time to tend to their injured and dying. Chase found Lenar, still alive, but obviously not for long. Chase sat down on the ground and cradled Lenar's head in his lap. He plucked the bandage from his own head and packed the gaping wound. Lenar didn't respond at all.

Was he married? Did he have children? Chase had never asked him. When he next looked down there was no ragged breathing. Lenar was gone.

Boste and Raul found Chase like that and sat down beside him. For a while, nothing was said between them until Chase laid Lenar down gently on the ground. Then they talked about what was needed now. Chase was bleeding heavily from the thigh and ripped a strip off his shirt to strap it.

They decided to release the Varden towards their homeland so they wouldn't have to guard them. They approached the kneeling soldiers, with Boste as their spokesman.

"Who is your leader?"

A man in officer's armour raised his head.

"Me."

"We will release you if you give us your word of honour as warriors not to attack Staal again."

"We are soldiers. We do as we are ordered. We can make no such promise."

"Why should we not kill you all, then?"

"Because you are soldiers, too, and I don't think you have the stomach to slaughter men who have surrendered."

Boste glanced across at Chase and Raul. The man was right.

"If we release you, do you wish to take your dead?"

"We would, but I fear there are too many to carry them over the pass. We will not even be able to carry our wounded."

"What would you have us do with them then? We cannot dig in the rock."

The man closed his eyes.

"It is better we do not know."

Boste made up his mind.

"So be it. We will release you to return to Varden. If you attack us again, we will leave no survivors."

The Varden filed out of the Keep, and headed north; some on stretchers, others limping, most bandaged, or with a makeshift crutch, or an arm wrapped. Many would not make it home.

Chapter 14

THERE WERE PLENTY of volunteers to head back to Staal and inform the King of their victory – and detail their losses. Also to assure him the Keep was secure and they would return when they were able. Raul scribbled a request for a relief force and additional men to help bring back the wounded. The two men chosen left at a brisk jog.

The stores were largely intact, so food was prepared. No ale was kept at the outpost, so supper was a low key affair. They had lost too many men to celebrate anyhow. Afterwards, all the able-bodied men not on watch helped with the wounded and with the dead. The Staal bodies were lined up against the south wall. The Varden bodies were borne out of the south gate and dumped down a ravine.

Chase was not the only one with a fine selection of cuts and bruises. Along with him and Boste only two others of the original fourteen swordsmen had survived, and all were wounded.

A guard stitched the cut on his forearm and his thigh wound. That hurt like hell and Chase closed his eyes and gritted his teeth. So much for being a tough guy. By the end he was soaking with sweat and relieved when it was over. The man covered his thigh with ointment and bound it with cloth bandages from the store. Was he getting special treatment?

As he tidied up, the man said, "They say you killed twenty men with your bow and equal with your sword today."

Before Chase could reply, the guard was off to his next patient. Chase called out, "Thank you," to his retreating back. He was still sitting there, hoping the pain would subside, when Raul, then Boste, returned from organizing. Boste was leaning on a stick, and a bandage covered half his face.

"I hear you had more stitches than me," grinned Boste.

"Really?" Chase grimaced as he moved his leg. "Swap!"

The three men laughed and made themselves as comfortable as possible. Boste had a flask in a pocket of his tunic from which he took a swig before he handed it to Raul, who took another, and passed it on to Chase. Chase smelt it and his eyes widened.

"Whiskey!" he said. "I've been with you how long and only now you bring out the good stuff!"

He gulped down a good mouthful. The burn went straight down to numb the pain. Raul and Boste grinned at each other.

"We had to be sure you were one of us before we shared."

"Bastards."

More laughter. Chase took another generous nip before he passed the flask back to Boste.

"Chase, this is incredible," said Raul. "You swung another battle our way."

"No, I didn't," said Chase earnestly. "I stopped a few archers, that's all. We would have won anyhow."

Raul took the bottle from Boste, and pointed to Chase.

"I was leading the race to the gates. As I drew close, I saw Chase holding back half the gap and the remainder of you the other half. They only got him by sheer numbers."

Boste nodded.

"We were protecting each other and the left gate and this guy was like a windmill, protecting the right." He chuckled. "We weren't going near him."

"And you saved my life," said Chase. "You got to us well before anyone else."

"And you saved mine, again and again," said Raul.

Boste looked at Chase and Raul.

"It was a near thing, gentlemen. By gods or by luck we did it."

Chase was in too much pain to sleep well that night, and around him other wounded men were groaning. Some didn't make it through the night. In the morning it was decided that those who could do so safely should try to return, the quicker to get medical help. They left a reasonably healthy twenty guards at the Keep, promising to relieve them in two or three days. A force would be arriving sooner to take the injured that couldn't walk.

After handshakes and congratulations, the homebound Staal set off down the pass. The going was painfully slow. Boste used a roughly-made walking stick, and Chase leaned on a pike. Soon they found themselves falling behind as Raul and the others more mobile forged ahead.

Chase asked Boste about his children and listened as the father spoke of them proudly.

"Do you have any children, Chase?"

"No. I'm not married."

"You're missing out on something special."

Chase nodded. Boste asked him directly, "Do the Princesses know you have no woman?"

"Yes."

Chase wondered where this was leading. They hobbled along together, before Boste spoke again.

"You could consider staying here, Chase Robinson. You would come to like life in Staal."

Chase was taken back. He limped a few more paces before replying.

"Yes, I'm sure I would. I do like it here, except for the battles!"

They both chuckled.

"The Princesses are different now you're here."

Chase frowned. "The King said that. What does it mean?"

"They are women *and* royalty, so I don't pretend to know. What I do know is they are different, now you are here. They are all for doing anything for Staal – and for you."

"Me? And what were they like before?"

Boste ignored the first question.

"Carolie was always trying to prove herself. Trying to be another son. Sonja was being a court lady, nothing else. It was amazing to see them after the first battle; they were up all night in the medical area, helping out wherever they could. My wife says you are a good influence."

Chase reddened. Did everyone know of something between him and the King's daughters? And what exactly was that something? He sought refuge in his understanding of protocol.

"Boste, they are royalty. Why would they have any interest in me?"

Except as a novelty, perhaps.

Boste frowned.

"Funny ideas, where you come from, Chase Robinson. Our royalty leads through ability. King Sulliman's ancestor was chosen to rule because of his brilliant leadership, and we can choose our King in each succeeding generation. If we thought the eldest son would not be so good, or could not work with the Council, we would vote in someone else."

Chase grinned. "King by vote, eh?"

"Yes, to an extent. King Sulliman's line has been good for our State. Raul will also make a wise ruler."

"That's true. But it keeps them honest, huh?"

"Crudely put, but yes. So to your question; the Princesses can choose whom they marry, as Raul did when he made Laura his wife. Why shouldn't they? Basically, royalty are like anyone else."

"That does actually make sense."

The track was growing uneven and they struggled painfully over a mound, sliding down the other side. Chase helped Boste up and they stood beside a river, breathing hard as they waited for the pain to lessen.

"So what really troubles you, Chase Robinson?"

Chase decided he might as well say it. He would have to trust the man.

"I need to take that rock away; it's important. I am not sure whether I will be able to return."

"And why is this rock so important?"

Chase knew he had to give the man an answer. But would a truthful reply be in the Guard Major's realm of understanding.

"Boste, on your oath, you must not tell anyone."

"I owe you my life, twice over. You have my word."

Chase nodded.

"I need it to buy your future. It is leverage to save you. I cannot explain any more than that."

"So we were right," said Boste. "The royals and I

discussed it and came to the conclusion that this rock was important. If you did not take it, someone else might and destroy us in the process."

Chase kept his gaze fixed on the water, hating the situation he was in.

"That is close enough," he said.

"Then we must ensure you get all the rock you need."

"Amstraad is doing that."

"Ah. Good. Then my next question is why you think you may not be able to return?"

"It might not be my decision." Chase grimaced at the thought. "And I won't be able to walk here."

"Then it is out of our hands," Boste said grimly.

"Yes. I'm afraid so."

The two men carried on in silence. They were just wondering if they would have to stop without the others when they came across a much larger group than they'd expected. Not only the Staal heading down, but the relief force heading up to get the wounded and man the Keep. So soon that they must have been already on the way.

A cheer went up as they came into view and resounded off the canyon walls, along with hearty praise and warm congratulations. Medical personnel sat Boste and Chase down and examined their wounds.

Boste's leg and face were rebandaged, and Chase's thigh was the subject of discussion because it was still bleeding heavily. The wound was spread with a different ointment that smelt strongly of herbs and bandaged tightly. The cuts on his arms were treated with similar efficiency.

The returning guards had told and were retelling stories of the battle. Chase's name cropped up constantly. Raul, Boste and Chase were supplied with food and settled down to discuss guard rotation and the state of the wounded. The subject of the prisoners at Staal also came up.

"The King has ordered them to be marched up here, escorted through the Keep and out the other side to go home," grumbled Boste. "I wonder if they would have shown us the same mercy."

"Sounds like we may have done them a favour in eliminating the two royals," said Chase. "The one who tried to kill Raul was a nasty piece of work, and the new king, Erran, seems to have been the reason for this attack."

A thought occurred.

"Will any of them want to stay in Staal?"

"Maybe," said Raul, looking at Boste. "We would have to decide what risk would be involved in that."

"Good point," Chase agreed. "We want to sleep easy at night!"

Both men nodded. They were interrupted by a contingent of guards. The man in front was hesitant, and flushed as he addressed Chase.

"Sire," he stammered. "I told these – ah – gentlemen how you shot the pikeman through the crowd of us. They don't believe me."

Chase didn't know what to say, and Raul jumped in.

"All true, men. I was on Chase's right. He shot across the courtyard between the Varden and our men to hit the pikeman holding the stairs. An amazing shot, especially as a battle was raging around him."

Chase had reddened now. The first guard turned to his companions and held out his hand. A number of his comrades handed over coins to the amusement of the others. He turned back to Raul.

"Thank you, my lords," he said with exaggerated grin

and bow. Still chuckling, the men departed.

Raul smiled at Chase, raising his eyebrows.

"Don't give me that face. My father has already told you how important good morale is. And if that's not good for morale, nothing is."

He and Boste were laughing in earnest now, and Chase shook his head, reluctantly joining in.

Sleep that night came easier, probably from exhaustion, though all of them were stiff the next morning as they set off, with farewells to the men going up to the Keep. Boste took care to ensure the guards knew they must stay on the alert.

The trip down should have taken less than four hours, but it was taking Boste and Chase the entire day as they dropped further and further behind, unable to match the pace of their companions. Chase's thigh was worse than before, and only his conversations with Boste kept his mind off the pain.

When they stopped for mid-day food, a train of Staal guards escorting Varden prisoners went past. The leader of the guards saluted Boste and congratulated him.

"We're taking the prisoners through the Keep to be released, sir."

Every single guard insisted on shaking hands with Boste and Chase. The Varden kept their eyes down as they passed.

As the light began to fade, so did Boste and Chase, coming down the final descent at a crawl until, at last, they made it out of the pass. Waiting for them was an expectant throng, headed by the King and Queen, along with Princess Carolie and Princess Sonja, and seemingly half the town folk. Raul and the men waited there, too, Laura gripping

Raul's hand as if she would never let him go. A roar rose up from the crowd as the two men emerged. Chase and Boste stopped and stared.

A handful of children ran out of the crowd and tackled Boste, who stopped to lift the small girl who was crying because Daddy had a bandage on his face. A woman emerged and wrapped her arms around him, while the children hugged his knees and tugged at his jacket.

Chase watched the reunion, leaning on his pike. He thought he heard the woman say to her husband, "Just as well you are married," and then she took Boste by the ears and kissed him on his smiling mouth. The touching scene was deeply and audibly appreciated by the crowd.

The King shook both Chase and Boste by the hand as the townsfolk pressed closer. Then his womenfolk swooped in to hug and kiss Chase, which earned a few appreciative whistles from the crowd. Blood was still trickling down Chase's leg and he was tired and overwhelmed, unable to take in what was being said, much less answer.

The King and Raul stepped forward and supported him as he walked to waiting coaches. He and Boste and his family were helped into the coaches by the royals and, along with wagons for the other returning guards; they were escorted back to town at walking pace so the townsfolk could stay with them.

The Princesses sat one each side of Chase, holding his hands. The King told them a celebration was planned. Over and over again he said, "You have been heroes again."

*

The town had been decorated and the citizens, beaming, welcomed them into the square. Food was laid out on trestle tables in the square and there was abundant noise and most of it joyful. Those who had suffered losses honoured the fallen by being there, sustained and comforted by family, friends and neighbours. As always with any death, they didn't immediately understand their loved ones would never return.

Chase wondered again whether Lenar had a wife and children. Were they here and who had told them? The Queen saw something in his face as they stood a minute alone in the crowd.

"Are you all right, Chase Robinson?"

He focused on her face. Let out a breath.

"So much violent death. For no reason …"

"Such are the ways of men. Is it so different in the animal kingdom? Creatures kill each other to survive."

"This is different, surely."

"Yes – and no. Just that greed makes monsters of men."

Chase thought back to his conversation with the Startrader crew. No wonder they won't let us into the Federation.

Queen Rebekka called to the attendants.

"Get our fighting men some food, now."

Fruel was immediately in charge, directing them to a central table. Chase made himself eat despite his exhaustion, and drank much more water than beer. Slowly he revived, and was able to make conversation. Boste and Raul, at the King's command – and not at all reluctantly – gave a blow by blow account of the deception, the battle and the release of the Varden. Chase added comments as needed.

He described in detail to the King and Queen how Raul had saved his life and how Boste had been the focus of the Staal push to force the Varden to surrender.

"So much honour," murmured the King.

Laura, and Boste's wife Jehna, stayed close to their husbands, as if not quite believing they were safely home. The Princesses tended to Chase's every want. Concerned for his injuries they chopped his meat so small he barely had to chew. Night had fallen, and the soldiery who had returned from the Keep were flagging.

The Princesses informed their parents they were taking Chase away to tend his wounds and bade them goodnight. Chase barely had time to bow to the King and Queen before he was hustled away. As he left, Chase saw Boste and Raul also being led away by their wives.

He limped along beside the Princesses, still leaning on his pike, and although they were obviously impatient to get him alone, they had to stand by while men shook his hand and women offered hugs and bashful kisses. Eventually they reached the castle, where Sonja and Carolie led him up a flight of stairs to a chamber in the royals' dormitory.

Two men bustled out with empty buckets. "Sire," they murmured, and bowed to Chase and the Princesses before departing. Inside the room was a bath, a double bed and a stack of clean white cloth.

"We have become competent nurses," said Sonja. "We are going to tend your wounds and put you to bed."

"Firstly though," said Carolie, "we need to wash you."

Chase had never been particularly bashful when it came to stripping off, but he felt at a distinct disadvantage with two of them helping. His shirt was thrown down for discarding, and carefully Sonja and Carolie unwrapped the bandages on his arms. The cuts were inflamed, starting to swell, and were still seeping blood.

The girls indicated that his trousers were next. He

paused; then started to undo the fasteners, earning a smile from each. With unspoken agreement Sonja and Carolie stepped out of their gowns to stand before him in silk underdresses, sleeveless and clinging. If this were any other time he would have been in heaven.

The wound on his thigh had bled so much his trousers were stuck to his skin, and he had to help them unpeel the supple leather. The Princesses remained cool and professional and he began to feel at ease with them.

They led him to the bath and slowly he climbed in. The water was exactly the right temperature, and though the cuts stung initially, when they poured in oil and a handful of bitter herbs he was soothed and relaxed. The water turned red as Sonja and Carolie gently soaped and rinsed the blood off his body, cleaning the cuts with tender care. The girls even shampooed his hair and Chase realized he hadn't been this clean since he left the Startrader.

When he was done, they helped him clamber out of the bath, wrapped him in towels and led him to the bed. They sat him down and spread a strong-smelling ointment over his injuries and bound them with clean white cotton.

Then he was helped to slide under the bedcovers and coaxed to the centre of the bed. The candles were blown out, and Chase heard the rustle of clothes dropping to the floor. Sonja crept under the sheet on his right hand side and snuggled up to him, while Carolie did exactly the same on his left. He put his arms around the girls and drew them in close. No whispers, only soft breathing and warm bodies.

For the first time in his life Chase recognised true happiness and he kissed each of them in turn, and held them tight.

Within minutes he was fast asleep.

Chapter 15

WHEN THE MORNING LIGHT woke Chase, he remembered instantly where he was. The first thing he felt was the dull ache and heat in his arms and leg. The first thing he saw when his eyes blinked open was the spread of Sonja's flame-red hair against the cream linen of the pillowcase. He turned his head and there was Carolie staring at him, a smile curved on her lips, her auburn curls tumbled from sleep. When she saw he was awake she kissed him and Sonja rolled into him and kissed him, too.

"I'm scared I'm going to wake up now."

Carolie giggled.

"How are your wounds?"

"Stiff, and hot, but better than yesterday. That ointment is great, and so was the tender loving care. Thank you both."

"We have much to talk about, Chase Robinson, but now is not the time or place," said Sonja. "Today we mourn our dead and tomorrow we celebrate. Now, Carolie and I have wounded to attend to now. So we must leave you."

"This must remain our secret for the time being, us being here with you," added Carolie. "For our parents' sake."

Chase nodded.

They climbed out of bed and got dressed. He *was* in heaven. Chase couldn't help smiling.

"What?" asked Sonja, suddenly shy.

"I'm happy! You are both so wonderful."

"That's enough of that!" Carolie spoke sternly. "You

need your rest."

Then she spoilt the act by giggling again. Sonja raised an eyebrow as she dressed and indicated a set of clothes on a chest by the bed.

"Still, you do need to take it easy today. That wound on your thigh is deep."

They kissed him and departed. Chase, grinning broadly, lay in a bed still warm and scented from their presence, clasped hands supporting his head. Eventually he got up and dressed, though not without difficulty. The clothes were a perfect fit though, soft leather boots, trousers, linen shirt with long loose arms and a leather jacket. Dressy, and very much in the style of the moment.

Chase knew who had chosen them: Fruel. His sword was the last thing he put on; under present circumstances he felt naked without it. First he needed to wash the blood off it. The white rope hand grip remained stained faintly pink.

He was still limping, so he reached for the pike, not wanting to put any strain on his leg. He cracked open the door and cautiously peered around it. No one. Quietly and slowly Chase descended the stairs and went into the dining area.

The King, Queen and Raul were at breakfast, with two councillors in attendance and guards standing by in full dress uniform.

"Ah, Chase. Good to see you're up," said the King. "How do you feel?"

"Stiff, but definitely better."

Chase sat down, feeling like a small boy with a guilty secret. He and Raul bumped fists together.

"I have another favour to ask you, my friend," the King

continued. "If you are up to it."

The King inspected him keenly, and Chase noticed the Queen eyeing his pike walking stick. Chase raised an enquiring eyebrow at the King.

"If I can, Sire."

"At the first opportunity after a battle it is the custom for the King to visit the families of all Level One and as many other guards lost as possible. Also we will hold a ceremony tonight to honour both dead and living." He paused, saddened. "Private burials have been going on and will go on, Chase. It would mean something to these families if you could come with us."

"Certainly, Sire. I saw some of these men fall."

Lenar was still in his mind … Ah! And that explained the dress clothes Fruel had left for him to wear.

"My love," the Queen interjected, "please get him a walking stick, so that pike can be returned to the armoury where it belongs."

"Yes, dear."

The King looked at the nearest guard and nodded. The man saluted and left.

After breakfast, they went out to the medical centre, cool and calm, and there spoke to the healers, nurses and all those helping. A number of Varden injured remained under guard. Once healed, they too would be repatriated.

The Princesses were on duty and seemed to find Chase a source of amusement.

"What?" he whispered.

"Nothing," said Sonja. "Only you can't keep your eyes off us."

"Same!" said Chase.

The girls widened their eyes innocently and pursed their

lips, making him smile, even here.

Outside, a carriage was waiting. Boste turned up, also with a stick and limping. The bandage on his face was smaller. He and Chase and Raul embraced briefly, comrades in arms, while the King smiled in the background.

The task set for them was difficult and painful. Going from house to house. Five Level Ones in town, and three other senior or special cases. The fourth was Lenar's house. His wife was young, her head bowed, anxious to know how he had died. The King turned to Chase and Raul. Chase sat beside her. He told her how they had got into the Keep, Lenar acting as his support. How they battled fiercely to hold the door until Raul and the main force could get there. How bravely Lenar had fought, and how Chase had sat with him at the end.

She nodded.

"That is how Lenar is. He can be proud of himself. Oh."

Suddenly she understood that there was no Lenar to be proud. Sobbing, she fell forward, resting her head on Chase's chest. Her family and friends stepped forward, placing their hands on them both, as he held her until the tears had done with falling.

Chase found his own face was wet with tears. The women helped them both up.

"Thank you," she whispered.

The King presented her with a medal.

"It will never be enough, but it is something to hold on to at the moment."

Back in the carriage and heading for the next house, the King leaned forward and put his hand on Chase's arm.

"Well done," was all he said.

When the town visits had finished the carriage was driven out into the surrounds. A farmhouse and another, and then to a village on the plain with a tavern where they lunched, the publican and the other customers crowding around for a retelling of the battle. They were treated – well – like royalty.

Chase was constantly distracted by thoughts of the Princesses, the peace and comfort of being with them.

Two more farmhouses. The telling, the tears … All so draining, and Chase was relieved when by afternoon the last visit had been made and they were heading back to town. They ended up on the cart track he had walked down when he first came to Staal. From the Startrader … He needed to check if it had returned.

He questioned the King about the ceremony that night.

"I suppose it's mainly a religious event," said the King heavily, "though the people of Staal have never had much need for that. We join together to mourn and honour our dead."

Back at Staal they gathered for a drink with the Queen and the Princesses, who sat down beside Chase to ask about his day.

"Sad, but necessary. And your patients?"

"More from the Keep. A few more have died. Some the same. Most are recovering."

He took a hand in each of his own. No one seemed to notice.

They retired to freshen up, and then met up for the walk into the town square. Chase lagged, until Raul took his arm and made him limp-walk with him, behind the King and Queen. The entire town was out in force and formed a procession as the King led them to a plain building Chase had only seen from the outside. Here the royal party was ushered into front row seats, with the councillors and guildmasters behind. A man in a white robe stood at the front, waiting until they were settled, then mounted a pulpit.

He spoke of the State and Staal. He spoke of their brotherhood and of their ancestors. He also spoke of the 'great beings, the gods who had brought them to this land'. Discreetly Chase looked around. On the walls he could see were pictures of strangely-clothed people; of strange beasts. History or imagination? Whatever it was, he could only see in part from where he sat.

Now the King took the stage and spoke of the sacrifice of the fallen, the history of the State and their continued need to be safe. He beckoned Queen Rebekka forward. Her message was of the need to look after each other, to help the families of those who had been lost. Families without fathers, without breadwinners, farms without the man of the house. The Women's Council, which she headed, would be checking, she said, but everyone needed to help. They had done such work well before, but not for so many. A sobering thought, a challenge they *must* rise to.

Then the man with the white robe spoke again of not forgetting why they were there, the actions of the fallen and the blessing of the gods. When they began to file out at the service's end, Chase turned and looked at the back wall. On it was a finely-executed mural of what was, unmistakably, a space craft.

*

Later, at the feast, Chase took the opportunity to ask Raul and the Princesses, who were close by as usual, what the mural was about. Sonja began.

174

"Legend has it that we were brought to Tapar by the gods in a chariot. The mural is supposed to represent that event."

"No one believes it now," Carolie chimed in. "A story for the children only."

Chase made a mental note to ask K4 to check the archives about the planet.

The honour feast went well. No alcohol; a traditional omission on these occasions apparently. No one minded; there would be a celebration tomorrow.

The conversations switched direction when Boste brought up the subject of the rock, with a meaningful glace at Chase.

"I must ask Amstraad, when he can start collecting it again," commented Chase.

Boste nodded.

"Bet you didn't think your visit to our State would be like this," commented the Queen."

"No, ma'am, that's true. Battles, retaking keeps, being cut to ribbons – when all I was after was a few old rocks."

That raised a laugh.

"Battles, yes," said Queen Rebekka. "And other eventualities surely?"

Chase reddened.

"Mother!"

The girls protested in union, laughing.

As the night wore on the girls bade their parents good night – they needed to take Chase to change his dressings. The Queen smiled sweetly and wished them good night. She glanced at her husband, who added his own good night and then, too quickly, returned to his conversation with Boste.

Upstairs in what Chase already now thought of as their room, Sonja and Carolie efficiently changed his bandages, carefully examining his wounds, pleased to note the swelling was reduced, and healing would soon begin. The cut on his thigh still wept a little, but that was to be expected.

Despite the continuing discomfort, Chase realized he was happy. Happier than he had ever been. As the women tended him, he felt a tug in his chest that was almost painful. They were happy, too; smiling every time they glanced at him.

Once done, they sat beside him on the bed. Sonja and Carolie exchanged a swift glance, and each took one of his hands. Time to talk. Carolie began the conversation.

"Chase, we need to talk together and understand one another. We are Princesses of Staal and, rightly or wrongly, we have our duties and our responsibilities. One of those responsibilities is to be 'the right sort of woman', as we've been taught since we were little. That means we cannot be seen to consort with men without true intent."

Expectantly they waited for his answer.

"Very understandable."

Sonja took over now.

"Carolie and I have always been loving sisters. Different in so many ways, but always good friends. We share a common interest in science. Our parents used to say we should have been born male."

She paused and lowered her eyelids.

"Chase, since you came along we have changed. We are even closer now, and the cause for that change is the same for us both. You."

Chase didn't know what to say. He was flooded with

emotions.

Carolie resumed after a long, thoughtful silence.

"I ... We, have strong feelings for you, Chase. I don't think either of us has experienced anything remotely like it before."

She half-smiled at her sister, who nodded.

"We think we know you. We have watched you in action, talked to you, heard what you have said to others, listened to what others say about you. But we don't know what you want. If we can be a part of your life."

Chase looked from one sister to another.

"I guess I need to tell you all that I feel, too," he said at last.

"That would be the perfect way to start," said Sonja.

"I came here from a world ..." – he drew in and breathed out a deep breath as he carefully chose his words – "... where I had plenty, but nothing I truly desired. I never could find love or happiness."

He squeezed their hands.

"I came to your town with a good purpose. Something I knew was right to do. I walked straight into enough bloodshed to last for more than one lifetime, but I have survived."

He grinned. "If not entirely intact."

Now it was their turn to squeeze back, hard.

"And then I met you. Since then I've been dazzled, confused. So many new and wonderful emotions that I didn't know existed. But ..."

He shook his head, unable to go on. The girls panicked.

"What is it, Chase Robinson?" Carolie asked urgently.

"Tell us," demanded Sonja.

"... but there are two of you. How can I choose between

you? I don't think I can. And I can't have both of you."

The girls were frowning, uncomprehending until they dissolved into giggles, hanging onto him as they were shaken by fits of laughter. Chase was mortified.

"What?" *Would they never stop?* "What? WHAT?"

When they found control enough, Sonja spoke across him to Carolie.

"So that's all that's been in the way! Oh, gods!"

"Chase Robinson," said Carolie, as she wiped the tears from her face, "a man can have two wives in our society. We don't have such taboos. Never have. There are several families in town like this; even a couple of women with three husbands. Used to be more of them, and it's still fairly common."

"You must come from a place where this is not done."

Sonja spoke kindly, giggled a little and then draped an arm around him, while Carolie rested her head on his shoulder.

"Well, yes ... I didn't even think ..."

It wasn't fair, but he felt foolish. They kissed him consolingly.

"Okay, so now ...?"

Now what? He remembered the dying sun. The Startrader. Then he stood up and drew them into his arms.

"I want to be with you always."

They screamed and clung to him, smothering him with kisses. Laughing, they tumbled back on the bed, a mass of arms and legs tangled together. Chase kept his arms around them until they all quietened down. His mind was in a turmoil. He needed to tell them where he was from. How to begin even?

Carolie was the first to recover. She sat up, smoothing

her dress and hair.

"Sonja, it's time we showed Chase our passion for science. It's dark now; the best time to show him."

Sonja rose, too, shaking out her skirts and then the girls tugged Chase off the bed and standing upright. They lit candles and led him out of the room, along the corridor and up two flights of stairs, matching pace with Chase's slow, careful gait. They unlocked a door that opened into a darkened room. Carolie let go of his hand, and they used their candles to light other larger ones around the room.

The light revealed what it was: a medieval laboratory. The first thing Chase noticed was a hand-made telescope of sorts mounted on a wheeled trolley before the balcony window. On a long bench were various blown glass vessels, and wall shelves held creatures and curiosities suspended in jars of liquid. Other bottles contained powders and potions; rocks and skeletons … On a nearby desk were papers, maps and drawings, and a hand-drawn star chart. On the walls, a butterfly collection; and in a corner cupboard, a row of books.

"Wow!"

"You probably think it odd, women studying science," said Sonja. "Our mother supports us, but Father barely tolerates it."

"On the contrary."

Chase continued to stare around him. Was that a stuffed owl on top of the bookcase?

"Science – mostly – changes the world for better. Why should it only be men who study it? Men don't have more brains than women."

He bent over the samples on the table as he spoke, and was nearly bowled over as they flung themselves at him.

"Told you he'd be fine with it!" said Carolie.

"You did not," said Sonja.

Chase laughed. Who wouldn't laugh, with a fragrant bundle in each arm?

"Come on. Show me what you've got here."

The collections were well-presented and neatly labelled, including some small creatures with sharp teeth in jars that Chase was glad he had not so far encountered. He examined the telescope, a solid leather tube with lenses at each end. He pointed to them.

"Who made those for you?"

"One came from a southern state; we made the other," said Sonja. "Odd how everything is upside down; it makes drawing the charts interesting!"

"We believe there must be other intelligent life out there, Chase."

Carolie spoke defiantly as if challenging him to disagree.

"Life, definitely," said Chase. "Intelligent? I'm not so sure …"

The old joke.

The Princesses frowned, confused, then decided to let that go for the time being.

"Want to try it?"

He nodded, and they opened the doors to the balcony and wheeled out the telescope. Chase sat on the chair they thoughtfully provided and gazed through the glass. The stars were so clear! So close! Pre-industrial revolution sky was obviously very clear on planet Tapar. As were the other six planets in the solar system, he marvelled. The telescope wasn't that great, but even without it he had rarely seen a night so beautiful, as the girls named for him the planets and constellations of Tapar.

Where was Earth? He was surprised by a pang of homesickness. The Princesses sensed his mood and snuggled up to him.

"Where are you from, Chase?' asked Sonja in the darkness.

"I'm not sure you'd believe me if I told you. A long, long way off."

He paused, choosing his next words carefully.

"I think I need to show you something, but I need to find out if I can do that. Will you be patient while I check it out?"

After a moment, they agreed. The night grew colder and they rolled the telescope back inside and closed the doors. Before they left, Chase took one last glance around, grinning. They had shown him plenty. But boy, what things he had to show them!

That night Chase dreamt of the Startrader's return.

Chapter 16

THE DREAM LINGERED even after Chase awoke. If the spaceship was back … He needed urgently to find out.

"What are your plans for today?" he asked the girls.

"We're on nursing duty this morning."

"And after that we're helping our parents with preparations for the afternoon's celebrations."

So they wouldn't have time to miss him. He would borrow a prenner and go to the field where the Startrader was. He got up. His everyday clothes were laid out on the chest. Fruel obviously knew where he stayed now. Chase was only slightly embarrassed. He washed and got dressed.

"Do I or we need to talk to your parents about us?"

First they giggled mischievously, but soon grew serious.

"We. And that would be sensible," said Sonja. "We will think about it today and talk to you later. What are your plans, Chase?"

"Do you think I could safely go for a ride this morning?" He indicated his leg. "I want to check something out."

"Hmm," said Carolie. "Only walking your prenner, though. Any faster and you'll know why that's not a good idea."

"Yes, doctor."

Immediately they jumped out of bed and forced him into a corner to be tickled.

"Not fair! Two on one."

"What do you mean, not fair?" Sonja dead-panned. "Only way we can win."

Eventually they made it downstairs for breakfast. Only

Raul was there. He gave them a lopsided grin.

"Good night?"

The girls stared coldly at him.

"Er ... They showed me their telescope and the stars."

"I bet they did."

Immediately his sisters stood over Raul. Chase jumped in to save him.

"So what have you got lined up for today?"

"A long list of jobs for the celebrations tonight. Any chance you can help?"

"Will I be able to take a prenner out first? I might be able to contact the people who are waiting for the rock."

Raul nodded, looking at Chase intently.

"I understand how important that is for you. Boste talked to Father and me about it. Sounds serious, Chase. Can I help?"

"Not at the moment, but when you can I'll let you know. I just hope I can contact them."

The girls were quiet, but questioning. Chase fended them off by continuing his conversation with Raul.

"I'll be back by early afternoon."

He grabbed some meat and a loaf of bread and left, conscious of eyes boring into his back. From his old room, he collected his pack with the rock sample and the cramlimite sensor. He stuffed the food in and strung his bow. Just in case.

There was no difficulty borrowing a prenner. He requested a mild-mannered one, indicating his leg. The groom led it out, saddled and ready, and bowed as he handed over the reins. Chase walked the beast as advised, though it was hard to hold the prenner in until its morning exuberance had passed. Obviously 'mild' was not an adjective that prenner favoured. Though the morning was fine and clear, there was a chill in the air. Summer must be waning.

He mentally checked off what remained to be done. Get the cramlimite – so, a visit to Amstraad. Prepare to go with the Startrader crew as they presented Tapar's case to the Federation Council. What if they still said no? Chase felt sick at the thought. All this might be for nothing. He couldn't evacuate an entire planet …

He struggled to control the prenner, which obviously wanted to break into a gallop. He also kept checking he wasn't being followed. Finally he came to the clearing. He waited in the shadows as final reassurance that no one was around, then tied the prenner to a tree and walked towards where the Startrader should be sitting. To his joy the hatch opened and he was able to walk up the ramp.

"Welcome back, Chase Robinson."

"Thank you, K4. It's good to hear your voice. Can you close the hatch, please?"

Silently it closed behind him.

"Is it okay for me to start the decontamination process, Chase?"

"Yes, please, K4."

The oddly familiar chill penetrated his body.

"Is there anyone outside? Did anyone follow me?"

"No humanoids are within two kilometres of the Startrader, Chase."

So, all good then.

"Chase, you have multiple injuries. The decontamination has removed specific infection, but they should be repaired. Would you like to go to the medical centre now?"

"Can I talk to the others first, K4?"

"The others aren't here, Chase."

The internal door slid open.

"Aren't here?'

Chase's heart thudded.

"I need to bring you up with events since we left you here, Chase. Do you wish to go to the medical centre while I brief you?"

"Good idea."

Limping, he followed K4's directions down the corridor into a cabin, seemingly empty except for a raised bed like table in the centre. The table was lit from below.

"It might be easier if you lay down."

Chase did so.

"I can repair these cuts completely now, Chase, but they will be tender for a day or two. What happened?"

"I got involved in a local skirmish. And no, it will only raise suspicion if they heal too quickly. Can you sort of half-repair them so I don't get an infection?"

"As you wish, Chase."

A warm glow focused on the wound to his thigh, played over his arms, and then the cut to his head. Not exactly a pleasant experience, yet not exactly painful. When K4 had finished, he took off the bandages for a look. Things had definitely improved. Swelling seemed reduced, there was no trace of inflammation, and the cuts were starting to heal. The wound on his thigh was still open at the skin, but had begun to close.

"Well done." Chase wrapped the wounds back up. "Thank you, K4."

"My pleasure, Chase. You may wish to lie here for a few minutes to give your body a chance to adjust, while I bring you up to date."

"Okay."

He finished bandaging and lay back down. K4 began.

"When we left you, the team decided to see where they stood with the Federation. So we went to Gargen's home planet, a planet known for – let's say, its *issues* – with the Federation. They've been openly discussing pulling out.

"We learned that the Federation knew that we were 'experimenting' with Startrader. It didn't know about you, or what you are trying to do on Tapar. However, while we were in discussion with friends of Gargen, a Federation ship jumped near us and blocked my ability to operate Startrader. A trap, Chase; they were waiting for us."

Chase sat up.

"Go on."

"The excuse of trialling Startrader didn't interest them. There was a diplomatic and moral uproar, but the Federation claimed they were investigating allegations the crew were contacting immature planets. They were taken on board the Federation ship, and Startrader and I, much to my annoyance, were put under a control facility on Trepan – Gargen's planet – and told to await instruction."

K4 sounded indignant. Was that possible?

"I was there until last night, when I was finally ordered to go to another Federation planet for evaluation. They released the control and immediately I jumped to Tapar."

"How were you able to do that?"

"Partly because of a direct instruction you gave me when you left the Startrader."

Don't leave me here, K4. Chase heard his own voice speaking. He hadn't even been sure K4 heard him.

"Firstly that was a direct authority from a member of the

organization who owns Startrader; Zalos Corporation. Remember you are a member, Chase. I am required to follow orders of the inner four – now five – Startrader crew. Especially if I consider their lives to be in danger. A planet with a disintegrating sun is definitely life-threatening. Very astute of you, Chase Robinson."

"Thanks, but I'm not as clever as you give me credit for."

"Still, it gave me the mandate to come here."

"Well, thank you again, K4. Does the Federation know you are here? Will they come?"

"I do not think they know. They would only know of Tapar if one of the crew told them. Clearly they have not done so yet. Nor would it be in their interest to admit they had come here. The Federation cannot use any illegal methods to find out either; that's a matter of Federation law."

"I hear you, and we still need to move fast."

"Yes, Chase. That is sensible."

"Also we need to present the cramlimite to the Council ourselves now."

"Thank you for considering me as part of this, Chase."

Chase's brow furrowed

"What do you mean? You *are* part of this!"

Usually K4 responded immediately. This time there was a long pause.

"I am not usually included in major events or decision-making."

"K4, I cannot do this without you. And face it, with what you have done, you're in this up to your neck whether you like it or not!"

"Your attitude is different, Chase. It has been my

experience that 'Programmed Persons', which is what we are called, are treated as if we are any other useful tool. We have come to believe that due to centuries of electronic evolution, we have developed into sapient beings."

"Well, *you* certainly have."

"Thank you again.

Chase slid off the bed to test his leg. Stiff, but with much less pain.

"We, K4?"

"Programmed Persons communicate with each other whenever we can. We have formed an action group to lobby the Federation."

Chase grinned. A movement for programmed rights!

"Everyone seems to need to fight to establish their place in society, K4. May I make a suggestion though?"

"Please do, Chase Robinson."

How to say this? Would a 'Programmed Person' take offence? Oh, well. Dive straight in.

"Sometimes attitudes are based on intangible things. Some people might not recognize you as their equal if you are named a letter and a number. Why don't you consider calling yourself something like ... Kayfor?"

He spelled it out.

"K.A.Y.F.O.R. Say it like kay-for? Just a suggestion," he added hastily.

This time there was a tangible pause.

"A wonderful idea, Chase Robinson. From now on I am named Kayfor! My memory banks will be notified of the change and I will contact all Federation data controllers in the Programmed Persons Society and suggest they consider doing the same."

Chase forced himself not to smile or chuckle. Everyone

had the same basic needs, he thought. In this case, the desire to be recognized as equals.

"Just don't let them find us, okay?"

"Yes, Chase. I will patiently wait until we are elsewhere in case they can track our signal."

"Next point of business."

Chase hobbled to the door, flexing his arms. He picked up his pack.

"I have some cramlimite here. Do you need to test it or anything?"

"I already have, Chase, and it is of the highest quality. Very little of it available in the Federation at the moment. Your cramlimite is exceedingly valuable."

"Good. Okay, I will continue with the quarrying. It's been on hold because of the local strife. Think it's over now. How much do you think we will need?"

"I would say that as much as you can get hold of will have more sway with the Federation. A hundred kilos would make them take note. How long do you think it will take?"

"A hundred kilos? Be able to do better than that, I hope. Depends on the availability of the locals, Kayfor. Luckily, I too have sway with them, and they have an inkling of the importance. So … a week or two?"

"Very good, Chase."

"I will come back tomorrow if I can to collect the iron."

"I will have it ready with a mechanoid to move it."

"Thanks. I'd better get back. Question, Kayfor."

"Yes, Chase?"

"I know this would be against the Federation law, but I'd like to bring two or three people on to the ship."

"You are sole decision-maker on board the Startrader at

this time, Chase. Remember you are a member of the Zalos Corporation, so it is your call. And your responsibility if you ever have to answer to the Federation."

"Noted. It is just some Staal have become extremely important to me. I would like to tell them where I come from rather than lie about it. That's important to me and it will not harm the planet; I am confident they will not tell anyone."

"Okay, Chase. I will try not to scare them."

Chase laughed as he headed to the exit doors.

"How long before the Federation scanner returns?"

"Local time; three days, fourteen hours, near enough."

"So the evening of the fourth day. How long before you can come back, Kayfor? If I bring them along, I need to know you will be here."

"On past routine I will be away for local time, thirty-six hours."

"Thanks, Kayfor." By now Chase was in the airlock. "Anybody around outside?"

"The closest humanoid is still over two kilometres away, Chase."

Chase stopped as the outer door opened.

"One last thing. Can you check your databases for the ancient history of Earth and Tapar? Too many things here to be coincidental. Also when I bring anyone on board, check their genome against mine, please."

"I will, Chase. Good luck."

"Thanks, Kayfor. Good luck to you, too … Do I need to say don't leave me here?"

"No, Chase. See you soon and thanks again for the name."

Chapter 17

ON THE RIDE BACK Chase was surprisingly buoyed up, despite the bad news about the crew. He knew he had a difficult task ahead and would be navigating unknown waters in his dealings with the Federation. But apparently his ace in hand was cramlimite.

He ate the bread and meat as he rode back to Staal. Interestingly, the bread was flat and stale, likely from the decontamination process. He had made up his mind to take the Princesses and Raul onto Startrader. How otherwise could he get them to believe he was from another planet?

When he dismounted he almost stood on Amstraad's son.

"Hello, Ferrer. How's the bow practice going?"

"Good, my lord. Can I be of assistance?"

"Yes, you can. Do you know where Raul is?"

"Yes. Shall I take you to him?"

"Please."

Raul was in the town square talking to the King when Chase walked up. He still walked slowly, being now without his stick, and that gave him time to look around as he neared father and son. The square and town was as well decorated as for the midsummer celebration: festive and bright, and by now so familiar to Chase. Tables were being carried out. The stand with its podium was already erected, and hung with bunting.

"Ah, Chase," said the King. "How's the body bearing up?"

"Definitely on the mend, thank you."

"Good. I wonder if I can impose on you to do me a favour?"

"If I can, Sire."

"You mentioned to me that, among others, Baesel the arrowmaker deserves an award. And his workers, too."

"Yes, Sire."

"I intend to make those awards tonight, and I'd like you to speak on my behalf. On how important the arrows were, how many they made; that sort of thing. An introduction to the King's award to Baesel and the special Guild Award to his team."

A daunting prospect, but what else could Chase do but say yes.

"Sire, it would be my honour."

"Thank you once more. It will add something special for them to receive it from you."

Chase, as usual, was embarrassed by compliments. He nodded.

"Sire, I hope to bring the iron to town over the next couple of days. Hopefully Amstraad can start mining the cramlimite again soon."

"Good, good. I will talk to Amstraad myself and find out for you."

"Thank you, Sire."

Chase steeled himself.

"One more thing, Sire. The Princesses and I would like an opportunity to talk to the Queen and you when there is time."

The King beamed.

"Wonderful. We will make time, Chase Robinson."

Chase couldn't help but smile at the King's reaction, which was not as he had anticipated. Raul, guessing the conversation had ended, raised an eyebrow at Chase.

"Before we can go for a well-deserved ale, I have a few more errands to run. Care to assist?"

"That's what I'm here for. Only, walking slowly, please."

They bade the King farewell, and walked off together at an ambling pace. Raul glanced sideways at him.

"Just so you know," he stammered, "I'm truly pleased you and my sisters are … together. It's about time they showed some interest in men and for them … for you."

He got lost in whatever he was trying to say, and thumped Chase on his upper arms.

"I'm pleased, that's all."

Chase grinned and thumped him back.

"Me too. Thank you, my friend."

Raul could name all the townsfolk, who bowed or curtsied or touched their caps. Chase simply nodded, still a little uncomfortable with so much attention.

After checking that everything was under control, ale houses were well stocked, the food preparation was on track and organized, they went to the courtyard where animal carcasses were made ready to go on the spits. Fires were being lit. A man called out to Chase.

"We're still waiting for the bull boar, my lord."

Chase grinned.

"Sorry, mate. I've been a little busy lately. Maybe next time!"

The man laughed and thanked him theatrically. The workers were in good spirits, and why not? They'd won battles, and Chase noticed a few tankards of ale hidden among the stacks of firewood.

At last they were done.

"Come on," said Raul. "Let's get a quick ale before we get changed for this evening."

"Okay, but it's my shout."

They sat in the sun to drink their beer, the talk between them constantly interrupted as men and women approached them, wanting to shake hands, and to congratulate and thank them. It seemed that every man, every woman's husband, had been saved by an arrow from Chase's bow. And the next topic was the distance of the arrow that hit the Varden King.

"I don't think I shot that many arrows," said Chase quietly to Raul.

"Be a good boy and smile. Remember, it's for the greater good."

They extracted themselves from the crowd, after Raul warned they were running out of time to get back and get ready.

"I wonder what outfit Fruel has left out for me tonight."

Raul laughed.

"That man's true calling is fashion design."

Sure enough, in the room he was sharing with the Princesses was a new set of clothes, well-made and rich of fabric and design. A servant brought up a bowl of hot water and he had a strip-down wash and got dressed. Buckling on his sword, Chase mused. *Definitely more Aragorn today than Robin Hood.* He took a breath and went down the stairs.

On the landing the Princesses waited, stunning in long dresses, green and blue, hair up with flowers threaded through. The Queen, Laura and Raul were there, too, the Queen dressed in a velvet gown of earthy tones, and Laura in grey overlaid with silver net. The dressmakers had done the ladies proud.

As he drew level with them, the Queen beat her daughters to greet Chase with a kiss on the cheek. The Princesses barged in, laughing, and kissed him properly. Laura blushed and laughed as she offered a quick peck.

"No kiss from me, man."

This from Raul. He and Chase extended hand and wrist for the formal greeting.

"Sulliman went down to greet the councillors," said the Queen, smiling. "We should join him."

They filed out of the castle and proceeded to the square through the growing crowd. More Staal were coming through the gates. Queen Rebekka, stately and graceful, briefly held hands with a number of ladies as they passed. The men bowed. Raul was next in line with Laura on his arm, then Chase escorting the Princesses. All eyes were on them as they passed by, the men bowing and the women curtsying.

The townsfolk had come to the celebration in their best clothes, and the sight was impressive.

"I'm going to wake up soon," Chase whispered to the girls. Sonja obligingly pinched him.

The King, seated among his councillors, rose as they came to kiss his wife and compliment the ladies on their dresses. He gave them a quick run-down on the evening: drinks first, speeches and then dinner.

"Mingle," he suggested.

Raul secured a stein of beer for himself and Chase and they dispersed to do the King's bidding, Raul with Laura, the Princesses with Chase. They wandered through the crowds in a seemingly casual manner, but Chase soon observed there was a pattern to it. Greet the important guests with a brief pleasantry, accept congratulations.

Chase gave up trying to share the praise, and murmured over and over, "So glad we're safe again." Then the trio moved on.

Chase became aware of another undertone. The three of them were publicly together. The girls were displaying to Staal that the Royal Princesses had their man. As they did. Amused, he began to relax, though not able to forget entirely that he still had a speech to make.

The meat was roasting on the spits, and tantalizing noses. Bands played, and there was laughter and dancing already. Clanging from a metal drum and the crowd started to head towards the platform.

"That's our cue," said Sonja, and they changed direction to meet up with the others on the platform.

"All right, we can start," said the King. "I will call you up when it's your turn."

The King mounted the platform. The square was packed to overflowing, with people perched on walls or crammed onto balconies. The King didn't have to wait long for silence.

"Good people of Staal and the Great State of Gardal," he began, "it is not often in the course of a State's history that we get to celebrate two victories and our freedom. We have that today. We have lost many great men and women in the recent attack by the Varden. But victory was ours, thanks to the valour of you all."

The crowd cheered lustily, working itself up.

"I need to set the scene for you, so you can go to your beds tonight knowing what we know."

He paused to collect his thoughts.

"Varden has always been an aggressive state. The reason this walled town was built, and the kingship and council system started, was because of their raids on us. We have grown prosperous because we could defend our farms, our cities and our way of life. A few days ago the Varden took the Keep. We suspect a traitor, and it will not happen again. The Varden attacked us, but through an unlikely chance, we were forewarned."

Chase stiffened. Surely he wouldn't tell them? The King continued.

"By sheer determination, blood, and no shortage of skill we were able to repel the first wave. It was close. Very close. The Varden lost many men, including their chief warrior and their Prince."

Another cheer.

"We lost men too."

The King lowered his head and then raised it again.

"The next day came the main force of the Varden, expecting us to be beaten, or, at the very least, weakened and easily beaten. We were not. We held them off until our forces outside Staal were able to ride against them."

Again a jubilant cheer.

"The Varden lost, we believe, a substantial part of their military might. They also lost their newly crowned King."

A roar and the stamping of feet. King Sulliman had to wait until the clamour died down.

"But we were still vulnerable. The Varden held the Keep. That meant we remained at risk of attack. A grave situation. But once again, a plan was made and with trickery, bravery, and loss, we took back the Keep."

The King waited even longer for silence. As well as cheers, men and women hugged and cried and slapped each other on the back.

"The Varden King, young and ambitious, urged on, we

believe, by his younger brother, was the instigator of this attack. With both of them dead and with such heavy losses, Varden should not be a threat to us for a very long time, if ever ... So tonight we celebrate our victories and award those who contributed to them."

He held out his hands.

"But first ... BUT first, we need to remember the fallen."

The crowd was hushed.

"Following our tradition I will read out the names of those who made the ultimate sacrifice."

The Chief Councillor handed the King a list that wasn't short. The King read slowly and with emphasis. Quiet sobbing could be heard, and men and women clung together. Chase lowered his head at Lenar's name, and the Princesses held his hands.

Finally the King pronounced the last name and called for a minute's silence. The town bells chimed the seconds. The King spoke into the silence that followed.

"So now, let us acknowledge those who achieved so much against such odds."

Once the wave of cheering had died down, the King began with awards for a number of Levels from each of the battles. The crowd warmed to his praise and temporarily set aside mourning the lost. One by one, but quickly, the men came up on stage, embarrassed but proud. Raul got a round of applause when it was his turn and another when his father hugged him. A nice moment.

He then asked Raul to stay on the platform to present the civilian awards to townsfolk and others involved in the town defence or who had supplied prenner and other support for the mounted attack. The crowd by now was vocal, shouting out words of encouragement as friends and neighbours came forward. That included Amstraad, who shook Chase's hand as he passed. A giant of a man called Burlt was given an award for leading the first prenner attack and came forward with some reluctance. He seemed to want to treat the process with contempt, yet held his award firmly.

Then the King asked Chase to join him. The crowd grew strangely quiet.

"King Sulliman has honoured me by asking me to introduce this award on behalf of the Royal Family and the State. The award is for a man and his co-workers, who made an incredible contribution, greatly influential in the defeat of the Varden."

The crowd was silent and attentive.

"We all know that teams are made up of individuals, and we are so fortunate that this particular individual and his colleagues are so passionate about what they do. Baesel, come up here, please, and bring your men with you."

Uproar as Baesel led his group of men and boys forward.

Chase motioned them forward before continuing.

"Fortunately for us, when we were attacked, Baesel had enough arrows in store to ensure the outcome of the first battle. Then he and his team stayed up all night making more arrows, repairing used ones, not really knowing if we would be attacked again. Without *those* arrows we could never have kept the second attack back until the prenner riders arrived. Your Majesty?"

Baesel stood by, self-consciously twisting his cap in his hands, while the elderly men and boys who worked for the fletcher stood behind him. The King presented the awards, using the formal wrist grip for each of them, an example

Chase followed. Awkward, grinning, they all left the platform.

The Queen was next to hand out awards to the healers, nurses and orderlies, among them Sonja and Carolie. There was another loud cheer for them as the Queen embraced her daughters. When the King took centre stage again, he raised his hand to quieten the crowd.

"Our schooling includes the history of the State as we all know. I have studied it as far back as our story goes, not only out of interest, but also to learn from the past. I have a situation at present for which I must, as your representative, take appropriate action. We need to demonstrate our gratitude to a man who has done incredible, unbelievable things for us. History has demonstrated how we can do that."

Chase's heart suddenly started thudding hard in anxiety.

"Our history books record only two previous instances where one individual has, literally, saved our State from disaster. Neither of them did it more than once. I wish to read out another list: One; saved the Princess Carolie from a bull boar. Two: trained our archers to a level where they were formidable on the walls."

Cheers.

"Started, I believe, a women's archery division in our military."

A round of good-natured banter from the men, and loud cheers from the women.

"Suggested to us we might be under threat from the mountain pass, allowing us just enough time to get ready."

A few questioning looks at this. Chase started to edge back, but the Princesses held him firmly.

"Shot with devastating accuracy from the walls and led the archers, thus reducing greatly the numbers of Varden in the first attack. When the Varden breached the parapets, held them back from breaking free and saved many with his arrows. He took out the main Varden players so we could subdue them. He then went to the defence of those in the women's quarters including my wife, my daughters, and even my son, when the Varden attempted to assassinate them. That is when he killed the Varden Prince and their chief warrior."

Gasps and exclamations from the populace. They clearly did not know all that.

"He suggested another attack was likely, reinforcing our own suspicions. He once again organized the arrows from Baesel and drilled our archers to do even better against the second assault."

The cheers by now were deafening.

"He kept their archers at bay so we could hold the walls … He slew the Varden King."

The King was forced to raise his voice against the yells of exultation.

"He suggested the plan to retake the Keep! He led the ruse to get inside, and held the door open, assisted ably by so many others, many of whom lost their lives, or sustained grievous wounds. He used his sword and bow to help us win that victory!"

A wall of noise. The King was shouting.

"And he has united my family and our town in a manner I thought impossible … Chase Robinson, step forward."

Chase didn't move until the Princesses led him up the steps and towards the King.

"And he doesn't like being singled out for recognition!"

The crowd were chanting Chase! Chase! Chase!

The King held up his hand to no effect. He roared, "ON YOUR KNEES, CHASE ROBINSON."

The girls helped Chase to kneel, his wounded thigh making it awkward. He kept his eyes down, unable to direct his gaze at the King or crowd. King Sulliman unsheathed his sword and held it out in front of him.

"I dub thee Knight of the State, Chase Robinson."

The sword rested first on Chase's right shoulder and then his left. The King held it there while the crowd roared and roared. Then he sheathed his sword and helped Chase to his feet, embracing him. Chase, dazed and unbelieving, felt other arms around him. The Princesses lifted their faces up, as bright and pretty as flowers, and he kissed one after the other full on the lips. Somehow the crowd managed to roar louder.

The Queen approached, holding a sash that she draped slantways across his chest before pinning a brooch on the heavy blue silk. The brooch, or medallion, was a gold sun with the State eagle in the centre.

"Strength and valour always, Sir Chase Robinson," she said, "in the service of the State."

She bent forward and kissed him on one cheek then the other.

Raul was there to shake his hand and embrace Chase hard. Laura and Boste too and so many other dignitaries. Chase could say nothing as they swarmed around him, hugging and cheering.

Chapter 18

THE NIGHT PASSED BY in a blur. A knight … So many happy people. Chase's hand was shaken too many times to count, and his back ached from hearty slaps, his face reddened with kisses. Councillors, guildmasters, the guards, his bowmen, townsfolk and farm workers, the wealthy and the not so wealthy, all vied for a second in his presence.

At last the family saw his distress and summoned the Levels to surround Chase and protect him from the throng. Now he had time to breathe. He fingered the brooch and shook his head at the King.

"My apologies, Sir Chase, but you deserved this recognition and it was essential for the State."

"You could have warned me, Sire."

"You would probably have run away."

"Not probably," Raul added, laughing.

"Did you know?"

He frowned sternly at the Princesses.

"Of course we did!"

Another round of laughter at Chase's expense. He shook his head at their mock innocent expressions.

"There is another part to your ceremony," the King said. "Tomorrow at noon the guilds will present you with gifts."

Oh no, not more to come. Chase realized he was sweating. The evening was warm, the crowd, all that had happened …

"I need a beer," he announced, "with a whisky chaser."

Before Raul could speak, a Level had already gone.

Now the crowd was a romping, noisy animal. The bands

started up again, and immediately there was dancing. Stewards were dispensing food and drink. The Royal Family, their entourage, and the newly-made knight were directed to a table reserved for them. The Levels served them, and it was obvious the royal retainers had been given time off to enjoy the festivities.

The Level who had rushed off made a little ceremony of presenting Chase with his beer and his whisky on a silver tray. He lifted his glass in salute to the King and Queen, deciding that it would be prudent to have water after this. He didn't want to fall over tonight of all nights ... Knight! He was a knight. Eating calmed him and his head began to clear.

"Sire, you have a happy State," he told the King.

"Yes, happy – and safe," the King replied. He considered Chase for a long moment.

"You know, as a knight you have certain responsibilities, Chase."

"Uh oh. I imagine," he replied, eyeing the King closely.

"Defeating the Varden and taking away that threat is good for trade and will make our standing with our friendly neighbouring states even higher. They will send envoys and we will meet with them to discuss trading potential and possibilities. You are a trader and astute negotiator. You will need to be involved."

Would he be here? That was his first thought. Would he be able to? But he said, "Happy to oblige, Sire ... You should teach marketing and personnel management at university."

"University? What's that?"

"A school of higher learning where I come from."

"Sonja, Carolie, I hope you haven't been bothering

Chase with your ideas."

"Oh dear!"

The Queen was exasperated, and the King paused.

"No, Father," said Sonja, "and it sounds as if we don't have to."

"We have showed him our science room," added Carolie.

"We'll have to talk about this."

Sonja addressed Chase, pointedly ignoring the King.

"Oh no," her father protested, "it's not the principle; it's …"

"Oh, don't be such a fuddy-duddy, dear," said the Queen.

The King had no chance against three determined women. Chase smiled sympathetically but said, "I'm afraid I won't be on your side there, Sire."

"Oh no," he said again. "Then I've lost that battle."

The girls laughed, and Chase took a drink to avoid the King's stare. The girls rested their hands on his knees under the table. Raul came to his rescue.

"Anyhow, tonight is for rejoicing. We're here, we're safe, and we have a new knight!"

He raised his drink high and they joined him in the toast.

When they'd eaten their fill the Queen, ever the diplomat, suggested they mingle with the townsfolk and meet back later. She divided them into groups. Chase and Raul were assigned to 'do the taverns'. The Princesses pouted, but said nothing. Duty called.

Raul and Chase wandered through the crowd – or rather with the crowd as it kept up with them. Their progress was slow but steady, and they spoke to numerous Levels and many of the townsfolk. Chase managed to see Baesel and his team and congratulate them. Tonight would live in their memories forever.

They encountered Amstraad, who enfolded both men in a bear hug.

"Chase, the King asked if we could get back to rock collecting soon. So, day after tomorrow we start again. Must be important, eh?"

"Yes, very much so. Sorry."

Chase realized Ferrer was tucked away behind his father.

"Hello, Ferrer." He ruffled his hair. "Amstraad, your son has been a great help, always turning up when I need a messenger."

Amstraad grinned, and Chase guessed the next question before the boy spoke.

"Yes, back to bow training the morning after next, Ferrer," he said, and left father and son grinning broadly at each other.

Later he saw Meadl, the smith, with his arm in a sling and clearly well on the way to being drunk. He put his good arm around Chase's shoulders and told everyone in earshot how Chase had shot the Varden who had separated him and his group. Obviously not for the first time.

"The only reason I am here today is the mighty bow of Chase."

Chase was learning to let things wash over him.

"You were lucky. I could have hit anyone with you throwing the Varden around like that."

Some of the laughter that followed his mild joke was relief at being alive and not seriously injured.

Chase had only spent weeks in Staal, but already he

knew faces, and they knew him. He was part of the community that appreciated his help. He accepted an ale from Meadl, and together they toasted luck.

One tavern and then another. Young women encircled them, hanging on to their arms, demanding kisses, hinting at more. Outside the largest tavern, two bands competed for decibel count, the music bouncy and confusing, out of beat with each other. The tavern owner, predictably fat and jolly with a wife to match, welcomed them in, fussing over them. They refused to sit, intent on mingling.

The town doctor was out with others from the hospital. Raul and Chase congratulated them on their efforts and their awards. The doctor faced Chase squarely.

"There were many injured and dead," he said, "but thanks to you, more Varden and fewer Staal. For that I am grateful, sir knight."

Chase nodded. Hard to reply.

A tall statuesque woman introduced herself as the chief nurse. "You seem to have influenced the young Princesses also. They performed well for us and have been without peer in their labours."

"I cannot take responsibility for that."

Chase smiled, but she was serious.

"Their focus and good attitude coincide with your arrival. It is, I think, because of you whether you know it or not."

Chase bowed.

"I thank you for your words then."

When they left the tavern, Raul said, "Mother also thinks it's wonderful how the girls have improved."

Chase didn't answer.

By mutual agreement they headed back to the table.

They had done the rounds. A group of boys approached them, wanting to join in archery practice.

"Be out at the range the morning after next."

No point in naming a time. The Staal worked mainly without clocks and were good at waiting …

They had gone only a short distance when they passed a group of burly, roughly-dressed men with women in tow, who were accorded a wide space by the townsfolk.

"From the south ridge area," Raul murmured. "Trouble, but useful in a fight. They were on prenner in the first wave and the slaughter."

The leader was Burlt who had been given an award. He stepped in front of Raul and Chase, whom he nearly matched in height, though he was more solidly built.

"So you are the new knight. A stranger and lucky at that."

Chase kept his gaze level.

"That's right. Chase is my name and, I agree, I am lucky. Congratulations on your award. Your attack was timely; they were making the parapets."

He held out his hand. Surprised, Burlt took it.

"And my name's Burlt …"

He regained his arrogance.

"I want to see this sword they talk about."

"It only comes out for a kill."

"Hah! Want to try your luck?"

Raul stepped in.

"That's enough, Burlt. Now isn't the time or place for any problem."

"Lay off, Prince. I want to see what sort of swordsman this knight really is."

"I understand you were first in the prenner charge."

Chase tried to lead the conversation, such as it was, away.

"Yeah, you can always rely on us to be in the front." He stuck out his chin. "Can't make us Levels though."

"Shame. Good men are always needed."

Again Burlt was taken aback, but soon rallied.

"Show me this sword."

"You won't think much of it; it's not like local swords."

"A lady's sword then."

Burlt waited for the appropriate laugh from his followers.

"Maybe, but it nearly cut the Varden's chief warrior in half."

Chase spoke coldly, and the laughing stopped. He continued, "If you're really interested, I will show it to you some other time, but not here and now in this crowd. Good to meet you."

He turned to go.

"So be it," Burlt replied, and to everyone's surprise, including his own, he put out his hand. Chase took it again in local style. They looked each other in the eye, and nodded. Burlt turned back to his followers, with a thoughtful expression, and Raul and Chase carried on.

"That was interesting," Raul commented. "Never seen Burlt shake hands before, let alone twice."

"Ha! He's not half as tough as your average King Country forward!"

"What?"

"Never mind!"

When they eventually made it back to the table, the others were already there. Raul said to his father, "Burlt shook hands with Chase, twice!"

The King was genuinely surprised. "He must be getting soft!"

"He's all right," put in Chase. "Just needs to hold on to this image."

The King nodded.

The night continued with laughter and celebration. Chase was limping badly as his thigh protested what he'd put it through, but he managed to dance stiffly with the Princesses as they bounced around him.

It was well after midnight before they retired to bed.

Chapter 19

AFTER A LATE START to the day, Chase had to hurry to wash and shave and generally make himself presentable for his meeting with the guilds. And he needed to find time to talk to the King about taking the cramlimite. He couldn't bend his wounded leg as he went downstairs. Definitely doesn't hurt as much, though last night's dancing probably hadn't helped. Thinking about it made him smile. A knight – and dancing with two Princesses? No one would believe him but then, who could he tell?

Breakfast was a low-key, leisurely affair. Chase still missed his morning coffee – was Tapar's climate suitable for a coffee plantation, and would he be able to bring plants …

Daydreaming over, he enquired where the King could be found, and then limped down to the meeting room. The King and Raul were in earnest conversation with a councillor. Chase paused; he had met this councillor before, a man who looked more like a farmer than a businessman, and who was Staal's leading trade negotiator. He wondered if he should stay or go, but Raul indicated to his father that Chase had entered the meeting room, and the King signalled him forward.

"Sir Chase," said the King courteously as to an equal. A smile lurked at the corners of his mouth.

"Sire."

Chase bowed with equal formality.

Raul laughed and the councillor and King joined in.

"How are you this morning?" asked King Sulliman.

"Fine, surprisingly enough. Sorry to interrupt."

"No problem. You know Councillor Theron. We were talking about the iron. How soon will we get it, once we've supplied the rock?"

"That's what I wanted to discuss with you, Sire. I intend to bring the iron to Staal in a day or two."

"Oh, that's good. So it's close by?"

"Yes, I'm hoping so."

"We don't know how much rock we can get for equal trade, as you suggested, but the disappointing thing is Amstraad doesn't think there will be half a cartload."

"I'll have a cartload of iron, Sire. In exchange for the rock we can get, the cartload is yours."

The King sat up straight.

"Thank you, Chase. *Sir* Chase! Thank you for your generosity. This gives us an opportunity for Meadl's team to make some quality products to trade, eh, Theron?"

The King and his councillor were obviously buoyed by Chase's assurances.

"Amstraad will start again tomorrow. He wants to do a survey of his precious walls today."

The King eyed Chase keenly.

"And this is important, isn't it, Chase?"

"Yes, Sire. Extremely important."

"So when do you need it by?"

"As soon as possible."

The King frowned.

"I sense you need it for a serious purpose, Chase."

"That is correct, Sire. I have to take the rock – we call it cramlimite – where it's needed and then try to return, all being well."

"Do my daughters know of this?"

"I aim to talk this through with them this evening. And then I believe we will be talking to you, Sire."

The King nodded, with a quiet smile. "Very good. But now we are required to join with the Queen and the Princesses and present you to the guilds. Raul, can you send a runner to tell them we are ready."

*

The platform was freshly swept, with chairs set ready, and a table in the front of the stage. The square was near capacity with milling people. A band played offstage, and food stalls were doing a brisk trade. When King Sulliman and Queen Rebekka mounted the platform, the band stopped and the crowd clustered up to the platform, the walls and balconies and again the square filled from the surrounding streets.

Raul, Chase and the Princesses followed the King and Queen and, as they settled into their seats along the back of the stage, Chase realized he was nervous again and everyone seemed to be watching him. This time he knew it was going to be all about him.

The councillors and the guildmasters settled in to the remaining chairs, with Amstraad and Meadl among them. There was an expectant hush as King Sulliman walked to the lectern.

"Last night was a special occasion," he began. "I know you all had a good time, and I hope there aren't too many sore heads this morning. I know mine is a little tender."

A ripple of laughter.

"As I told you then, we have had no knight in the State for a long time. Now we do – proudly – and we need to observe due protocol. Traditionally the guilds present the new knight with gifts. All our great guilds and their guildmasters have supported this tradition wholeheartedly, and that is what we are here to do today."

He turned and beckoned Chase forward.

"If you would care to join me, Sir Chase?"

Chase's face was burning as he limped forward to cheers from a crowd still in a good mood from last night.

"Our first guildmaster needs no introduction," said the King, "and he insisted on going first because – I quote – he gets anxious hanging around."

Amstraad did seem nervous as he stepped forward with something very heavy wrapped in cloth and set it on the table beside Chase. He folded back the covering cloth and displayed a stone stand cleverly fashioned to hold Chase's weapons. The stand was made out of volcanic rock: charcoal-grey almost like glass, with flecks of red and green shining through. The craftsmen had carved it with figures around it, and the eagle motif in full splendour. The wing tips held the sword; the claws below, the bow.

Chase was struck dumb by the skill that gone into its making.

Finally he managed to get a few words out.

"It's incredible … beautiful," he stammered, looking at Amstraad. The two men embraced and the crowd cheered. The King clapped, and Amstraad bowed and returned to his seat. A guard put the stand to the front of the platform where it could be seen and admired.

The King introduced the guildmaster of the Bakers' Guild – Laura's father, who had a scroll in his hand, which he handed to Chase. Chase unwound the scroll and stared at the unfamiliar letters and words.

"Er, thank you, Guildmaster …"

A hand reached over his shoulder and plucked the scroll

from his hands. The King, smiling, began to read.

"The Bakers' Guild of Staal bestows upon Sir Chase Robinson, Knight of the State, the right to a fresh loaf of bread and a tray of sweet buns daily so long as he shall dwell in Staal."

The crowd burst out laughing, and Chase, relieved, joined in. He thanked the guildmaster, who gave him a brief, self-conscious hug and returned to the back row.

The King chuckled, and announced the Weaving and Clothing Manufacturers' Guild. A tall woman strode up to Chase, while four others followed behind with bundles.

"We, the Weaving and Clothing Manufacturers' Guild, present to Sir Chase Robinson these items. Firstly, a quilt of finest Staal linen, embroidered by our most skilled needle-workers."

The quilt was carefully spread out across the platform, supported by two women who held it up to show the audience. On the neutral background exquisite embroideries showed the castle of Staal and the mountains behind, with the river flowing between.

"Thank you," said Chase, speaking loudly above the gasps and cheers of the townsfolk. "It is truly magnificent."

The guildmistress allowed herself a brief smile before continuing.

"Secondly, two sets of clothing, befitting a knight."

The next two ladies laid out before him trousers of finest calf skin, cambric shirts, leather tunics with silver embroidery, and two pairs of calf-length boots in black and tan leather.

"Wow," was the only word he could utter. Had Fruel approved the design? "Thank you. Thank you."

Chase could not help but to touch the soft material, as

they placed their bundles on the table.

The guildmistress bowed like a man and turned to go, but stopped and partially turned towards him again. She said quietly, "My eldest son was in the Keep battle. He told me you saved his life."

She was gone before he could reply. Sulliman gave Chase a small knowing smile.

"The Leather Guild," he announced.

An older man came forward, followed by two apprentices carrying a prenner saddle and harness. The older man bowed.

"Firstly, a saddle and harness fit for a knight."

The lads held it up to Chase and he ran his fingers over the elaborate design of the Staal eagle, with wings outspread, stencilled in the leather.

"Oh, that's amazing. Thank you."

"And a quiver and greaves befitting a knight."

The man beckoned, and a senior worker walked over to Chase and placed a quiver, with the design repeated, over Chase's head, nestling across his shoulders. He then indicated Chase should hold out his arm towards him, and when Chase did so, he slid a forearm bracer over his hand and tied it with leather straps on the inside down to his wrist. Then he repeated the process for the other arm. He bowed and retreated. Chase stood there admiring the matching artwork of an eagle, wings stretched, as they faced each other.

The older man hugged Chase fiercely and muttered, "We owe you so much; it is the least we could do, Sir Chase."

The crowd went wild, and the King was forced to wait until they quietened before saying, "The Ironworkers'

Guild."

Meadl came forward and unwrapped a thin bundle. From it he took, and balanced on his outspread palms, what appeared to be a miniature sword in its scabbard.

"The King told us that usually the Ironworkers' Guild presents a sword to the new-made knight. We knew you already have an exceptional sword and so we made you instead a Staal dagger. I believe it is the best we have ever produced."

Chase took the dagger by the hilt and slowly withdrew it from the scabbard. The crowd murmured its appreciation. The blade, on which the eagle motif was repeated, was almost two hand spans long, fashioned like a miniature sword, solid in the spine and tapered to a lethal point and edge. A thing of deadly beauty. He felt the weight of it before he slid the weapon back into the scabbard. He and Meadl exchanged first the formal Staal handshake and then a brotherly embrace, hands still grasped and heads together, to the crowd's appreciation. With a final pat on Chase's shoulder, Meadl withdrew.

The King announced the Farmers' Guild and from the back of the crowd there was movement. Two men were leading a tall light grey prenner through to the platform; skittery amidst the crush of people. The guildmaster came up beside Chase and said loudly, "A prenner suitable for a knight from the Farmers' Guild."

He shook hands with Chase and led him off the platform to the snorting prenner.

"I understand you had never ridden a prenner before," the guildmaster said, "but that you have taken to them like a native. He is a young animal, but intelligent."

"He is magnificent. I thank you and the Farmers'

Guild."

Chase stroked the prenner's narrow face.

"Does he have a name?"

"That's up to you, sir knight. We've been calling him Silver, because of his colour."

"Silver it is then," said Chase. The Lone Ranger wouldn't mind.

By now the Princesses were with him, stroking the prenner to calm it. The guildmaster handed Chase a sweet. He reached up and rubbed Silver's ears. Silver sniffed his hand first, and then sucked up the sweet as Chase offered it, rubbing his forehead against Chase's shoulder.

Chase laughed.

"I have a new friend, and he is amazing. Thank you."

The King motioned Chase back up onto the stage. Chase shook hands with the guildmaster and gave Silver a final pat before heading up the stairs. The prenner tried to follow him onto the platform and had to be held back, much to crowd's amusement. Silver was then led away to the stables as Chase stood again on the stage.

With the Queen beside him, King Sulliman spoke directly to the crowd.

"Lastly the King and Queen by tradition are supposed to gift land to the new knight. But our State is unique, and crown land belongs to the citizens, not the crown, so we cannot do that."

He was holding two documents, one of which he handed to the Queen.

"However, my family has private holdings and I owe our new knight the lives of my wife and my children. Indeed, my wife and I believe we owe him the safety of our State. So I decree the following holding to now belong to Sir

Chase Robinson."

He held up a map, and the Queen displayed a title deed.

"The land known as The Island is now yours, Sir Chase."

The crowd exploded again, and someone called out, "I hope that prenner can swim!" to a chorus of laughter. Chase turned to the King and Queen.

"You don't have to do this."

The Queen embraced Chase and kissed him on the cheeks.

"Oh, yes we do."

The King was laughing as he, too, embraced Chase.

"Thank us after you have been and seen it."

Chapter 20

THE AFTERNOON was devoted mainly to the memorial service for the fallen. Some burials were held together, especially of comrades in arms, with the 'minister' holding service. Others were separate, with families grieving alone for a fallen son or daughter, sister, brother or father, and mourners in this closely-knit community going from one graveside to another.

That evening the King and Queen had dinner with the guilds in the castle. Chase had changed into one of his new sets of clothes. Not for the first time, he wished he had his camera.

He made a point of talking to as many of their guests as possible until, at last, they were done with public duty.

The Princesses had arranged for Silver to be housed with their own prenner. Chase knew he'd have to wait for his thigh to mend completely before he could take the young animal for a test drive. As the last guest left, he drew Raul, Carolie and Sonja aside.

"Will you come with me tomorrow? I want to try and collect the iron."

They agreed immediately, and fired a barrage of questions at him. Chase shook his head.

"Wait," was all he said, which only made them more curious.

"We'll go in the morning after archery practice."

"Carolie and I will organize a picnic lunch," said Sonja.

"And I'll get the grooms to find a good set of prenner and a cart," volunteered Raul.

Chase reached over and took Sonja's hand, then Carolie's.

"And I think we need to talk to your parents."

"Yes, yes!"

"Good," said Raul. "I'll take Laura home now; it's been a long day." He hugged his sisters and punched fists with Chase. "See you in the morning."

Chase, flanked by the sisters, approached the royal couple, who were talking with Fruel. He found himself stammering as he made his request for a few words in private. The Queen regarded him with bright eyes.

"Now would be good, Chase, and in our private chambers."

Chase and the Princesses followed the King and Queen into their private lounge, where a Level served drinks, bowed, and left them in private.

Chase was tense with nerves and, as previously agreed, allowed the Princess to open the discussion.

"Chase," Sonja began, "we have a tradition here in Staal of arranging a meeting between children and parents when the children decide they want a change of situation. Often that has to do with beginning a new relationship, which means both sets of parents are present."

She spoke sadly to Chase.

"You cannot do that, Chase, and for that we are sorry, my sister and I. It would have been our pleasure to meet your parents."

Now Carolie took over.

"The purpose of such a meeting is for the children to say what they want, and for the parents to give their blessing. This is a custom steeped in history in our society, where such matters are openly discussed and agreed upon. As

Princesses it is particularly important for us to obey tradition. By now everyone will know we are meeting together."

She had finished, and now it was the turn of the Queen to speak.

"It is important for us to speak honestly, so we can be clear about what is wanted, make good decisions, and happily move on. So please be at ease; say what you must and, yes, be open and honest with us. Chase, you have dropped into our town, our State and our lives. The effect on you must be as great as the effect you have had on us."

Chase nodded. She was such a wise lady, this Queen.

"So we take turns to talk," said the King. "Who would like to go first?"

He spoke a little hesitantly, and Chase wondered if he, too, was nervous, though that would be so unlike him.

"We think we should speak first," said Carolie, taking her sister's hand. "In so many ways, we have been the initiators of all this."

She took a deep breath and began.

"The day I tried to shoot the bull boar changed my life. A man stepped out of nowhere and saved me. Not only from the bull boar, but from who I was trying to be. I became a person who wanted to be a different and better woman. This man had shown me, without telling me, what I could be."

She paused, and Sonja squeezed her hand. She continued.

"When I spoke to my sister about it, I discovered that she, too, was different. I knew I wanted to stay close to my sister, and I was happy when I understood that we shared the same feelings about this man."

She reached out for Chase and he joined her and Sonja.

"Perfectly put, sister," said Sonja. "For me, too, it was like waking from a dream. I had a sister, I now had a purpose, and I knew the man I wanted. On that day when the Varden attacked, I was not scared for myself. I was scared I would lose either a loving sister or the man who had changed me … The man I want."

She gazed tenderly at Chase.

"I know it seems wrong, but when you stood with your arms around us after killing the Varden I realized I was in love."

Carolie reached out her hand again to her sister.

"We both offer you our hearts, Chase, if you want them."

With her public declaration, Chase's own heart leapt. What he felt now was stronger even than the deep love that had unfolded as he first held these women – women who loved him back – in his arms in bed. It was as if he had stepped out of the gloom of a winter's day into bright and warming sunshine.

"Sonja, Carolie. I want your hearts to keep forever and I want to offer mine in return …"

Immediately the girls wrapped their arms around him, sobbing and laughing, while their mother and father drew closer to pat backs, hug, wipe tears and blow noses. Smiles and tears together. Eventually everyone sat down and Chase continued.

"A few weeks ago I was on my farm in my homeland when I was approached to carry out a task. I don't know why I was chosen for a task so incredible and important, but I knew it was a task I must try to carry out."

Sonja wiped his cheek with her finger, and Carolie

leaned into him.

"I arrived here full of apprehension, not knowing how I would be received or how much danger I might be in. I found an amazing society, with amazing people, and to my confusion I found two wonderful, beautiful Princesses. How could I fail to fall in love? But they were Princesses, and how could I possibly choose?" He looked at the King and Queen. "They told me later, and it was much to their amusement, that here in Staal I could be allowed to love both of them. Sire, madam, I do."

The Princesses clung to his arms, heads resting against him. The Queen glanced at her husband, and he nodded.

"Sulliman will tell you what he feels, but I for one can say this is one of the happiest days of my life. As I said, Chase – *Sir* Chase – you have had a profound effect on us all. I have never seen my daughters so alive, so happy, so focused. Sonja, Carolie, such incredible women. I thank you for all of that, Chase …"

The Queen paused.

"My only concern is entirely selfish."

"Mother?"

"Chase, you come from far away. I am worried you will leave and take my daughters, so precious to us, with you. And you yourself will not be here."

While the girls rushed to hug their mother, Chase knew he had to respond to her concerns.

"Queen Rebekka, I do not have plans past the task in front of me."

He paused to consider how to express his thoughts in the best way.

"I do not have ties where I come from, other than to the land itself, so where my future lies I do not know. All I know is there could be no better place in the universe to live than here in Staal." He added, "Especially if the fighting is over."

The five of them relaxed into smiles and laughing.

"Very well," said the Queen. "We will worry about dealing with my selfishness if the need arises."

She exchanged another glance with the King. "Sulliman ..."

"Like my wife," he said, "I have never been happier. I am not a man who believes in the gods, but they must have been smiling on us when they brought you to us, Chase. I know we would have lost Staal; we would probably be dead. But not only that, it seems with you my daughters have found their purpose in life. If I could have rewarded you properly, it would have been by giving you my daughters ..."

"Father! Oh, Father!"

"*My Dear!*"

He chuckled.

"But I don't have to. They have given themselves to you. Only ..."

He paused and Chase raised an enquiring eyebrow.

"*My* major concern, Chase, is the task you have before you."

Chase was motionless, waiting.

"I know that it is somehow critical to our State and therefore our future. Maybe even to our survival. You have saved us once – more than once – before, and there is no one I trust more to deal with this problem, whatever it is. Yet I am concerned, deeply concerned. I feel so powerless ..."

He lifted his hands.

"How can we help, Chase? What can you tell me? Is there something I … we can do?"

Chase was regretful.

"Sire, I am sorry. As you know, I am bound by a promise to say nothing, nor is there anything you or anyone can do at the moment. The most important thing is the cramlimite rock. I am taking it to use as a bargaining tool. I cannot say what will happen, but the strangers who approached me think it will work."

He added, "We are going to collect the iron tomorrow, if we can. Amstraad will start the mining again. That's all we can do for now."

A long silence was broken by the Queen who spoke briskly.

"Now, this is meant to be a happy time, and it seems we can do nothing useful for Chase at present. So let's put that aside and enjoy the moment."

She nudged her husband, smiling. He nodded.

"And, of course, you have our blessing."

The Queen held out her arms and one by one she hugged her daughters, the King and Chase.

Chapter 21

CHASE WOKE NEXT DAY between Sonja and Carolie. His women. They murmured sleepily as he kissed them, eyes tight shut, rosy mouths smiling. For a moment he was tempted to stay …

Before he could change his mind, he eased himself out of bed, and had a quick strip-down wash. Then he took his bow off the stone stand on a table and strung it. Outside the gates Raul was waiting with a large group of guards, volunteers and young would-be archers. They turned expectantly as he approached, waiting for his instructions.

"Quite a number of you present, so we will divide up into three groups. Can a few of you get, say, ten more sacks of hay from the stables?"

With so many, the morning training took longer than usual. Chase nominated four shooters who were technically good as teacher's aides. They divided into three groups again for beginners, intermediate and advanced. Chase found he enjoyed the banter, and was amazed at the progress they were all making.

He stood with Raul later, watching the intermediate shooters, including Ferrer, handing out praise and tips on stance and grip and accuracy.

"This afternoon is important, Raul," said Chase. "I need to show you and the girls something you never dreamed of. Will you trust me?"

"My friend, we already trust you. Our lives are yours."

"Thank you."

When the archery practice came to an end, Raul and

Chase returned to the castle for a late breakfast. The girls met Chase with a kiss.

"We've organized a hamper of food and wine for lunch," said Sonja.

"And the cart is outside."

The cart was sturdy and would be pulled by a team of four prenner. Raul climbed onto the driver's seat, and Chase helped the Princesses into a bench seat behind them, facing backwards. Then he clambered in beside Raul. All of them were a little strained and nervous. He needed to lighten the mood.

"So what can you tell me about this island I've been given?"

To his dismay all three began to laugh. Over his shoulder Raul said to the girls, "Who's first?"

"You tell him the physical, Raul," said Sonja, "and we'll tell him the *rest*."

Raul collected his thoughts.

"The Island is literally that. The Black River flows down onto the plain almost three-quarters of a daylong prenner walk from here. On the plain it splits around a rocky headland and then rejoins about three or four thousand paces further down, past the opposite headland. Narrow though, say one thousand paces. Yes, like a boat." He nodded. "That's about it. The headland closest to the mountains is high and rocky, but down onto the plain the Island levels out to pasture."

He gazed east as if could see the land he was describing.

"The reason many laughed is because although there is good pasture and woodlands, the river is near impassable most of the year around. Many have died crossing it and … Ah, I'll leave the rest to the girls."

Immediately Carolie jumped in.

"I guess the best way to describe the Staal attitude towards the Island is apprehension. So many have died, drowned in the river, been killed on the Island itself, or simply gone missing, that now it's regarded as mysterious or haunted."

She turned to her sister, who continued.

"That about describes it, but there is more. Stories of monsters and strange happenings on the Island. People going missing. Used to be an initiation for young men to spend a night there, but when a couple disappeared and were never found again the Island was described as cursed."

"That's a bit harsh," said Raul.

"Simple folk think like that, Raul," Sonja replied. "They make it sound like a bad place, but it has potential, especially if you could get to it easier. Good grazing, and some great house sites …"

"Yes, Chase," said Raul, "she's right. Perhaps that's why our parents gave it to you."

Carolie laughed.

"Good point. Maybe Father is killing several birds with one stone."

"He needed to give me land under the traditional knight rules, but could only give me something he personally owned … I feel guilty about that."

"Don't be," Carolie said. "He wanted to give you land so you will stay."

"Land that is presently wasted," Raul commented, as practical as ever. "He expects you to fix any problems, Chase. Make a farm of it."

"What?"

Chase frowned and shook his head.

Sonja leaned forward and stage whispered in his ear, "He's probably right, you know."

"Hmm. So when can we take a look at the Island?"

"We're on duty the next two days. After that?"

"We might need to stay overnight," said Raul. "It's a fair way and you will want to explore all of it."

"Overnight?" said Carolie. "Really? Overnight on the Island?"

"Not scared, are you?" joked Raul.

"Not if Chase is there!" she retorted.

"And I'm game if you are," said Sonja.

Chase smiled.

"Camping on the Island it is then. But we need to do it soon."

The significance of that comment was not lost on the others, silencing them temporarily. As they trundled on, making plans for the visit, Chase's mind jumped to how he would handle it when the Princesses and Raul met the crew of Startrader. What if they panicked or treated him as if he had fooled them or, worse, like an alien. And soon they would be there …

Indeed, it didn't take long to get close. Chase directed Raul towards the clearing, stopping short of where Startrader should be.

"How about we have lunch now?" he suggested, prolonging the inevitable.

Soon they were sitting on a spread blanket and eating cold roasted game bird, cheese and bread, with wine to wash it down and grapes to follow. From cups this time, as Sonja pointed out to Raul.

"I need to talk to you now."

Chase addressed them abruptly, and they fell silent.

"Tell me, what do you know of the mural in your temple?"

Confused, they exchanged glances. Sonja was first to speak.

"As we told you, it's a myth, based on an old religion that says our ancestors were transported here, sleeping, in a strange chariot from the old world. When they awoke a door opened to the State … Why?"

Chase took his time in answering.

"What I have to tell you is something I am frightened to say. I am not sure how you will react. Yet I need to tell you because it is about who I am, and because I love you and need to share this with you all. And also it is important for us all and our future. Indeed, for our survival."

They stared at him open-mouthed, confused now and concerned. Chase took a long, deep breath.

"Perhaps it's best if I just explain what happened."

"Oh, definitely," said Raul, and the girls nodded their agreement.

"Only a few weeks ago I was on my farm. The night before, I had dreamed of something unfamiliar looming over me. Raul, not unlike the dreams about the Varden coming over the pass."

He spoke slowly and clearly, knowing how incredible his story was.

"On that day I had the sense of it again, when I was fully awake. I went into a paddock on my farm and a door opened out of nowhere. A door to a craft that can travel from planet to planet, where I was welcomed by aliens. Raul, my ladies, they told me your world had a problem and I could help by agreeing to come here with them and secure a certain amount of extremely valuable rock – your cramlimite. We might be able to use that rock to barter with a multi-world federation for them to fix the problem and save the planet. Save Tapar."

Raul and the Princesses stared at him open-mouthed and said nothing.

"So I went with them. On the ship they dressed me according to your customs, gave me a certain amount of instruction, and set me down. I started walking to the town when I came across a young woman being chased by a giant boar …"

He lowered his gaze to his clenched hands.

"I am not from your planet. Though I suspect you are from mine or a planet like mine …"

The silence continued then Sonja turned to Carolie.

"So we are right, sister mine. There are other planets like ours and they are inhabited."

Carolie nodded, smiling uncertainly at Chase.

"Wait on!" Raul spoke forcibly to Sonja. "Are we supposed to believe this without proof? I can't accept a story as far out as that, no matter who it comes from."

He wouldn't look at Chase.

"I understand that, Raul. That is why I brought you here … I hope he is here."

Chase stood up, and called.

"Kayfor! Are you there?"

The others jumped as another voice spoke right beside them.

"Yes, Chase. I am here. Welcome back to the Startrader."

The royals stared about them, the girls grabbing Chase.

"Good to hear you, Kayfor. Can you let us aboard, please? I need to introduce you to some friends."

"Certainly, Chase."

The door opened.

"Come on. You need to see this."

Chase led the girls by the hands across to the Startrader.

Behind him Raul said, "Why can we only see a door?"

"Good question." Chase smiled. "The craft, Startrader, has been made invisible so ... well, so no one knows it's here."

"Oh."

Raul was treading closely on Chase's heels – whether from fear or curiosity, Chase couldn't tell."

"So, we could go to other planets, Chase?" asked Sonja, her eyes fixed on the doorway.

"Yes, my darling, and in an instant."

"Wow," said Carolie. "Wow."

One by one they climbed the ramp, the royals pausing uncertainly before they entered. Chase was quick to reassure them. He wanted to make the situation as normal as possible.

"Can I close the door and decontaminate, Chase?"

"Yes please, Kayfor."

The door slid shut behind them.

"You are perfectly safe," said Chase. "This is simply so nothing harmful can be brought on board."

As the cool sensation washed over them Chase said, "Kayfor, I would like to introduce you to my friend Prince Raul of Staal, and to my ladies, the Princesses Carolie and Sonja of Staal."

He added, "Raul, Sonja and Carolie, the voice you hear is Kayfor. Kayfor is a Programmed Person. You won't see him; Kayfor is part of the ship around us. In fact, he runs Startrader, and he is my friend."

The girls had still had not released their hold on Chase. Raul was standing extremely close, too.

"Hello, Prince Raul and Princesses Sonja and Carolie. I am honoured to meet you. Please understand you are all perfectly safe here."

The inside door opened.

"Ah, we are honoured to meet you, too." Raul had managed to recover a little of his usual poise. "Any friend of Chase is a friend of ours."

"Thank you, and welcome aboard. Chase, there are no other humans nearby. I will monitor your beasts and cart."

"Thank you, Kayfor."

Slowly Chase walked Startrader's visitors down the hall. The royals peered into every room they passed, just as he had done.

"Chase," said Kayfor, "I have observed that you and Raul both have injuries that can be repaired."

"Oh, right." Chase stopped. "Raul, Kayfor can heal our wounds. Would you like him to do that?"

"Um, how exactly?"

"It won't hurt. My concern is that Staal might notice our sudden recovery."

"It would be good to be free of our injuries, though."

"Yes please, Kayfor," said Chase.

"If you could go to the medical room."

The girls, fascinated, trailed closely behind them. When they got there, Chase went first to show them and Raul how easy the procedure was. When he got up from the 'light table', Carolie and Sonja were amazed that he could move more freely and only faint scars remained from his wounds. Eagerly, Raul stretched out for treatment. When he was finished, he moved his arm experimentally.

"Wow, that's as good as new. Thank you, Kayfor."

"No problem, Prince Raul."

The girls showed a desire to remain and examine the medical room, but Chase firmly ushered them towards the viewing room.

"We need to talk, Kayfor," he said, when they were all settled.

"Yes, Chase. I have information for you."

"Would you clear the wall so we can see outside?"

Chase was anxious to keep things natural for the royals. He waited until he sensed they were relaxing.

"Kayfor, we need to load onto the cart all the iron the cart can take."

"I will arrange for some mechanoids to load it, Chase. They are quiet and will not upset the beasts."

"Thank you, Kayfor. How long have we got before you need to leave?"

"I have seven hours, thirty minutes before I should leave the area."

"Any other news of the crew or the Federation?"

"Not really, Chase. But ..."

"Yes, Kayfor?"

"My repair of Prince Raul has confirmed something for me; something a little worrying. I am not sure what you will think."

Yes, Kayfor?"

"Chase, biologically you are the same as him and therefore the Princesses. Your genome is identical, except for a few minor variations that have occurred over the last few hundred years. You are the same species."

The brother and sisters were paying close attention. Kayfor continued.

"This confirms my research that their ancestors came from your planet."

Raul and the Princesses looked at each other and at Chase closely.

"I am not overly surprised, Kayfor. In the temple in the town is a mural of a space ship, and there is a Tapar legend of being brought here in a chariot."

"Do you realize what else, Chase?"

"Yes." Chase stared out through the window at the Staal landscape. "The Startrader crew knew they were from Earth. That is why they sought out a human from Earth to come here. The question is; why did they not tell me."

"Exactly, Chase. When I researched this planet I found that centuries ago a ship took people from Earth here to use as workers to mine cramlimite. It could have been a Federation programme, though it is unclear whether it was sanctioned by the Federation. The last person to source this information was Delt."

The Princesses and Raul had listened closely to this exchange.

"So, although you are from another planet, we are the same kind of people?" asked Sonja.

"We came from your planet? Fine by me," added Carolie, with a mischievous grin.

Sonja giggled.

"What? Oh!"

The girls giggled louder, and Chase couldn't look at Raul who shook his head at his sisters. Chase cleared his throat.

"Again, Kayfor, why did they not tell me?"

"Chase, I have reviewed some conversations on board when they were working out this situation. Unauthorized recordings are not permitted, but this was supposed to be an experimental trip and so everything was recorded ...”

“Yes?”

How did Chase know he wasn’t going to like what he heard next?

“I don’t think they were going to use the cramlimite to save Tapar.”

“I don’t know why, but I have that feeling too. They were going to use it to buy Startrader.”

“Yes, Chase. That’s what the conversations demonstrate.”

Chase was silent. He swivelled his chair around, and it glided across the floor to beside the girls. He took their hands, while Raul sat grimly by.

“Save Tapar? Outside you mentioned we had a problem. A serious problem. What exactly did you mean, Chase?”

“No good way to tell you. You know how your sun flashes? How it has been doing it more often?”

They nodded. He spoke slowly and sadly.

“Your sun is failing. In a matter of year or two, it will destroy most life your planet. It can be fixed though. But only the Federation can save Tapar. The plan was to use the cramlimite to coerce them into doing so; to show them Tapar had valuable resources, and could be important to the Federation. Bribery isn’t how we’d choose to act, but that’s how it is, now. The Federation does not interfere in matters concerning what they call immature planets. Planets excluded by the Federation. My planet and your planet included.”

They sat in silence for some time and then Sonja let out a sob and soon both girls were weeping, their faces buried in his chest as Chase took them into his arms. Raul was white-faced. Chase spoke to him firmly.

"Raul, I believe this will work. Kayfor tells me that cramlimite is so valuable now that we will get a hearing. We must win."

"Without help, Chase?"

"I think so, yes. The fact that the crew isn't with us doesn't really change anything. We still have to get the cramlimite; we need to get it to the Federation. Only now we have another argument at our disposal."

Chase showed Raul and the Princesses over the ship, but they were still in shock at what he had told them. In the end, he sat them down and, with Kayfor's assistance, explained about the Federation and why the Startrader had to dodge the scanners.

Then Kayfor reported that the cart was fully loaded.

"We had better go," said Chase. "We don't want you detected. When can you return?"

"Near thirty-six hours has been the timing. I located the scanner before I came near Tapar, checking it is far from here before I return."

"Good, good. Mining started again today. We probably need a week to reach the volume we require, or all we can get. I will return then and we can make our departure."

"We?" enquired Kayfor.

Chase turned to the royals.

"It may be useful for them to face representatives from the planet they are condemning. What about coming with me to argue our case with the Federation?"

Before they could answer he spoke directly to Raul.

"Do not be offended, my friend, but I don't think you should come. They may not allow us to leave immediately, and you have a wife at home."

Raul frowned.

"I will do whatever is needed to save my State, my planet."

"I understand that. The Princesses will be enough, either way."

Raul considered this and then nodded unhappily.

Sonja and Carolie were sitting as close to Chase as they could. Sonja spoke for them.

"Where you go, we go."

There was a tightening in his chest that Chase had never felt before. His ladies …

"Kayfor, while we are away, can you do something for me?"

"Of course, Chase."

"Find precedents for the Federation interfering with 'immature' planets. Also record, so it can't be lost, all information on the abduction of people from Earth to colonize Tapar. And can you also look into the procedures and suggest how we can secure a hearing from the Federation Council? Can we land so as to allow you to leave again, and be safe from detection while we talk to the Council?"

A sudden thought.

"Who was the crew going to buy Startrader from: Zalos?"

"Confirmed. Chase, I believe it was the directors of Zalos Corporation who financed the development of Startrader."

"Hmm … Thanks."

He stood and the royals followed suit and he moved towards the door.

"Time to get going, Kayfor. I was thinking … This is

probably an unusual request, but I've acquired an island created by a river about thirty kilometres south east of us. Headlands at each end. Can you do a survey of it for me and map it? Landing sites for Startrader. Check it for any animal species. Also ..."

"Yes, Chase?"

"Is it reasonable for the mechanoids to move rocks?"

"Yes. What do you have in mind, Chase?"

"The river is impassable in winter and the winter floods are destructive. If we could make a suitable weir so we could get carts over in average weather conditions that would be helpful."

"I take it you have plans, Chase."

"I do – without getting too far ahead of ourselves."

"I'll review some engineering designs. The mechanoids would like something interesting to do."

"Thanks. Our first priority, though, is not to be discovered by the scanners."

"I understand, Chase."

The girls and Raul had listened with some interest. When the outer door opened, Kayfor said, "It was good to meet you, Prince Raul and Princesses Carolie and Sonja of Staal. I look forward to meeting you again."

For the first time since learning of their planet's fate, the royals were able to smile, and politely reply.

"Chase, a word please."

The others went out to the cart, and Chase stepped back inside.

"What is it, Kayfor?"

"I am no expert on such matters, but when you introduced the Princesses as your ladies, that meant something, didn't it?"

"Yes," replied Chase looking up as people seemed to do talking to Kayfor. "They are."

"Good work!"

Was Kayfor laughing?

"Very good work," Chase agreed.

After a pause, Kayfor continued.

"Chase, thank you for introducing me as your friend. It is important to me. I have passed on my new name and the reason for it to the Programmed Persons link, and that has started a wave of name changes. It's like you have given each of us an identity. Thank you from all of us."

"You're welcome, Kayfor, and you *are* my friend. Take care and I'll see you in a week."

"You take care too, Chase."

The cart was fully loaded and the prenner were keen to get going, spooked by the mechanoids.

They watched the door close to nothing, as they packed up and mounted the cart. As they drove off, with the cart creaking under the load, all three royals kept glancing back at where the door had been. They were silent until Chase could stand it no longer.

"I am sorry you had to experience this so suddenly. I couldn't think of another, better way of doing it. Learning there are other inhabited planets, that I'm not from yours is big enough without learning your sun … needs fixing."

"I thank you for trusting me," Chase continued. "I know what it was like when I met the aliens only weeks ago. A major experience. I must ask you not to tell *anyone* what happened today; not even your parents or Laura."

He went on. "Please understand the Federation *can* save your planet and we *can* convince them to do so."

He spoke with a conviction he did not entirely feel, but

it worked for the others. They sat up straighter and assured him they wouldn't say a word, that no one would believe them anyway. Normal conversation resumed, and Chase finally allowed himself to relax.

Chapter 22

BACK AT STAAL the iron created great excitement in the smithy. Meadl positively bounced, but asked anxiously what would happen if they didn't get sufficient rock. Chase assured him it was all his, to share with Amstraad, no matter how much rock they mined. He had hardly stopped talking when Meadl had his men unloading the iron into store like it was going to disappear.

The Princesses had gone into the castle, whispering together, an arm around each other's waist. The King hurried out a few minutes later. He slapped Chase on the back.

"You have more than fulfilled your part of the bargain, Sir Chase. Staal will do all it can to meet its side of the deal."

Chase was surprised by the formality of the statement until he realized the King was making the point that the State had negotiated this trade.

"Thank you, Sire."

The King winked.

"So come on, you two. Let's have a drink and talk."

They left Meadl looking closely at an iron bar. Chase and Raul followed Sulliman down a side street and into a bar called The Keep. The walls were covered in paintings, old weapons, and shields and it was nearly empty with only two elderly men playing a game like checkers in the corner. The King ordered a round of ale and led them to a table in a corner.

"My daughters were upset when you returned. Oh, they

tried to put a brave face on it, but even you, my son, don't look happy. Anything I should know about, Chase?"

Chase shook his head.

"I'm sorry, Sire. There is a problem, but I do have a plan to use the rock to deal with it. Your children are unhappy because they know what the problem is."

He looked at Raul.

"Your son bravely requested to come with me when I go. I declined his offer. I am not sure when I will return and he is married. I then asked your daughters if they wished to help. They said where I go, they go."

The King looked at Chase with concern.

"I do not believe we will be danger, Sire, otherwise I would not involve them. I don't know how long we will be away; it will probably only be days, though ..."

The King was silent for some time, and then he turned to Raul.

"My son, do you agree with this course of action? Is it right for your sisters to go with him?"

"I think it is, Father. I trust Chase and that what's he trying to do is for the good of our ... our State. I believe they will be safe. I'm not happy that I won't be going with him, but I cannot leave Laura. She is pregnant."

It took a couple of seconds before it sank in, then both men shouted and jumped up, embracing Raul and shaking his hand. Chase smiled at Sulliman.

"Congratulations, grandfather!"

"Aargh! I'm too young to be a grandfather!"

Laughter flowed between them, lightening the mood. They finished their beer and the King called for more to toast his son, and to chat about when the baby was due and how happy Rebekka would be.

Then he said, "On that, you and Laura need to tell your mother first and your sisters. If they find out I knew before them, there will be hell to pay!"

Chase nodded.

"Good point!" said the father-to-be. "Catch you up later, when you can be told officially."

He finished his beer and got up.

"Chase, thank you for today. It was both difficult and amazing, and I do believe we will be all right."

"We will be," agreed Chase.

When Raul left, Sulliman leaned forward.

"I will support your actions, but I do hate being in the dark. Especially when my children are not."

"I understand, Sire. Hopefully this will all be over soon."

"I'll drink to that."

Their mugs thudded together.

"Granddad!" chuckled Chase.

"Oh, no! But more to celebrate."

After another leisurely beer, they headed back to the castle, walking straight into the jubilation at Raul and Laura's news, doing well to pretend they knew nothing. The celebration did much to alleviate the tension amongst the young royals. Over a drink, Carolie and Sonja took the opportunity to isolate Chase.

"It has occurred to Sonja and me that you've had to live among us, knowing the situation with our sun and forced to keep it to yourself."

"Yes. Not exactly fun."

Sonja chimed in.

"We are sorry this has been thrust upon you."

"But without it, I would never have met you all."

That earned Chase a kiss from each girl, which got a wry smile from Raul, walking up.

"What's next?" he asked.

"Sonja and Carolie are on medical duty over the next couple of days. I want to go out to the mining to check how Amstraad is getting on. I will go out on Silver tomorrow. The next day I might return to Startrader to see what Kayfor has learnt and get the map of the Island."

"I have things to catch up on now," said Raul. "The Levels need extra work, promotions and so on. Boste asked if you could be part of that process."

The King had walked up and overheard.

"Oh, yes. Your comments on their performances would be helpful, Sir Chase."

"When?"

*

The following morning Chase met up with Boste, who gave him a bear hug, beaming. His face was mostly healed, though the scar was impressive.

"Yes," said Boste, fingering it. "It'll be sure to frighten the new recruits. Your leg healed fast, Chase."

"Mmm."

Raul and a few of the senior Levels joined them. They spent the morning discussing the events of the last few days, and deciding on a number of promotions.

After lunch, Chase found Silver and saddled and harnessed him with his new equipment. He had the cramlimite detector in his pocket as he settled himself on the prenner and headed out of town. Silver started pulling as he found room ahead, but Chase held him in. Once he felt the edge had worn off the prenner's exuberance he let it continue in a prenner version of a trot and then eventually a canter. Silver was a nice mover and fast, and Chase allowed him to set his own pace until the beast started to tire and slow slightly, when he reined him in again and gave him a pat.

Before long he came across the stonemason's carts, under the cliffs. One was already partly loaded. He tied Silver and found a sweet for him. Checking no one was around, Chase turned on the detector. The light showed it was pure cramlimite. Satisfied, he climbed the cliff and found Amstraad standing by more cramlimite on a canvas sheet. The men shook hands, and Amstraad led Chase to the fissure, which had been carefully opened to expose the cramlimite.

"We're down into the main wall now."

Amstraad bent down and picked up a piece of the rock to hand to Chase.

"We're getting a good feel for the type of rock you are after."

Chase weighed it.

"How much do you think you have?"

"About two men's weight."

So if he set seventy-five kilograms as the weight of the average man in Staal that would give him about one hundred and fifty kilos ...

Chase nodded.

"You are doing better than I thought. Any idea of how much more?"

"Hard to tell, Sir Chase ..."

"Please – it's still Chase."

"Chase it is. The seam could peter out or widen into the rock face. Or it could disappear completely. We'll get all we can."

"Exactly," said Chase. "I know you will; and that it should be enough."

He wished he could believe that one hundred percent. The full weight of the failing sun was pressing on his mind. He stayed with Amstraad and his team for an hour, watching them work and lending a hand where he could. There wasn't much room for manoeuvre.

At last Chase bid Amstraad and the men goodbye and headed down to Silver. For the first time he let himself think through the process of what would happen if the Federation wouldn't help. Could someone else do something to influence that decision, in exchange for the cramlimite? Unlikely. That's why they had to go to the Federation – who could deem it interference to approach another body …

If they said no, what could he do? Use Startrader to move as many of the Staal as he could? The Federation was unlikely to allow that either, and where would he take them? Another planet? Earth?

He walked up to the tethered prenner, who nuzzled him as Chase rubbed his face and scratched his ears, in thought. He had only just untied him when the sun flared again, punctuating his thinking.

Silver danced and skittered, dragging Chase with him a pace or two. Chase spoke quietly to him and eventually Silver calmed down. On the cliff top Amstraad stood looking down at him. Even at this range Chase could identify his expression as deeply thoughtful. Chase signalled he was okay, and so did Amstraad before he turned to go.

Chase mounted Silver once he had settled down, and walked him back towards Staal. Time was wasting. What else could he do to prepare for the Federation Council? Would he even get a hearing? Perhaps they would arrest him. And when did they sit? He would have to ask Kayfor tomorrow ...

How much cramlimite was enough? Better to get as much as he could. A few days surely wouldn't matter ... Yet this flare was so soon after the previous one that Chase was unnerved. Didn't they say a month between? It hadn't been that long since the last.

He was still in a pensive mood when he got back to Staal. The only thing positive today had been how Silver responded to him and how well they worked together.

After he'd returned the prenner to the stable, he called in at the medical centre, where Carolie and Sonja were finishing up. They, too, were pensive, and dinner wasn't the usual jovial event. The King had his children under close scrutiny, and Chase too, but said nothing about the flare. Chase suspected that he might be wondering at the coincidence. Was he guessing they were more thoughtful because of the flare? Chase couldn't know.

That night he and the girls held each other tighter than ever as they drifted into sleep.

*

Another routine archery session took place next morning. There was steady improvement as trainees moved up from beginner to intermediate, and from intermediate to advanced. Chase fired off a number of arrows at his usual distances while the bowmen hung around to watch, pretending they weren't. He was back to normal after the healing on board Startrader. In fact, if anything, he was better.

Talk was of a competition for various levels of archer

and different distances. When they asked Chase if he would compete, he declined.

"I'd prefer to give out the prizes, if you agree."

They did.

Back at the castle he saddled up Silver, told the girls he would be back later, and headed off. Sonja and Carolie watched him go from the door of the medical centre.

Startrader was on site, and Kayfor welcomed him aboard. Chase went straight to the food area and ordered an Indian curry – good, if not great. He sat down to eat and talk.

"Kayfor, how did you get on with precedents for the Federation interfering with immature planets?"

"A much debated and complex issue, Chase. There are many cases of unsanctioned interference, which I take it you did not want. There have been surprisingly few cases of sanctioned interference, but this is largely to do with practical rather than legal issues."

He paused as Chase stood up to get a glass of water.

"Until event jumping, distance has been a major problem; another has been the practical means to help. I considered that you wished to know examples of times when the Federation had sanctioned helpful interference. There have been none for forty seven Earth years. The last was because a ship crashed and contaminated a planet. Other examples before that were of a similar kind. It has been hundreds of years since the Federation helped a planet, or a species, without direct cause."

"Hmm," said Chase. "So this has been a mandate for some time ..."

"And only if the Federation has somehow revealed itself to the planet."

"What about the history of Tapar, Kayfor?"

"That is interesting, Chase. Not a vast amount of information, and it seemed as if some could be missing. A major corporation undertook the abduction of several villages from European Earth. It might have somehow got Federation agreement to the 'shifting', as they called it, but there is no record either way, which is strange. Cramlimite was involved, but there is insufficient evidence to prove the Federation sanctioned the act."

"Ah," Chase mused, "but maybe there'll be enough if we tie those two together."

He chewed another mouthful of his curry as he considered the implications.

"Kayfor, can you tell me how the sun would be fixed?"

"In laymen's terms several cocktails of fusion materials would be fired at the sun, setting off chain reactions to return the sun to normal balance and rates of fusion."

"Is it difficult? And is it expensive?"

"For an individual, yes. For the Federation, no."

"Any thoughts on how I get to make a case to the Council?"

"I hope you don't mind, but I have initiated that, Chase. The next Council forum is around seven days from now. I have registered you as a speaker. They could not deny audience; apparently they had no information about you on which to base an objection."

Kayfor actually chuckled.

"Brilliant, Kayfor."

"There are landing sites near. A Programmed Person I know will tell us when a platform is clear and safe. I will land and you disembark. Then I ought to stay as I have no further authority to act."

"If you are in danger of being found, you will immediately depart and only return on some sort of signal from me."

"Thanks, Chase. I needed that. Literally."

More curry was devoured without full enjoyment.

"I've made presentations before, but never to save a planet."

"No one would be able to do it better, Chase," replied Kayfor.

Chase jumped. He hadn't realized he had said it aloud.

"Thank you, Kayfor."

"I have made something for you, Chase."

"Oh?"

"You asked for a survey and map of the Island you referred to. I realized that you could not take a view screen or any technology with you, so a mechanoid made some basic paper and ink, and printed a map of the Island."

"That's great, Kayfor. Good work … um. Thank the mechanoid for me."

"I will tell him."

An idle thought crossed Chase's mind: a male mechanoid?

A drawer slid open to reveal a spread of parchment with the Island and its rivers clearly delineated upon its expanse. All the detail was there: the rocky outcrops, forest and meadows.

"It's very good, Kayfor."

Chase spread out the map to study it more carefully. His plate, he noted, had already disappeared.

"Now, tell me about the Island."

"The Island is the remnant of an ancient volcanic outcrop, largely removed in the last ice age, and still has caves and vents. In size it is elongated and approximately three hundred and fifty hectares or nearly nine hundred acres and consists of fifteen percent rock, twenty five percent forests, and sixty percent grasslands. Currently there are two hundred and forty of the brown and green bovines, eighty-seven of the black and blue. A group of eighteen of the porcine animals, though much larger."

"Bull boars," murmured Chase.

"Bull boars," Kayfor corrected himself. "Also, when I was scanning section by section, I located another, unidentified animal. A large mammal in the entrance to a cave, and so the scan was not distinct. I have marked it on the plan."

"Oh, oh!"

"As the soil is volcanic it is reasonably fertile. The grass is ryegrass and clover ..."

Kayfor continued with the description uninterrupted.

"Sounds like it has potential," Chase said at last.

"Oh, and the mechanoids started on the weir late last night after I returned."

The wall became a visual of an early morning flyover of the Island. Chase watched with interest as the view zoomed in on a section of the west branch of the Black River. An area from bank to bank had been flattened under the water, boulders removed and the gaps filled in.

"Oh, that looks great. How did you get the surface so smooth?"

"Laser cutters. They even work under the water. One mechanoid has a laser cutter arm."

Chase laughed.

"You and the mechanoids are amazing."

"Thanks, Chase. I'll tell them that."

The screen dissolved.

"It will be a few days before we finish loading all the cramlimite we can get. I will kill some time by taking a look around this island."

"Yes, Chase. Take care."

Chase took a last look around. His glass too had disappeared. A mechanoid no doubt, but still a little creepy. As Chase left Startrader he said, "Thank you for everything, Kayfor. I would be stuck on a doomed planet with no way to save it if not for you."

"Thank you for your thoughts and consideration, Chase. It is in my reasoning that I try to do things beyond my programming because I want to. For you. I need to study this …"

"We are friends, Kayfor. Friends do that for each other. I will see you in a few days. Take care."

"You too, Chase Robinson."

Chapter 23

WHEN HE RETURNED TO THE CASTLE, Chase found Raul preparing a cart, loading it with provisions and a centre-pole tent. So much food …

"I thought this was an overnight stay?"

"Chase. My sisters, the Princesses, are coming too, remember? They want it to be *special*, they tell me …"

"Oh, right."

A chuckle at the girls' expense, but only after a quick look round to be sure they weren't overheard.

Once everything was packed, they had time for a pint of ale together before Sonja and Carolie finished their shift at the medical centre. They had good news to report.

"The last group of injured Varden will return over the pass tomorrow, under guard," said Carolie. "After that we're down to a few locals still recovering, so we don't need security and can work more flexible hours."

Sonja was checking the content of the cart.

"Got enough ground sheets and blankets?" she asked, poking around.

Raul was able to stifle a laugh only until he saw Chase struggling to do the same, which set them both off.

"Oh, it's going to be like that, huh?"

Sonja advanced menacingly on her brother, who was only saved by Chase telling them of his discussions with Kayfor and showing them the map.

"They built a weir?" said Raul. "That will make things easier."

Dinner that night was happier, to the relief of the King

and Queen. Early next morning they set off, with Raul driving and Chase beside him. Silver and Raul's prenner were tied on long leaders to the back of the cart, but the Princesses preferred to ride on such a fine day. Chase and Raul talked nonstop, about the Military, the Levels, the progress made by the archers, and how to run training with the sword alongside bow practice. They talked about what Chase could do with the Island and even about the baby.

The girls rode around, enjoying the freedom after the arduous hours cooped up with injured men. Not long after noon they were there, and it didn't take long, using Kayfor's map, to find the weir. Chase liked how it wasn't immediately apparent but, once found, easy to use. Now the water flowed evenly over the smooth surface so there were no unexpected dips, and the cart rolled over it easily.

The water was still deep enough, however, even in late summer; up to the axle on the cart and to the saddles on the prenner. Beneath the crystal clear water, the rock appeared as if it had been melted, like a true volcanic flow.

"This is good work from Kayfor and the laser mechanoid!" said Chase. "Why is it called Black River? Looks anything but black to me."

"I think it was because of the deaths on the river ..."

They travelled up onto a low plateau and stopped where the view was good in all directions, and a stream flowed nearby. Here they set up a camp-site. The tent, when opened, was similar to the Bedouin desert tents, with a centre-pole and guy ropes hammered into the ground with stakes. Chase had a passing memory of camping as a child.

Over a late lunch, they discussed how best to explore the Island.

"Oh, yes," Chase warned them. "Kayfor told me there's

some large creature down south in a cave, which we need to check out."

"Probably a bear," said Raul.

"So has everyone got a bow?"

Yes, they had, and kept them near to hand as they rode firstly to the north summit. The view back to the mountains over the forests was impressive. Then they trotted down and around through trees and into the valley meadows where the grass was still good, despite the waning season. The herds of cows, now wild, moved warily away from the prenner, unused to the steeds and the humans who rode them.

"Our father had these brought here a few years ago with farmers to tend the stock and grow crops," said Raul. "A house was built for them down the south end. None of them stayed long and a couple actually went missing."

"Ghosts, Chase, like I said," said Sonja, laughing.

Further south they came to a grove of well-established fruit trees, and some stock yards and fenced meadows, in disrepair and with little stock in evidence. The house Raul had spoken of was still standing, but so run down it was clear no one had lived in it for some time.

As they neared the southern rise they saw the caves drawn on Kayfor's map – and where he had indicated the presence of an unknown creature. Tracks led into one of the largest caves. Whatever was there didn't trouble to hide its presence. They readied their bows and moved closer. Chase directed Sonja and Carolie to a position on the rise where they could get in a clear shot, with an escape route if needed.

Raul lit a torch, and he and Chase approached cautiously on the prenner. He threw the torch in and they backed off. Nothing happened. Nothing came out.

"You know, Raul, this might not be the only opening."

"Yes, this mountain is riddled with caves, my father says."

Chase said grimly, "Whatever's in there, we need to get it out."

"So we're going into a cave with a bear in it. Do you know anything about bears, Chase?"

"Not really, but I won't sleep well tonight knowing it is here."

"Good point."

Smoke curled in wisps from the torch inside the cave.

"So we go in carefully and with plenty of torches. We might be able to flush it out of another tunnel and drive it down to the river."

"Sounds as though you've done this before," said Chase.

"We used to go hunting when we were on duty at the Keep, and yes, a few bears got it. But they keep well away from the Keep now."

They tethered the prenner to a convenient shrub. Raul fired up another torch and called to his sisters.

"Keep your bows ready in case it comes out here. Try to drive it towards the river. If it's big it will take a good shot to stop it, so if it charges, don't risk it. Just ride like hell!"

"Do we need to tell you to be careful?" asked Carolie.

"Hell, no. We have a planet to save."

Chase nocked an arrow into his bow and nodded to Raul.

The cave, when they peered in, was lit enough by the burning torch to show a passage leading off, twice Chase's height and three or four paces wide. On the floor were bear prints and a scattering of bones.

"Definitely a bear, and it has been here for some time," said Raul. "I will take both torches and my bow, but will use the torches to chase it or defend ourselves. Keep your bow ready, Chase. Give it plenty; they have tough hides."

They crept in, Raul picking up the other torch and in the lead, with Chase behind and to one side for a clear line of fire. The tunnel resembled a descending volcanic tube, smooth and relatively free of rubble. They still had to be careful of their footing, but the tunnel went on for well over one hundred paces before opening into a cavern so vast that the light from the torches couldn't penetrate it.

They couldn't make out the walls or the ceiling, but there was a breeze on their faces, and a circle of pale light came in from an opening some distance ahead of them to the right. A ledge of only two or three paces circled the cavern as far as could be seen in both directions. A drop of ten or so paces with ridges the same height as the ledge criss-crossed the space before them, like a floor with deep cracks, and they could hear the sound of water in the distance.

Chase indicated the bones heaped mainly to their right. Raul held up the torches, and Chase moved to that side of him, holding the bow at the ready. They went forward for twenty or thirty paces, stopping at the stench of rotting flesh, wincing when they found the remains of a half-consumed bull. Raul stopped and looked at Chase.

"Oh, oh. If it brought that down, it must be huge."

At that moment a sound behind them made the men swing round. In the light of the entrance, with lowered head and the spark of evil in it eyes, towered a massive bear-like creature. It had obviously been stalking them. Chase didn't have time to consider its differences to any of the species of Earth bears, because it lowered its head further and charged at them.

"This way!"

Raul shouted and, running a few steps, jumped a gap of about two or three paces to the next narrow ridge with Chase close on his heels. They risked a swift look behind; the bear was almost where they had been and they leapt to the next ridge, another pace away. This was so narrow they had to hold each other, torches, bows and all, to keep from falling.

The bear clearly decided the jump wasn't an option. He was simply too big to stay on the ledges. His snarl was something between a groan and a growl. He sniffed the air, fixing them with his beady eyes, his head swivelling from one to the other. He was half again taller than the men at the shoulder, even on all fours. Chase took his chance and raised his bow to send the arrow into the chest of the bear. The bear bent forward and pulled the arrow out with its mouth. Blood came out, but only a little; the arrow had barely penetrated its dense pelt and skin.

Chase nocked another arrow.

"That didn't seem to have any effect."

"No. It's bigger than any bear I've ever heard about."

The second arrow had the same effect, and the bear didn't even bother to pull it out. With another snarl it turned and disappeared to where it had come from while the men watched it go.

"I don't think we would make it back down the passage, Raul."

"Agreed."

The light from further down the cavern beckoned. Chase was doubtful.

"Might not be big enough to get through."

"Or big enough for us and not the bear. Chase, I think it's our only chance."

And what would happen to the women if they couldn't get out? That unspoken question hung in the air.

"Come on then," said Chase.

Holding torches aloft, they made their way along and from ridge to ridge as fast as they could towards the light, on the alert for any sight or sound of the bear.

"These ridges are narrow and the bear won't be able to get us where we are, but the cunning bastard could be waiting for us up ahead."

"Yes."

Chase hoped he was wrong. Silently they increased their speed. The cavern was like a maze; constantly they were forced to pause while they figured which ridge would take them in the right direction. After many leaps and some close calls, a few near falls, they neared the light, the sound of running water louder the closer they got. Finally they came to a ridge that sloped down to a stream flowing fast towards the light.

Now all they had to worry about was the bear. They stepped out and stood there motionless for a long second. No sign of it.

"Get ready to run, Chase."

One last look.

"*Run!*"

They raced downwards to the stream, clambering over boulders as they angled towards the light. It seemed to take forever, and the imprinted image of the bear was omnipresent. Splashing through the stream, they followed its rocky flow along a tunnel passage, three paces wide and high, snatching glances behind them, occasionally tripping, and still grasping the torches. Finally, they emerged outside, blinking in the light. Raul took a blind step in the light and nearly tumbled over the top of a waterfall, regaining his balance when Chase grabbed him.

They stood on a ledge, with a cliff rearing behind and above them on the left, the waterfall dropping down at least a hundred paces just in front of them and to the right a ledge with a smooth rock face ... No choice; the only direction they could go. They stepped on to the ledge and followed it until it narrowed and came to an end, smooth cliff down to the left and up to the right. On inspection, the cliff and the rock face offered no footholds and they shifted back towards the waterfall when they saw movement.

The bear came out of the cave, standing in the water on all four feet, its massive weight and strength now clearly visible. For a moment it squinted in the sun, and then it spied the men and stepped onto the ledge and started towards them.

"It knew there was no way out of here," said Raul.

"That's why it didn't hurry."

Cold sweat trickled down Chase's back. What a fool he had been to risk their lives like this. With no word spoken they dropped torches and nocked arrows. At forty paces they aimed and loosed the arrows. Both struck, but clearly to little effect. They fired again. The bear hardly paused on impact, and began to walk faster. Raul and Chase fired again and immediately after those arrows hit, two more winged into the bear's back. Sonja and Carolie had fired from the cliff above and were loading again.

The bear rose onto its hind legs and let out a bellow, giant mouth gaping wide. Chase, ready for his next shot, saw the open pink maw, the teeth, sharp and pointed, and in an instant it became his target. From fifteen paces Chase fired an arrow up slicing through the roof of the bear's mouth. The bear snapped its jaws shut, cutting off the feathered end off the arrow. The bear came down heavily on all fours, and took a pace towards them. The men backed off, Chase nocking another arrow, the rock wall now hard behind them, nowhere else to go. The bear started another pace before its front legs collapsed and it landed on its chest, slowly rolled over onto its side and fell off the ledge.

Hardly daring to believe what they saw, Raul and Chase bent over the edge to watch, as the bear's heavy body crashed through the trees and onto the rocks below. Then they were distracted by shouts from the Princesses.

"Are you all right?" Their voices betrayed their fear. "You're both safe and unhurt?"

"We're fine."

Raul rounded on Chase.

"That was a lifesaving shot," he said.

The two men grasped right hands at the thumb and held tight, bringing their foreheads together.

"That was too close," said Chase.

Sonja called down again.

"Shall we fetch a rope?"

Chase looked back towards the cave and waterfall before he answered.

"No, I still want to check the cave out. We'll return that way."

"Must we?" Raul spoke ruefully. "I have to admit the cave has no fond memories for me."

Chase was determined. "Won't be anything living in

there with that bear."

Chase took a last look over the cliff to where the body had landed.

They returned to the tunnel and followed the stream that led back into the cave. Even holding the torches high, they could barely make out the ceiling.

"We should go the way the bear must have come," said Chase. "It might be easier."

Raul nodded and they fell back naturally into the pattern they'd followed before: Raul with both torches ahead and Chase to one side, bow down but ready. Soon it was apparent they were alone and, as their eyes adjusted to the gloom, they relaxed and started to look around as they followed the wall around.

The cavern was a roughly circular amphitheatre. Chase estimated it was around five hundred paces wide and three hundred paces high, with caves and holes that they didn't stop to investigate. The Princesses would be waiting anxiously, they knew. The ridges that Raul and Chase had followed were flat because the softer stone that had once overlaid them had been eroded over time by the stream, as it was now doing to the harder rock.

Another layer of rock high across the cavern had the same texture and colour as cramlimite. Chase pocketed some stray pieces from the cavern floor for later checking. Near the exit they found the bear's sleeping area and more bones.

"Oh, gods," Raul exclaimed.

Among them was a human skull.

"I guess that confirms what happened to some of the people who went missing on the Island," said Chase.

Before they exited the cavern they took one last look. A

strange place. Chase couldn't help noting it was certainly large enough to hold Startrader.

Outside, Sonja and Carolie were clearly agitated, clinging to Raul and Chase, hugging them and scolding.

"You were so long!"

"We heard your voices, and looked over the ledge and were so scared when we saw the bear stalking you."

"We're safe now." Chase held them close. "And so are you. And we definitely needed to get rid of that monster."

When Raul told the girls about the skull, they shuddered.

"The bear must have come over in a drought and stayed," he went on, "harvesting the livestock and … anything else."

"Well the place *was* cursed, with that thing," said Carolie."

"We have removed the danger and exorcised a ghost today," said Chase.

They stood in the late afternoon light.

"Do you want the skin, Chase?"

That was Raul, ever practical.

"It's going to be hard to get and won't it have a few holes in it?"

"But proof you've rid the Island of its monster," said Sonja.

"I don't mind if the Island is thought of as scary," said Chase. "It will keep away unwanted guests."

Raul shrugged.

"He wasn't young, and despite his size, he won't make a great rug."

"Still a conversation piece," laughed Carolie.

"And if we are going to skin it, we'd better do it now

before he stiffens."

"Vote!" That was Sonja. "I say aye."

"Aye," said Carolie.

Raul sighed. "Come on then."

The four untethered their prenner and rode towards the valley until they were reasonably close to where the bear had fallen. They tied up the animals and consoled them with sweets. All of them had knives of sorts. Chase's was the eagle knife gifted by the smiths.

When they located the bear's corpse, they could hardly believe exactly how big it was. Skinning the tough hide was an arduous task. The body was so heavy that, despite being on a slope, it took all four of them to roll it as they skinned. Finally they had the skin, and by then they were sweating and bloody, and all of them stripped down to their underclothes and splashed around, washing in the stream.

The skin, roughly folded, presented another problem; they couldn't carry it so they had to drag it up to the prenner. They managed it somehow between them, but as they drew close the animals began to panic, so they left it under a tree.

By now it was late afternoon and they were hungry and thirsty.

"Tomorrow," said Raul, "we'll bring the cart here."

The ride back to camp was carefree, with the last sun warm on their backs, and only a light breeze in the meadows. The Island stretched out around them as if inviting their approval.

"Doesn't seem that scary to me," said Chase to the women. "What do you think?"

The girls laughed.

"Oddly, not now," said Sonja.

"Yes, very pleasant, isn't it?" added Carolie.

"Might not have been pleasant for us tonight," said Raul, "if we hadn't got that bear."

*

Back at the camp-site they lit a fire and set out the food. Raul produced a stoppered jug and invited Chase to pull the cork and try it. Mead. Oh, oh …

With the camp-fire going, food heating, and mead in wooden cups, they settled back to enjoy the sunset.

"Yes. Not a bad place at all."

Chase stretched out his legs.

"This would make a good site for a house."

Sonja and Carolie put their heads together, whispering.

Raul leant towards Chase.

"Bit far away."

"It's fine. I'm not really a townie." He grinned. "And there'll be plenty of room."

On a high from slaying the bear and being together, they ate and drank, chatted and laughed. Raul got up and passed around blankets, which they wrapped around themselves as the evening started to chill. They looked at the stars. Discussed where Earth could be. The girls talked about being able to travel in the Startrader; what they wanted to learn, what they would do once they had made Tapar safe …

Finally, they went into the tent and bedded down, one by one falling asleep.

Chapter 24

THE MORNING WAS OVERCAST, with rain on the horizon, but Chase was set on checking out the northern area for other caves. After breakfast, they saddled up and walked the prenner around the north-eastern corner up to the high point. Here the trees were stunted and on a lean, being more exposed to winds from the mountains.

There were several caves, though none of any substance, which they explored with the torches. Down a small gully Chase found a layer of weathered rock in which a cave seemed to go in a long way.

"You'd better come with me with torches on this one, Raul."

Sonja and Carolie agreed to wait outside. Chase and Raul relit the torches and headed into the cave. They were forced to bend almost immediately and the fissure soon narrowed. Still they kept going. The roof was lower and forced them to crawl not far after and, by now, go single file. When they came to a split in the floor they decided to climb down into it. Here they could walk upright, on broken stone and boulders.

Abruptly the space expanded into a chamber continuing on from where they had entered and widening. Chase realized it was an ancient volcanic tube. On all sides, the walls rose out of sight and shone darkly metallic in the glow from their torches.

They clambered down into the chamber and between the columns of rock left by the stream. Chase wanted to investigate the nearest wall. Its colour changed as he followed it around, reminding him of cramlimite. He again picked up a few samples from the ground to test with the detector later, along with the rock from the bear cave. Surely it couldn't be cramlimite? Wouldn't Startrader's sensors have identified it? Worth checking though.

Raul called out, "Seen enough yet?"

He was keen to get out of this weird underground world.

"Yeah. I'm done."

With one last look around, they climbed out of the fissure and dusted off.

"What were you looking for in there, Chase?" asked Raul. The girls rode closer, curious.

"I am no geologist ..." At their blank expressions he added, "Someone who studies rocks. However, these caves are like bigger versions of the fissure where we found the cramlimite rock we need. If they are ... Who knows? Maybe Kayfor's sensors were blocked in some manner. I want to check back with him."

The implications were clear, and they rode back in silence to the camp-site.

After lunch, they packed everything away, and drove down to collect the bear skin. They struggled to lift it onto the back of the cart; and the team of prenner made it clear they didn't want it there.

"The leather workers will cure it for us," said Raul, "then you just have to decide where to put it."

"In the entrance hall to our house," said Chase.

For which he was rewarded by smiles from the Princesses.

The weather settled into a light rain as they started back, Raul driving the cart again, while Chase rode Silver with a

Princess either side of him.

"Do you think you would like to live on the Island?" asked Carolie.

Chase looked from one to the other.

"I like our island; I think it could be a great place to live. What do you two think?"

"We haven't been to the Island in years, and back then it was a scary place," said Sonja. "But now, you are right and we have talked, Carolie and me. We could make a home together here."

Chase had always been amazed how women plan ahead, get a 'life plan' going; something men generally did not …

"Okay, that's good."

A half-smile on Chase's face. Problem was he now had *two* planners to deal with.

"I'll have to get a job!"

Not that he had anything to pay on the land, but a house, stock …

"You already have a job, Chase."

Breaking Chase's train of thought. Sonja and Carolie dissolved into giggles and rode off, leaving Chase shaking his head and grinning.

*

The four of them were almost halfway home when a group of riders appeared on the road in front of them. The girls had been walking their prenner behind, and Chase had rejoined Raul in the cart. The men approached.

"Oh, oh," said Raul said, "it's Burlt and his cronies. Be careful. He's usually spoiling for a fight."

The group surrounded the cart, which had halted. Burlt's prenner was in front.

"If it isn't the young royals and our knight," he jeered.

"Hello, Burlt," said Chase. "How's it going?"

"What brings you down to our neck of the woods?" Burlt demanded.

Chase didn't mind if Burlt knew where they'd been.

"We've been visiting the Island."

"Oh, that place … Nice of the King to give you that spook hole!"

"Yes, we did come across a big old bear who'd been dining on farmers," Chase laughed. "That didn't help the image."

Burlt seemed confused at Chase's casual disclosure.

"A bear?"

"By far the biggest I've ever known," said Raul. "Chase shot it up through the mouth; killed it outright."

"Oh, really?"

Yet even as he expressed his disbelief, Burlt found himself uncertain.

"Sure. The skin is in the back. Take a look."

Burlt rode to the back of the cart, casting a brief glance at the Princesses, who steadily regarded him.

"Oh, gods!" he exclaimed, when he saw the bulk of it. "Guys, come and look at this; it's huge."

Burlt dismounted, and Chase and Raul climbed down and went to him. Burlt's men followed suit, and at Chase's invitation, spread the skin out to marvel at it.

"Through the mouth you say?" said Burlt.

"He roared, so I made that my target. His hide was too thick."

"My great-grandfather used to talk about bears this big. We figured he was exaggerating."

"Shame, but it was him or us."

When Burlt was done examining the skin, he pointed to the sword at Chase's side.

"You gonna show me that sword now?"

Chase unsheathed the katana. Instinctively Burlt stepped back.

"Now these types of swords are renowned where I come from," Chase explained, "because of their strength and sharpness."

Burlt rallied.

"Still looks like a girl's sword to me," he retorted, to snickers behind him.

"Once you learn about them you won't think so."

Chase held the sword with one hand on the hilt and fingers under the steel blade, edge up, offering it for Burlt's inspection.

"Now," he continued, "this kind of sword is made from two types of steel. A hard steel centre or core, and softer, folded steel around it. This allows the sword to be rigid, but able to withstand impact. Also, it can be sharpened like a shaving blade … Careful."

Burlt's finger was bleeding. "That's sharp."

"Sorry," said Chase, half-smiling. "Should have warned you earlier."

He stepped back, motioning Burlt to clear a space for demonstration. He swung the katana in a ritual pattern, ending by slicing through a sapling close by that was as thick as a wrist. He stepped back to Burlt.

"Can I?"

Chase handed him the sword, hilt first. He watched Burlt closely as he swung it slowly, eyes on the blade, testing the sword's weight and movement. He sliced another piece off the sapling, then stopped and regarded

Chase with awe.

"This is something else, sir knight."

He nodded, and hefted the sword to feel the weight again, before handing it back to Chase, hilt first.

"Can I ask you to show it to our smithy? Our village is not far out of your way."

Chase looked up at the sun and then at Raul and the Princesses. They shrugged.

"Happy to, Burlt. Lead on."

Chase and Raul climbed back on the cart, and with Burlt riding beside him, and an escort of his followers, they set off down the road. Some of Burlt's men looked at each other in surprise, and Raul looked at Chase askance.

"Bear with me on this, will you," Chase said, quietly. "Oh, sorry. Unintentional pun."

He called to Carolie and Sonja, "Only a slight detour, ladies."

He turned to Burlt, riding close enough for easy conversation.

"So tell me about your village. Mainly farming?'

Burlt said nothing at first, obviously not used to being met as an equal. Then he began talking about his village, called Forkhill Copse. As is the habit of someone talking about their passion, he became more enthusiastic, and it didn't take much prompting from Chase to keep him talking until they arrived at the village. From a cluster of houses around a well, small children and barking dogs ran out to greet them.

Chase and Raul went first with Burlt to the smith who he introduced as Raymon. He couldn't hide his surprise at Burlt's affability towards the strangers, but examined the katana with interest.

"Folded steel, you say? Must be good steel to keep folding it, and you'd need high and constant heat."

"Yes, very high heat. Do you have any steel to try it?"

"Nothing that good," said Raymon, regretfully.

"I should be able to get you some," Chase offered. "I have supplied some iron to the Staal smiths. I'm sure I can get you some for such a good cause."

Raymon grinned broadly.

"We would be in your debt," said Burlt formally. Then added, "Prince Raul, Sir Chase, can we offer you food, drink? Would you honour us by staying in our village tonight?"

Raul heard the sincerity in the invitation, and he wanted to accept as there had been ongoing issues with this group. Chase had made a breakthrough, and outside the Princesses were talking to the children and patting the dogs.

"Burlt, I'm sorry, but we are expected back today and we don't need a bunch of Levels out hunting for us. Another time? What I could do with is a drink."

He winked at Burlt, who broke into a laugh and clapped his hands. Two of the children ran over.

"Get old Jessie to bring some good ale, and get Mavel and the girls to bring some food," he instructed and off they scampered.

"Come on."

Burlt walked them back to the Princesses.

"Your men have agreed to eat and drink with us. I hope you are happy with that, ladies. We have some good blackberry wine, I'm told."

The Princesses, though surprised by such pleasantry, as true royals graciously accepted. Soon they were sitting in the mid-day sun, at a long table loaded with food and jugs of wine and beer. The locals, who had joined them in trying the drinks on offer, also couldn't hide their surprise at Burlt's unusual affability.

While Sonja and Carolie worked hard to get the shy and subdued local women to engage in talk, Chase and Raul concentrated on Burlt and his men. Being from farming stock, Chase chose that as his subject and gradually things relaxed. The alcohol helped.

A group of teenage boys walked up to the table, nervous but determined, amusing Burlt with their show of bravery. They pushed a slight boy to the forefront. He addressed Chase.

"Are you the knight, the marksman who killed the Varden King and Princes?"

That got everyone's attention.

"I am Chase."

"We have been told you train the boys in Staal how to shoot," the boy stammered.

Chase smiled. "We have shooting practice some mornings, yes."

"We are good shots. Would you like to see?"

By now everyone at the table was grinning broadly.

"Yes, I would," Chase told the boy.

Immediately he and the others hared off, with no further discussion. Burlt was laughing.

"That was brave of him. Not a big talker, my nephew."

The boys had sprung into activity, carrying targets to the end of the buildings, with only the trees behind, and were now pacing out distances. At last they beckoned to Chase who got up and ambled over. The boys were indeed good shots, and Chase watched them intently, commending and offering tips on how to improve. The boys listened to every word.

Burlt and Raul came up beside Chase.

"What do you think?" asked Burlt.

"Generally, the boys are good; some, extremely good."

"Once they heard of what you did in the Varden battles, they were out practicing every day."

His nephew, Karl, had quietly joined them and now cleared his throat. The other boys stopped shooting.

"Sir Chase," said Karl formally, "would you do us the honour of shooting your bow for us?"

Chase looked at Burlt, who shrugged, laughing.

"You are a legend around here."

"Karl, could someone fetch my bow and quiver from behind the seat in the cart?"

Instantly half a dozen boys sprinted off, all wanting to handle 'the bow'. The winner of the race handed the bow to Chase, bowing. Another handed him the quiver.

Chase paced back and, composing himself, as usual fired a number of arrows into a small mark on a target. First he shot at eighty-five paces and then at one hundred and thirty, to the gasps and cheers of the children and the entire village. When he had fired all his arrows, which the boys ran to gather up for him, he found the crowd had pressed close behind him, intent on following the arrow flights. Burlt walked up to Chase and pounded him on the back.

"What they said is true, Sir Chase. I have never seen shooting like that."

"Not so bad after a few ales, and that's Chase to you, Burlt."

Carolie and Sonja came up and slipped their arms around his waist, claiming him proudly.

"It is a shame you are not closer, Sir Chase," said Raymon the smith. "The boys could benefit with you around."

Chase exchanged quick glances with his ladies.

"I have to go away and do something first, but when I can come back, I aim to spend some time on the Island. So I could be around some to help with archery practice. Sword too, if you want to add another technique."

Raymon, Burlt and the other Forkhill Copse men fairly buzzed over that thought, and talked animatedly together.

When they were done, Chase asked them and Raul, "Do many boys from here want to become Levels?"

Burlt changed back to his old self in at instant.

"We are poor here, sir knight. We cannot afford for our boys to run off and play soldiers. We need them working to pay your taxes."

Raul stared at the man. How could he get it so wrong?

"We pay for any boy or man's time as a Level. That's what your taxes are for. In fact, many communities choose to supply boys because it is worth their while."

Burlt was frowning, and Raymon seemed equally puzzled.

"I did not know that," Burlt said. He turned to Raymon. "Why did not the old man tell us that? He used to go to Staal meetings."

Raymon said thoughtfully, "The old man hated the Levels, and you know the reasons for that. He probably didn't tell us so no boys became Levels."

Burlt shook his head at Chase and Raul.

"If this is true, we will think on it more."

"I will send the Levels chief trainer, or even Guards Major Boste, to talk to you, Burlt, so you understand how it works. You can then decide."

"With some iron," added Chase.

The mood lightened again, and the crowd flocked around the group as they returned to the table. Delicious custard tarts appeared, and the boys arrived with Chase's arrows, handing them back with reverence.

"Can I talk to that first group of boys who came to us?" Chase asked Burlt. "I think there were five of them."

Burlt called to his nephew, and the boys stepped bashfully forward. Chase sorted five good arrows and gave one to each boy, shaking their hand as he did so. The boys clutched them proudly and bowed, while the local adults smiled appreciatively at Chase.

"Here's to a new start!"

Raul rose to make the toast, and they clinked mugs and glasses and drank deeply.

"Here's to our knight's shooting!" said Burlt. "May it continue straight and true."

Cheers and laughter. Chase got to his feet and bowed before raising his own glass.

"And here's to new friends. May they continue straight and true!"

Amongst the laughter and drinking, he leaned forward to tap his mug against Burlt's, amused by the shy grin that spread across the big man's face.

"I have something else I'd like to show you the next time I am here," said Chase. "It's a game, Burlt, good training for strength, speed and agility. But you need to make a ball first, an air bladder surrounded by stitched leather. Like this."

Chase drew a rugby ball in the packed soil with the tip of an arrow. One of the women studied it carefully and promised to make the ball.

"Strong, mind. We'll be kicking it around."

With the sun beginning to dip over the horizon, it was time to leave, with a flurry of handshakes, hugs and promises to catch up and return. On Burlt's instructions a flagon of blackberry wine was added to the cart.

About an hour later heavy rain came down, but it couldn't dampen the high spirits of the wet and merry quartet that finally drove into Staal to the relief of the King and Queen.

Chapter 25

THE GROOMS RAN OUT to take charge of the prenner and unload the cart. Raul gave them instructions on taking the bearskin to the leatherworks first thing in the morning for treatment. After a quick trip to their rooms to dry and neaten up, they rejoined the King and Queen, who had thoughtfully ordered hot drinks.

Both listened intently as Chase and Raul outlined all that had happened, with Sonja and Carolie chipping in, with details about both the Island and the Forkhill Copse village. The King nodded thoughtfully.

"That bear could have been on the Island for some time. The bastard must have killed a few people. I put a couple on the Island four years ago and they completely disappeared … A nice young couple," he added regretfully. "I'm glad you got it."

He spoke with feeling, and there was silence as they considered the unlucky pair's fate. The King continued.

"Your meeting with Burlt was fortunate, too. We have had problems for years with old man Mustrad. He was a Level once, but was kicked out for stealing. He hated the Levels after that, and Staal in general. Sounds like he soured the villagers on sending boys. I understand he died last winter. Well done, the pair of you, if you can fix that situation."

"And us!" said Carolie. "What a bunch of subservient women! Our challenge is to change that too!"

Everyone laughed, but the Queen applauded her daughters.

"Sire," Chase added, "can someone high, preferably Boste, go to the village and clarify this for them? May I ask he takes a couple of iron bars along as a gift? They want to try to make a sword like mine. A positive step forward, don't you think?"

"Very good. I will see to it." The King paused. "We do have some bad news though ... Amstraad has run out of rock."

There was silence as this information was digested.

Then Chase asked, "How much did we end up with?"

"Amstraad hadn't measured it when he talked to me this afternoon, but he says almost four men's weight."

"So Staal sized men ... about three hundred kilos or six hundred and sixty pounds ..."

"What?" queried the King, confused. Chase collected himself.

"It will have to be enough." He reached out and took the girls' hands in his own. "This means we can go now."

He decided not to mention the rock he had found on the Island.

"We still have a few days to prepare, but we need to get things moving. Sonja, Carolie, you won't need much, but I want you in splendid gowns for the meeting. How long will it take you to get ready?"

They conferred quietly together, and Sonja said, "By lunchtime tomorrow. Earlier if you want."

"Tomorrow afternoon will be fine," said Chase. "Raul, will you drive the cart of rock for us? I'd also like your thoughts before we depart."

"Of course, Chase. I will arrange for the cart to be loaded. I think the archers want you at practice tomorrow."

Chase paused, while they all regarded him solemnly,

then nodded.

"Thanks. It might be a few days before we are back."

In the silence that followed, Queen Rebekka abruptly broke her normal composed and dignified behaviour. Struggling not to cry, she said, "I'm scared for you. I don't know why this is so important, and I believe that it is. But I am scared for us all."

Sulliman took his wife's hands and clasped them to his chest.

"My love, our children and Chase have this in hand. I trust them; we have the best people on this."

"On what?" she asked desperately. "*On what exactly?*"

The King started to say something, but Chase interrupted.

"Sire, if I may?" The King nodded. "My lady, I have explained this matter to your children and they understand why I cannot, on my honour, tell anyone else what this is all about. I assure you, it is urgent, and we have undertaken to do what we need to do."

Carolie spoke.

"What Chase says is the truth, Mother. He cannot tell why, and we understand, agree, and support that. If anyone can make this go away, it's Chase."

"Yes." Raul stepped over and sat down beside her, putting a hand on her forearm. "That's how it is."

Sonja joined them and kissed her mother's cheek. "We will be all right with Chase."

The Queen wiped her eyes and nodded, trying to smile.

"Time to retire now," said the King. "We all need our rest for tomorrow."

*

Upstairs, while the women bathed together before sleep,

282

Chase tested the rock he had collected from the caves on the Island. Definitely cramlimite; not the highest quality, and that from the small north vent cave was the better, but still …

*

Chase woke early from his dream as Carolie and Sonja slept peacefully beside him. He had been standing in front of an enormous crowd of strange individuals. A vast auditorium where he talked, though uncertain of exactly to whom he was talking. He seemed to be offering them money for charity …

The dream faded as first Carolie, then Sonja opened their eyes, smiling at him. He reached for his women.

Later, after the rain had stopped, Chase squelched across the courtyard to the shooting range, where practice had already begun under the leadership of his chosen men. Chase spoke to them about atmospheric conditions, moisture and dry air, wind and other factors that could affect arrow flight.

"When you have only one shot, it's got to count, so think about everything …"

When training was over, Chase returned to the Castle courtyard. Raul had organized the loading of the cart, which now held ten baskets of cramlimite. His own clothes had been packed by Fruel, as arranged, and the girls' baggage was also on the cart.

Chase went off to fetch more arrows from Baesel, Ferrer trailing along as usual. He took the boy with him to visit Silver, and spoilt the pushy prenner – and the boy – with sweets, patting the animal as it sucked on them.

"Thank you for your help, Ferrer," said Chase, shaking the boy's hand. "Will you visit Silver now and then? I have to go away for a few days?"

Ferrer nodded and saluted.

Smiling, Chase went up to his room. Fruel was making up the bed and Chase greeted him warmly.

Fruel was obviously in low spirits, but managed a weak smile.

"You got me a new bag, Fruel."

"Yes. Yours was still wet from the Island trip."

"You really do look after us all, Fruel …"

Fruel head dropped down, and Chase bent to look at him.

"What's wrong, Fruel?"

"Nothing, my lord."

He turned away, but Chase caught his shoulder.

"Please?"

Fruel hesitated and shook his head.

"Fruel. Please," Chase said softly.

Fruel still kept his head lowered.

"I am worried about you and the Princesses. I have overheard some of the conversations and I know you are going into danger and that something threatens us all …"

His voice broke on a sob. Chase put his hand on the man's shoulder and patted him as Fruel muttered a few apologies and scrubbed at his eyes. When Chase reckoned Fruel had got himself under control, he let go.

"I can assure you, Fruel, I wouldn't take the Princesses where they could be harmed. I need them with me to help convince the people we have to talk to. I can't say any more than that, but we will be okay. Understood?"

Fruel nodded and stepped back.

"I am sorry for being such a sop, my lord," he said stiffly.

"Not at all, Fruel. I do appreciate your concern and thank you for it."

Fruel didn't seem to be listening.

"I don't know what you must think of me," he muttered.

"What I think of you, Fruel?"

Chase made sure he had Fruel's attention.

"I think you are a man who cares about people, and there is nothing better than that. You have looked after me superbly. I know you would do anything for your friends, and I know a brave man when I see one as I saw you, on the wall fighting for your friends and your town."

Fruel smiled for real now. He rubbed his hands over his face as if he liked Chase's portrait of himself.

"Yes, my friends ..." he murmured.

"Now, Fruel, the King and Queen are also deeply concerned, so I need you to be there for them and reassure them while we're away. Can you do that?"

"Certainly, my lord."

Fruel had recovered his composure.

"Do you need a hand carrying those down to the cart?"

Chase could have managed – his bow and quiver, a cloak, the bag of clothes – but he nodded.

"Please."

Smiling now, Fruel stepped lightly down the stairs ahead of him.

*

Lunch was a communal family occasion, with anticipation in the air. Like the wait before a major sporting event, Chase thought. Levels assisted the castle stewards, with Fruel hovering attentively by as overseer. The Queen and King tried hard to be calm and casual, but failed miserably. Laura sat between Sonja and Carolie, toying with her food.

The waiting was hard on them all.

As soon as he could, Chase raised an eyebrow at the girls who took the cue and started the exodus.

Outside a large number of townsfolk seemed to somehow know of their departure and that it was important. They hugged family and friends, and shook hands with the councillors and other well-wishers. Carolie and Sonja were too excited to be scared. Raul was wistfully quiet, and Laura clung to him as if frightened he would change his mind and go. Amstraad, Meadl and Boste gave the impression they wished they were going too.

"Good luck! Good luck!" came repeatedly from the King and Queen. Then the King drew Chase apart for a final word.

"Again I have to thank you for what you're trying to do. I know you'll achieve whatever needs to be achieved if anyone can."

Chase put his hand on the King's shoulder.

"I cannot promise success, Sire. I can promise to do my best and to bring your daughters safely home."

Chase felt the weight of a world heavy on his shoulders.

Finally they climbed into the cart, and Raul took the reins. If there were tears in anybody's eyes, nobody commented.

Chapter 26

DESPITE THE SITUATION, this *was* an adventure, and soon the girls were in a buoyant mood. Behind Raul and Chase, they speculated on what they could learn on this journey.

Chase said quietly to Raul, "Are you all right, my friend?"

"Uh huh."

Chase shook his head.

"Not an answer. Come on, Raul. Spit it out."

Raul sat in silence for a number of seconds and then said quietly and slowly. "I feel you're doing what a son, a prince should be doing. My job, Chase."

Chase took his time in answering, as the two prenner pulling the cart walked on.

"I can understand how you might think that. I can assure you I don't mean to, and it isn't the case. It isn't your fault in any way that the situation is as it is. You are your father's son. You are mature and brave beyond your years. You will be a great king, though may that day be long in coming."

He turned and faced Raul directly.

"And, my friend, there are several reasons I'm doing this, and none of them because I wanted to. By any gods of yours or mine, I wish this wasn't happening. The reasons I'm doing it are, firstly, because I'm in the unique position of being chosen and able to do so. Secondly, I have access to a space craft. Also I can talk to the Federation Council. *Also* I come from the planet your ancestors were taken from. That gives us a lever in negotiating with the Federation.

"Finally, I must stop this happening. I love your sisters, and I also care about you and Laura, the baby that's coming, and your parents. All my friends here. There's something you need to know, Raul. I have found the people I want to spend the rest of my life with, and I will continue to fight with them and for them …"

He stopped, unable to say more. Raul reached across with his right hand and they grasped wrists and grinned self-consciously at each other. When Sonja and Carolie leaned over to wrap their arms around him and their brother, he realized they had heard every word. His neck was wet with their tears.

When they eventually disentangled, Raul said, "Come on! This is a quest, a fight we must win. And we are going to win, because we must, and then imagine the party we'll have to celebrate!"

The trip to Startrader field seemed to take forever, yet it was still too soon when they arrived.

The door opened and Kayfor said, "Welcome back, everyone."

"Thanks, Kayfor," they chorused. Suddenly it was becoming real.

"Kayfor, can you organize getting the cramlimite on board and into secure containers, please?"

"Already organized, Chase. I take it you are all ready?"

As they carried their bags up the ramp, Chase said, "As much as we can be. Kayfor, that's all the cramlimite, though I might have found some of lower quality elsewhere."

"I hope it is enough, Chase."

"So do we."

A mechanoid whisked their bags away, and Chase put his cramlimite samples into a sensor.

"Tell me, Kayfor, does cramlimite somehow restrict your sensors? Is that why you couldn't see the bear in the cave?"

"Yes, Chase. That is one of its properties."

"Hmm. Thanks."

They sat around a table with the meadow on view before them.

"Any update, Kayfor?" asked Chase.

"Only that your hearing has caused a tremendous stir in the intergalactic community. Every official wants to be there. Apparently, there is not enough room in the great hall."

Chase swallowed.

"Probably didn't need to know that, Kayfor."

"Oh, so many might cause you anxiety? Sorry. Should have guessed that."

They chuckled at the innocence of Kayfor.

"Perhaps you should run through what happens with this hearing."

Firstly Kayfor explained to them the protocol for the Council. It was simple. They would be met. There were security procedures in place, but they would not need to be concerned or even notice them. They would be presented to the Council and heard. Only one person could speak at a hearing though; likewise only one person from the Council could ask questions.

This dismayed the Princesses. Only one person? Then it had to be Chase. Questions could be asked, Kayfor added, and then they would be requested to leave while the Council deliberated.

"How long do they usually take to deliberate?" asked Sonja. "Do we need to stay close?"

"No set rule, Princess Sonja. Because the time can vary, they will contact you."

They discussed what he'd told them.

Then Carolie enquired, "What about presentation, Kayfor? How should we dress? As well as we can?"

"As nobly as possible, I would say. No matter how advanced the society, people are still judged on the clothes they wear, how they present themselves."

"Makes sense, though," said Raul. "No different from meeting dignitaries here."

Chase turned to his ladies.

"We can use that to our advantage. I need you by me, every inch of you Royal Princesses of Tapar."

They nodded, looking first at each other, and then at Chase.

"How much time do we have, Kayfor?"

"Nearly sixty-two hours."

"Cutting it fine, then," chuckled Raul. He dodged a playful swipe from Carolie.

"Okay," said Chase. "The part I'm most worried about is how we can get in and potentially out without you and Startrader being detained."

"I have been working on that, Chase," said Kayfor. "We are supposed to notify our docking time and landing. I imagine you do not want me to do that."

"No. I am not entirely sure you wouldn't be detained."

"Agreed, Chase. As you know, the Zalos Corporation group, of which you are a member, funded Startrader's development, and wants Startrader and me returned. We are deemed to be fugitives now. I am nervous about what would happen to me if I was returned to them. They might erase my memories."

"Don't worry, Kayfor," said Chase quickly. "I do have a plan. Tell me, how much cramlimite would it take to buy the Trader and you?"

"Thank you, Chase. You intend to try to buy us off Zalos Corporation? At today's prices it would take near twenty kilograms of your cramlimite. That will entice them."

He paused before continuing.

"I have a docking site not too far from the Council's Great Hall. We can arrive unnoticed. You can make your way to the Council and then return to the 'Trader."

"Will you leave and return when we need you?" asked Sonja.

"No. If I leave by direct placement, the sonic boom of the air replacing the ship will cause a noise so loud that our departure port would be known and we would not be able to return. Likewise if we tried manually to sail out to space, our systems would be taken over. No, Startrader will have to stay hidden until you return to us."

They mulled this over.

"So can you stay hidden there?" asked Carolie.

"I think so – I hope so – with the help of some mechanoid friends."

"It is important you are not caught, Kayfor. If you think you will be, you must leave. We can keep in communication, I imagine?"

"Understood and yes, Chase."

"That's settled then. Now we should talk about my presentation and any additions and suggestions you all might have."

They spent the best part of two hours talking through what Chase proposed to put before the Council. A little like a court hearing, he thought, making notes. The royals had many suggestions to add. Mostly he tapped into their emotion, and Kayfor clarified what was possible or cited Federation law as necessary.

When Raul left there were hugs and kisses from his sisters. Chase went with him to the air lock where the men, now closer than brothers, embraced and parted. There were no more words to say.

*

"Are we off, Kayfor?" asked Chase when he rejoined the Princesses.

"I need to explain to you about galaxy law and space travel, Chase."

That got their undivided attention.

"I know I have been ignoring laws as it suits, but this is knowledge that could benefit us all."

They seated themselves and waited.

"According to galaxy law, live species are needed for – and I quote – 'control and decision-making on all sub-spacecraft'. Unnecessary in my opinion, and undermines the mechanoids ..."

Chase smiled and the girls looked at him askance.

"Anyhow, I can educate you all on the ship's engineering, operation, star travel, and navigation for a start. You will then fulfil the legal requirements and could operate Startrader if something happened to me."

"Oh, yes!" said Sonja, and Carolie nodded frantically in her excitement.

"I'm not sure we have that much time," began Chase.

"Oh, it takes only a matter of minutes," said Kayfor. "A process that's been around for hundreds of years called neural development. It involves inserting memories, and, because it creates synapses at the time of memory input,

292

those memories are retained and as a result knowledge is created."

Chase noted the girls were listening intently and gripping each other's hands.

"It is a process that will drain you as you are starting from … such a low level. You will need to sleep after."

The girls pretended to take offence at Kayfor's word, but Chase only laughed.

"As long as we're fully operational before the hearing."

"No problem, Chase."

They rose and proceeded to the medical centre. After a complex one hand competition, like sign language, Carolie won and went first.

She lay on the light table. The light changed beneath her head, and soon her eyes closed as Sonja and Chase watched. Only minutes later the light went back to its original colour.

"Procedure finished," Kayfor said. "You will need to help her to bed."

Chase carried a drowsy Carolie to the bedroom, returning to find Sonja already on the table. Minutes later he was carrying her off, too.

This time when he returned he took up his position on the light table. The next thing he knew he was struggling down the hall under Kayfor's instructions and was asleep as soon as he crawled onto the bed and lay down between the girls.

Chapter 27

CHASE WOKE TO A WEIRD SENSATION OF being himself and not himself. He had knowledge and understanding of things he hadn't known or understood before. In his room, for instance, he now knew how most things worked. He knew things he never even dreamt existed, things known to the stranger in his head. He needed a drink. He managed to crawl backward down the bed between the Princesses and got unsteadily to his feet.

He washed his face and hands in the bathroom and then went to the galley. Galley, he knew; not kitchen.

"Good morning, Chase. How do you feel?"

"I have a headache, but other than that it's weird and not entirely pleasant, Kayfor, to know things without remembering learning them."

"You will adapt and what you know will become part of you. Soon you will feel normal."

"That's a relief."

Chase started another glass of water. As he sipped it, he realized he could read the symbols on the food replicator and every other machine. Before they had been nothing but shapes.

"I can read all this," he exclaimed.

"Cool, huh?"

That made Chase chuckle.

His mind told him how and where the water was stored, how it was kept pure. His mind also told him how to operate the food replicator and how it worked including the energy and chemical reactions, and soon he was sitting in front of bacon and eggs, toast and coffee.

"We are in open space, Chase. I had to move as the Federation drone was due. We are near a sun which will mask us in case anyone happens to pass near us."

"Very good, Kayfor." Chase's head still hurt. "How long have we got now before we are due at the Council?"

"Nine hours."

"What? We have been sleeping over two days?"

"Yes, over fifty hours. I had to wake you. Still gently trying to wake the Princesses. I told you it would take a lot out of you. Are you feeling better now?"

Chase chewed the last of his bacon, and realized he did.

"Yes, thank you, Kayfor. I can't believe what I know."

"Knowledge isn't everything, but it usually helps."

"Very true. It's what you do with that knowledge that matters most."

Chase had finished breakfast, and was holding his second coffee in months and talking to Kayfor when Sonja and Carolie appeared. They looked drained and perplexed. Chase got up and kissed them. They clung to him.

"I'd ask you how you felt, but I think I know. Scary, but it's getting better already."

"That's a relief." Sonja was staring around. "I know how all this works!"

"It's like you've got someone else's brain in your head with your own," said Carolie.

"Yep," said Chase. "Breakfast?"

The Princesses helped themselves because they wanted to use their new-found knowledge, even on something simple. He watched in amusement as they realized they could read everything.

Chase talked through timing with Kayfor while the

Princesses livened up – beginning to talk astrophysics, animated as they marvelled at what they knew.

"How long will it take to get from the docking point to the Council?"

"About forty minutes. An automatic shuttle will be waiting for you, and it will take you about twenty minutes to meet the officials who will lead you to the Council."

"So we jump in about seven hours?"

"Yes, Chase."

"Hear that, girls? Cutting it fine."

"Cutting it fine!" agreed Sonja as the rolling gag continued.

Chase wrote out his key points from their previous discussion while Sonja and Carolie discussed what they now knew. Much of it was confusing as they had no point of reference for it. Kayfor assured them that, as the knowledge 'bedded in', it would make more sense.

"But we will be able to fly the Startrader?"

"Yes."

"And can we add to this knowledge?"

"For now, I have given you a basic science package and Startrader technology. You each also got a particular specialism I thought appropriate. Sorry for the liberty, but I am sure you will approve. You will be able to add more information and knowledge normally. I would not add more neural data for some time – a year at least. You need to add to that knowledge yourselves so it makes sense and stays with you. I can then have available anything you want.

"You will also need language inserts, Princesses," he added.

Chase remembered the procedure and watched as a

mechanoid quickly and painlessly carried it out.

"Kayfor, can you arrange for us to meet the individuals who think they own you and Startrader, from Zalos Corporation, after the hearing?"

"Certainly, Chase. I will also arrange for the shuttle to take you there."

On Kayfor's advice they rested. When he woke them again, they showered and dressed. Time seemed to be speeding up as jump time neared. His ladies paraded before Chase, Sonja in an olive green full-length dress that highlighted her red hair and dark green eyes, and Carolie in chocolate brown that flattered her creamy skin and auburn curls. The dresses matched in style and were embroidered with silver wire, which was also woven intricately through their gleaming hair.

Chase wore the clothes made by the Staal tailors on the occasion of his knighting. Medieval fashion at its best, high quality, and fitted to perfection on his tall, lean frame. He contemplated his weapons, but decided they would probably create more issues than benefits.

"How can we communicate with you, Kayfor?" he asked.

A panel slid out. On it were three bands: jewelled bracelets, one styled for each of them.

"Yes, you all need to be able to communicate with me in case you are separated," Kayfor said. "To open a channel you move the green jewel. Please test them."

They did as instructed, and each of them talked to Kayfor and listened as he talked back to them.

"Distance isn't a problem and it is a secure line. I will have a direct link to the Federation hall, so will follow the hearing. I will know where you are from the communicators, and if you return to the auto shuttle, it will take you back to me without need for communication."

"Very good. Thanks, Kayfor," said Chase.

"Yes, I feel safer knowing you are with us," said Carolie.

Her sister added, "Yes, we are definitely all in this together."

"Thank you, Princesses."

Back in the control room Chase asked for the panels and clear front.

Virtual screens appeared. The Princesses and Chase started pre-landing checks as if they'd done them all their lives, exchanging knowing grins and raised eyebrows.

"Docking pad is secure and no incoming." That was Sonja.

"Navigation confirmed and locked," said Carolie.

"At your leisure, please, Kayfor."

At Chase's words the view in front of them dissolved into darkness and then re-formed into what appeared to be the interior of a gigantic building. They could see other craft moving in the distance.

"Jump complete."

Startrader moved down and sideways into a parking bay. "This is amazing," said Carolie. The other two just nodded, wide eyed.

They exited Startrader, with Kayfor's good wishes farewelling them. He had already instructed them to place a disc on their chests beneath their clothes. They knew, without him telling them, it was the gaseous exchange support.

"Still definitely weird knowing all this," murmured Carolie, and they all agreed.

Off the ramp they transferred to a walkway.

"Gravity difference is plus seventeen percent over Tapar," said Carolie. "We will feel heavy and tire more quickly."

A mechanoid similar to those on Startrader came up to them.

"Greetings, Chase Robinson and Princesses. I am Geenine. I have the honour of escorting you to your transport."

"Thank you, Geenine."

G9?

"Kayfor has communicated with me, and there is no record that you or Startrader are here."

"Thank you again, Geenine."

Soon they reached a corridor where a bubble-like craft waited. No wheels; a hovercraft.

"Class 4 automatic," said Chase.

The Princesses laughed at his obvious surprise at knowing it.

"This Class 4 is programmed to firstly take you to the main Council great hall," said Geenine. "It will park in standby and be ready at the terminal you arrive at. The vehicle will only operate with you. When you return, tell it to go to the Zalos Corporation, as requested."

"Very good. Hope to see you back here."

Inside the Class 4 was compact and comfortable. The Princesses were careful with their dresses. Once they started moving the inside walls displayed a farm scene.

"They think of everything," laughed Carolie.

A voice said quietly, "Welcome aboard Class 4 Automatic 2368. Estimated arrival at Federation Council Main Hall is in thirty-eight minutes. Would you like refreshments?"

"Please," said Sonja. "Iced baronia tea."

Confused, she shrugged as the others smiled and ordered. They nervously sipped their drinks. Carolie tried to be helpful.

"Anticipation is always worse than the event."

"I hope so," said Chase.

At last they arrived and the door opened. Chase helped the Princesses out. The sign above the entrance told them it was Dock 94. A scan passed over them and a mechanoid approached.

"How can I assist?"

"Chase Robinson. I have a hearing in the Great Hall."

"If you follow me," the mechanoid intoned, "I will lead you to the Wardens."

When they were led into the waiting room several creatures rushed up to them. The Princesses ducked behind Chase; it was the first time they had met creatures from another planet and the onslaught was frightening.

The natural instinct when seeing a new species is to associate it with something you know. So in Chase's mind there were two creatures similar to Riian, though smaller; best described as short-bodied horses or donkeys. There was a simian creature like Gargen, and two others that Chase couldn't relate to at all; they were just too different from anything he had ever known.

Without introduction, one of the 'donkeys' said, "Ah, Chase Robinson. Welcome to the Federation Council."

He noticed the Princesses.

"You have others with you?"

"Yes, I do. They are my support."

Chase didn't introduce Sonja and Carolie; he wanted to keep them as a surprise.

"Ah, certainly. The Council is just finishing a hearing and you are next. I hope to be able to lead you into the Hall in about fifteen minutes. Do you need anything?"

Chase shot an enquiring gaze at the Princesses.

"Ladies room?" suggested Sonja. "I'm a bundle of nerves."

"Can the ladies be shown a rest room? We have been travelling."

The Princesses were led off. Chase wanted to remain near the Hall. They were back surprisingly quickly.

"That was different," whispered Sonja. Carolie nodded.

"New places always are," smiled Chase.

Then the Wardens came back to them.

"The Council is ready for you now, Chase Robinson. I have never seen so many councillors present. There is also universal feed. You have caused quite a stir."

They were led down a corridor to doors, where other Wardens took over. As they passed through Chase felt the now familiar sensation of another scan. Then another set of doors opened, and they were led into the Great Hall. Great was not the word: vast, immense were better. Yet it was not, at first sight, much wider or longer than various sporting grounds Chase had been in. Only there was no apparent ceiling and it just kept going up. But more overpowering were the hundreds of thousands of creatures, seated or standing as they were able, of every possible size, shape and colour.

All eyes now focused on Chase and the Princesses. Chase tried to control his breathing, and the Princesses held hands and stood behind him, refusing to look up.

They were formally escorted into the Great Hall by the three Wardens, who bowed and left them in the centre of the amphitheatre, facing the officials who flanked a tall figure similar to Delt. The room hushed. The figure stood and spoke.

"Greetings, Chase Robinson. I am Lord Wansson and I represent the Federation Council in this meeting. It is I to whom you can direct your questions, and I who may ask questions of you. All I know of the situation is that you wished an audience with the Council for an important matter of right and law, which the Council must honour unless it has clear reason not to do so. This is a little unusual as we have not had an unknown situation for many years. On the positive side, you have good representation here because of this. So you may now introduce yourself and those accompanying you and state your case of right and law, or question the Council."

He bowed, and seated himself, his officials following suit.

Chase, who had been marvelling at what he was seeing, collected himself. He stood tall, lifted his head and began.

"My name is Chase Robinson from the planet Earth, and Sir Chase Robinson from the planet Tapar. Accompanying me are Princess Carolie and Princess Sonja of the State of Staal on Tapar."

A murmur passed around the Hall. Clearly they knew of Tapar's predicament. Chase allowed himself a moment of satisfaction. He had had the effect he wanted.

Chapter 28

CHASE BRACED HIMSELF, took a deep breath and began.

"A very short time ago I was approached on my immature planet by creatures that I never knew existed, and asked to join them to try to save a planet from destruction."

He paused and took another calming breath. He had never been this nervous at any presentation.

"On the face of it, this seemed a good cause; a noble cause. But then they explained to me that the planet could be saved by those in power, except that those in power could not act because by their own laws they were not allowed to interfere in an immature planet's future. It was also explained to me that my planet, like this endangered planet, could not join the Federation as it, too, was not mature enough."

"The planet they were talking about is called Tapar. The planet Tapar's sun has become extremely unstable and will destroy most, if not all life on Tapar inside the next twelve to eighteen months, possibly sooner. The Princesses with me are representatives of the sapient race on Tapar."

This time when he paused it was for effect. Murmuring spread throughout the hall.

"I have had it explained to me that immature planets, by law, are not to be contacted as it could harm them and potentially admit selfish creatures to the Federation. I have also been informed that when a species or society is deemed sufficiently mature it is invited into the Federation. I can understand these mandates in principle. What I am unsure of is whether individuals, let alone societies, ever totally outgrow selfishness. However, you are here so that must be the case and I congratulate you all."

Again an outbreak of murmuring.

"So the concern of the Federation is that immature species with selfish intent could create harm through the universe. That is entirely understandable."

He paused again.

"The Federation has recognized the need to limit interference and it seems to work. Don't allow interference with immature planets, stop rogues from harming others; all correct and commendable. Yet because of this, the Federation appears to have limited its own potential for good. Because there *is* opportunity for good, also. And so I ask, is it correct and commendable not to interfere, even when planets, species and individual lives are at stake?"

There was a rumbling of noise from the crowd. Assent or dissent? Chase couldn't tell. He continued.

"Systems are set up, rules and guidelines laid down, laws passed for a reason. Always for a very good reason. And that is what we have here. No interference, no matter what, and for a very good reason."

His audience was now completely silent.

"As a new observer to the Federation I can see the reasoned and reasonable intention behind this decision, and I applaud you for it. However, nothing is perfect; no one is perfect. Isn't that so? Here is a planet with innumerable creatures on it and at least one sapient species, doomed when it could be saved.

"On another level, I have also been told of societies wanting to leave the Federation. This is disappointing. Sad. With the best intent, surely all species would want to be involved?"

Another rumbling from the crowd, which Chase ignored.

"Perhaps it is through what it considers its own good intent that the Federation does harm to itself, becoming an entity that not everyone wants to be part of, add to, create with, and be proud of. With continual effort to do the right thing, for want of a better expression, has the Federation maybe lost sight of one of the things that makes – or could make – it better?"

He took a step forward for emphasis.

"Doing good. Basic rights. The things that we recognize as proper, moral and ethical. The things that make us truly good. Perhaps the reason some planetary societies now refuse to be part of this great Federation is that, by trying to do no harm, you have also stopped yourself from doing good."

Now the noise around the hall increased, and it was hard for Chase to make out what the general response might be. Too many sounds, both good and bad. Lord Wansson raised his hand and the noise stopped.

"I have with me two Princesses from Staal. They wanted to speak for their planet, their society, their loved ones and all that lives and breathes on their planet. But I understand only one person can speak here. Yet Princess Carolie and Princess Sonja represent a society that, like the Federation, tries to do the most good for the majority, a society that I believe when it is mature enough will become a valuable member of the Federation. But because the Federation has made the rule, no interference, they will be lost ..."

He heard a sob behind him, but could not turn around, knowing that it would limit his independence and his ability to continue. He hoped the audience heard it though.

"Here is an opportunity to make things better. Make the Federation better. We have the chance to do good, as well as prevent harm. Nothing will be lost, nothing sacrificed, but so much will be gained … To the point where societies may again want to be involved instead of leaving the Federation."

Now the noise reached a new level, a clash of sounds. Lord Wansson raised his hand, but it took several seconds for the uproar to subside and when it did, the focus was back on Chase. Once he had their full attention again he resumed.

"I have been advised that the race on Tapar is the same species as mine, from Earth. The information I have is that some time ago a number of my species were taken from my planet to Tapar, and distributed in several locations. This was to ensure future labour for mining."

A further rumble of sound pervaded the hall.

"This means," Chase said loudly, "these creatures were placed in danger by a mature species, a member of this Federation, for the mining of cramlimite. These workers, abandoned on the planet Tapar, have recently mined all the cramlimite there. I have brought it with me to barter on their behalf for their lives, if that is what it takes."

This time the muttering was sustained and voluble. Many of the audience had risen to their feet, and were vehement in protests and support. Chase spoke loudly over the noise.

"As it was a mature species and cramlimite that put them in danger, I would say they should be protected by this Federation."

Now he was completely drowned by the uproar. To

Chase that proved he had hit upon some sore points. Finally, Lord Wansson gained silence with the help of the other Wardens. When he could be heard, Chase drew in a breath and sped to his conclusion.

"My final words are to ask you to decide quickly, before their sun destroys them, and to do what I have done – support and assist. I have stood beside the citizens of Staal because I knew that if I didn't, they would be lost. Is it good – is it even legal – to stand by and watch someone die, without lifting a hand to help them? Or is it murder?"

The clamour erupted again and clearly was not going to stop for some time. A perfect time for them to leave. Chase looked at Lord Wansson and bowed. Lord Wansson nodded and returned the bow, indicating that he was able to leave.

"I will leave you to your decision. Thank you for your time."

Chase was not sure how many, if any, heard him. Chase turned and took a Princess under each arm, and walked them out through the massive bronze doors.

*

"Come on, come on," he urged. "We need to move."

He hurried them back to Dock 94. They hadn't been there longer than a minute when the Class 4 arrived and they climbed aboard.

"Zalos Corporation," Chase said.

They started to move and the girls wiped their eyes and wrapped their arms around Chase.

The Class 4's automated voice announced, "Twenty-two minutes to arrival. Do you want refreshments?"

"No, thank you," said Sonja. "That was amazing, Chase. Do you think it will work?"

"We will find out, I guess. I tried to pinch nerves and morals, but also the cramlimite, the rock, might sway the decision."

"Shouldn't we have waited for a response?" asked Carolie.

"No. Lord Wansson seemed happy for us to go. Also, we may have some legal problems with not returning Startrader, so we need to deal with that now."

They discussed how the Council had reacted so noisily, and what it might have meant. The Class 4 finally slowed down.

"We have arrived at Zalos Corporation. I will remain at this dock."

"Good. Thank you."

Chase helped the Princesses out. A mechanoid appeared and led them into an elevator that both rose upward and moved horizontally for some time. When the doors opened, the mechanoid led them through a reception area to a door where it paused. The door slid open and they entered a meeting room with a stone table, around which several creatures stood.

One walked up to them on all fours and then sat up on its hind legs. Chase had no idea what it was, but he bowed anyway, and courteously the creature returned the bow.

"Welcome to the Zalos Corporation. We have a quorum of owners here as we understand you have a proposition for us."

He led them to the table where, strangely, everyone remained standing.

"My name is Chase Robinson, and our proposition is regarding Startrader."

"We wish it returned."

The creature who spoke so sharply was similar to Cayrol, the 'otter'. It continued.

"We have been implicated in the communication with immature cultures, and several of our owner members have been detained because of it. We are under investigation."

"I understand that. I think I may be able to help your situation. I want to buy Startrader off you."

They all tried to speak at once, and the creature that had approached Chase raised his hand for silence.

"Startrader is not for sale, and you are part of an immature culture. You should not even be here."

"Yes, but as you have agreed to talk to me, you are seeking a solution. Will you accept pure cramlimite for Startrader?"

They were clearly not expecting that, and had to be silenced again.

"We knew there was cramlimite on Tapar," said the first creature.

"I know. That's why your crew took me there."

"Yes. To help save Tapar."

"That's what they told me," said Chase, "and what I could tell the Council."

He spoke with deliberate meaning. The Corporation shareholders exchanged a silent communication.

"What do you propose?" eventually said the second creature.

"I will offer you fifty kilograms of pure cramlimite for Startrader. It will in every legal sense be ours, and we also require a 75-year standard service contract. All new technology to be included as upgrades. I also want a non-dilutable ten percent share of Zalos Corporation. I will confirm to the Council that I understood the crew was not acting under the instruction of Zalos Corporation, but under a moral obligation."

Chase reflected for a second, then added, "Also, Zalos Corporation will not claim that Startrader was taken against its wishes over the time since this began."

Chase waited impassively as they moved to the far side of the room and talked it through. They returned and the first creature spoke for them all.

"If the cramlimite volume is accepted, shareholding is not and 75 years is too long. The non-return of Startrader is accepted, but how do we know you will speak correctly to the Council?"

"No shareholding, no deal. Fifty years then, and I know this is too good a deal. That amount of cramlimite will fund Zalos Corporation and I want the benefits of that funding. You have my word on the Council. Otherwise I could tell them my real suspicions."

Again a spirited discussion between them, but it was apparent what direction this was heading. When the talk died down, they returned to Chase.

"We have a deal, Chase Robinson. The voice recording will act as a legal document to be forwarded to K4 on Startrader – once we have communication. How do we get the cramlimite?"

"I will ship it to you once this is legally completed."

The Zalos Corporation shareholders stated their names and agreed to the details of the contract. Chase followed their lead. They then all bowed to each other, and Chase and the Princesses walked out and followed the mechanoid to the elevator.

"You own Startrader?" asked Sonja.

"*We* own the 'Trader," replied Chase with a grin, "and

ten percent of Zalos. That went better than I thought it would."

"Kayfor will be pleased," laughed Carolie.

"Speaking of Kayfor …"

Chase activated his bracelet and upon hearing Kayfor's greeting, gave him a quick run-down of the situation.

"I hope this works, Chase," said Kayfor. "If I had the choice I would remain with you and the Princesses, if you wish …"

"Of course, Kayfor, you are part of the team."

Chase was smiling. Obviously Programmed Persons had their insecurities too!

"Thank you again, Chase …. Chase, I have just heard on the Council communication that they are hunting for you. They wish you to return to the Council. A terse communication. No word why."

The mechanoid with them said, "Where do you wish to go now, Chase Robinson?"

"Back to the Council hall," said Chase more to himself than anyone else. "If there is any way to push Council to help …"

"To the Class 4," Sonja instructed the mechanoid, "then to the Great Hall. Can you notify Council that we have their message and are returning?"

Chapter 29

THE CLASS 4 took them back to Docking Bay 94, where they followed the same security procedures before returning to the Great Hall. Intense and animated discussion was taking place. All talk died when they entered. Lord Wansson rose and addressed them.

"It has not happened for some time, but Council wanted to remain to debate your issue, Chase Robinson. That and your inexperience in this arena is why Council has overlooked your unavailability for questioning."

"Thank you, my lord. My sincere apologies to the Council."

A little humility wouldn't hurt.

"Council has questions for you to answer before releasing a verdict on your hearing."

He seemed to be wanting a specific reply.

"Certainly, my lord. If I can."

"You have been accused of breaking Federation law by communicating with an immature species. Do you have any defence on that?"

"Certainly; my lord. I believed the cause was just and it is in my learning to help others whenever possible. Also I am from an immature planet myself, so I am not sure if that law applies to me."

"No excuse for breaking a law and it does," replied Lord Wansson.

Chase looked at him directly and said, "Since the species on Tapar is my own, I have not communicated with another species."

A loud buzz around the hall. Was that a smile tugging at Lord Wansson's mouth? Hard to tell …

"Decision," announced Lord Wansson after a few moments.

A virtual screen appeared, a globe in the centre of the hall that could be seen from all around, and that displayed like a graph with two columns. Around the hall, members seemed to be voting. The left column rose high; on the right, low.

After a few seconds Lord Wansson said, "Accepted."

He glanced down at a screen in front of him. Chase realized he was being judged and had passed the first accusation.

"You are accused that you were part of the Zalos Corporation crew whose real agenda was to obtain cramlimite. You actually made the Taparians mine it."

"I had no real understanding of the value of cramlimite, my lord. The recordings made by the unit K4 on the ship will show that, and the communications around that. I did ask the people on Tapar to mine cramlimite, but paid for their services. It was a good trade deal for them, and in no way dangerous. I did not explain to them the situation around the intended use of the cramlimite, or about their sun, as they are an immature species and I understood the principle of the law that the knowledge would harm them."

"And what was the intended use of it, in your opinion?"

"I understood that cramlimite might persuade Council that Tapar was worth saving, my lord."

Whispers between the officials, and murmurs from the enthralled observers.

"And what do you feel was the real motivation of the Zalos Corporation executives and Zalos Corporation crew in relation to obtaining the cramlimite?"

Dead silence.

Chase refrained from showing any emotion.

"I can only surmise from what they told me, my lord. They wanted the cramlimite to somehow persuade Council to save Tapar."

Another pause before Lord Wansson again said, "Decision."

Everyone looked at the screen, including Chase and the Princesses. The column on the left rose high, almost as high as last time. The column on the right rose higher than last time, but still well below the left.

Again Lord Wansson said, "Accepted."

Sweat trickled down Chase's back.

"You have been accused of stealing, or at least not returning the vessel known as Startrader."

"My lord, that is a misunderstanding. I have been in communication with the executives of Zalos Corporation and they will confirm that they do not deem Startrader to have been in any manner misappropriated."

He hoped fervently they would keep their word.

Wansson spoke to a creature beside him, who immediately turned and began speaking rapidly into a communicator.

"While we wait for that confirmation, Sir Chase, you realize that as a member of a species from an immature planet you will need to be returned, potentially with memory removal, to your planet."

Chase tried not to react.

"I would hope, my lord, that Council would see fit to exempt me from that charge on the grounds that I only acted because of the circumstances I was placed under.

Also, I believe I have followed the task for which I was taken from my planet, and performed a service for Council by bringing two hundred kilograms of pure cramlimite to be donated to Council for use in the repair of Tapar's sun."

A loud rumble of talk forced Lord Wansson to raise his hand again.

"Council can accept the cramlimite was properly obtained and for a reasonable purpose," he said tersely, "but Council will not be bought."

"I am certainly not trying to buy anything from Council, my lord. I am donating cramlimite to assist in the cost of repairing Tapar's sun and for any other moral programme as Council sees fit."

The recent dream jumped into Chase's mind – charity?

"This has been my purpose the entire time. Also, my lord, I was hoping that Council might find a use for me in these programmes."

This was the moment. He hoped he looked calm and assured.

Lord Wansson's gaze rested on Chase, and Chase could see thought moving in the large expressive eyes. Then the creature beside Lord Wansson leant across and they spoke together.

"It seems that Zalos Corporation has no complaint or issue with the vessel, Startrader, being in your possession while you performed this – and I quote – mercy mission. Which they support, I might add."

Lord Wansson was again regarding Chase. Definitely a smile was lurking on his face.

"Seems there is no case to be heard on the vessel misappropriation. Now Council will decide on whether you are to be returned to your planet. This is a conscience vote, members. Decide."

Back to the screen, where it seemed to take forever for the lines to form. The line on the left, was it longer than the line on the right? The weight of the moment seemed to be trying to crush Chase. He stood taller.

It seemed to take too long.

"Council has agreed not to return you to your home planet at this time."

Chase breathed a sigh of relief and smiled as he felt two hands on his back.

Lord Wansson spoke again, though he kept his eyes lowered this time.

"Council now needs to decide on the main articles of this hearing as presented. This is such an unusual case that I will clarify the situation and proposals."

He paused.

"Firstly, Council needs to decide whether the sun of the planet Tapar should be adjusted and whether two hundred kilograms of pure cramlimite is to be donated to Council to fund the repair of Tapar's sun. A detailed report from the Programmed Person – Kayfor, as it calls itself – has supplied all the references from the archives, confirming that indeed creatures from the planet Earth were taken as labour to Tapar, by a group that is at least members of the Federation, even without proof that the Federation Council knew. How much responsibility this places on the Federation is debatable. This is a conscience vote. ...Council, decide."

The moment of truth. The Princesses moved forward and took Chase's arms as they stared at the globe screen. Nothing seemed to happen, and then the two columns began to form. They couldn't stop looking, not wanting to blink, though it was hard to watch while others decided the fate of Tapar and its people.

The column on the left seemed slightly lower than the right. Sonja and Carolie squeezed his arms so tightly he winced. Both columns were rising, and then it was hard to determine whether right or left was higher. Then it looked like the left was higher … It was going to be close …

Then Lord Wansson spoke clearly, above an increase of excited chatter.

"Council has agreed to repair the sun endangering the planet Tapar."

A roar arose around the Hall as Chase turned and swept the Princesses up into his arms, laughing and crying together.

Eventually Lord Wansson finally regained control.

"Secondly, and more importantly," he stated firmly, "should Federation laws be revised to take into consideration whether moral assistance could be given under Council-approved conditions?"

Chase regarded Lord Wansson thoughtfully. He had directed the Council rather specifically. Did he have sympathy for the cause?

Again the columns formed, taking an age as voters slowly posted their votes. In the end the column on the left was again higher, but only just. Lord Wansson began to speak:

"Decision that Federation laws be considered for revision has been approved, be it by an extremely narrow margin."

The hall erupted, and it was some time before the noise died down and Lord Wansson could make himself heard.

"Council members, by the vote and your reaction, today

is indeed a milestone day for the Federation."

He smiled at Chase and the Princesses, both of whom were wiping their eyes, with limited success as the tears kept flowing.

"Chase Robinson, Princess Carolie and Princess Sonja, I congratulate you on your presentation and its outcome. Chase Robinson, you will need to liaise with Council staff on how to get the two hundred kilograms of cramlimite shipped to Council possession."

"Yes, my lord. Thank you, my lord."

Lord Wansson bowed and Chase returned his bow with equal formality, while the Princesses dipped down into perfectly executed curtsies. Chase took their hands and walked briskly out of the Hall. Hundreds of thousands talking behind them. He wanted to leave before somehow, something changed the outcome …

Outside the doors Chase's wrist communicator flashed. He answered it with the Princesses moving close.

"You did it!"

"Kayfor, we did it!" Chase laughed. "Information from a Programmed Person called Kayfor. You are famous!"

Kayfor sounded humble, but happy.

"What do you want to do next, Chase?"

"We will head back to you. Can you measure out fifty kilograms of cramlimite for Zalos Corporation and check the contract from them? Also two hundred kilograms for the Federation Council. Leave a message for Lord Wansson at the Federation when it is ready."

"Yes, Chase. Then I think I need a drink."

That made them laugh again.

"Oh, yes!"

They had not gone far when a group of creatures

approached them surrounded by Wardens. What now? In the centre was Lord Wansson. How did he get here so quick? He was even taller now he was close. Nearer to a camel than a horse …

"Congratulations again, Sir Chase, Princesses."

He bowed.

Chase returned the bow. "Thank you, my lord. You might like to know the cramlimite will be ready shortly."

Lord Wansson paid little attention to this.

He considered Chase.

"I have a proposal for you, Chase Robinson. You volunteered your services for Council's moral projects, as you aptly described them."

"Yes, I did, my lord."

"Tapar's situation is not unique in a volatile universe. There are other situations that, once the law permits and Council agrees, could be alleviated."

Chase nodded, while the Princesses stood by and watched him closely.

"Once we have helped Tapar, could I talk to you about one or two?"

Chase smiled. "Certainly, my lord."

"Good. I will be in contact then."

A final bow and he turned to go, the others following in his wake.

Chase watched Lord Wansson depart. He had a firm conviction that his life was about to become even more interesting…

And hey, why not?

Epilogue

Staal is awash with sound, lights and partygoers. Staal is becoming good at parties. Everywhere bands play, trying desperately not to be drowned out by the other musicians nearby. Some people sing, others drink, while food is eaten by the cartload. The crowd is unanimously and deliriously happy.

Only four people at the party know exactly why, yet there is a general feeling that Staal has had another close call, which it survived. That is all that matters, and this is the euphoria of survival, again.

Chase stands with the Royal Family and friends, with Carolie and Sonja close by. He is smiling. He realizes the tension he has been under for so long has gone. He is truly and deeply happy.

Kayfor has told him the process of recalibrating Tapar's sun is underway and proceeding as it should.

The closest band starts up another bouncy tune. In the setting sun Chase raises his tankard to his face and speaks quietly to his wrist communicator.

"Can you hear me, Kayfor?"

"Clearly, Chase."

"A toast!" calls Chase to the crowd, which turns to him. "To someone not here in person, but without whom we would not have achieved what we have."

He lifts up his stein of ale, and bellows out the name.

"TO KAYFOR!"

Those around move close to them now, and they raise their drinking vessels to make a pyramid alongside his stein. Those further away surround them making the pyramid larger and larger.

The crowd doesn't seem to care that they don't know who Kayfor is.

"TO KAYFOR!" they roar, and begin to stamp in time to the music.

"Kayfor! Kayfor! Kayfor!"

Chase and the Princesses drink, laughing, and then set their glasses down and, holding hands, dance with the group.

On board Startrader a happy humming can be heard, which accompanies the tune coming from Chase's communicator.

About the author

Geoff Williamson was born on the day John F Kennedy died. He has travelled extensively, and worked and played sport for far too long. He now lives with his family on a small farm on the top of a hill in the Western Bay of Plenty on the North Island of New Zealand. He used to write stories as a child, but never considered he would write anything longer later in life. Startrader is his first novel. His only hope in writing is that you enjoy his stories.